ISBN #: 978-1-950279-11-1
Library of Congress Control Number: 2019911941

Follow Us on Social Media:

Join Author L. Leigh's Email List:
www.authorlleigh.com/links

ISBN #: 978-1-950279-11-1
Library of Congress Control Number: 2019911941

Follow Us on Social Media:
Instagram: @AuthorLLeigh
Facebook.com/AuthorLLeigh
Twitter: @AuthorLLeigh

Join Author L. Leigh's Email List:
www.authorlleigh.com/links

Carol,
Enjoy the book
Thank you

The Lekki Club

a novel by

L. LEIGH

L. Leigh

18/1/2020

Acknowledgments

I would like to say a big thank you to my family for bearing with me while I got this book off the ground.

To my father, you showed me distance is not an obstacle to show support and encouragement. Thank you.

My grandmother thank you, I hope I have done you proud.

Prologue

He could hear his heart beating as he placed his hand on the handle of the door. He breathed in deeply, trying to steady his nerves as he walked into the room.

The gloom of the surroundings was lightened by the scented candles dotted around the place. Lavender and vanilla assaulted his senses. The scents were relaxing and warming, drawing him into its embrace.

He looked around as the door clicked softly behind him. The room was empty, confirming he was alone.

Enormous potted plants were all around helping soften the starkness of the room. The table, roughly six-feet lengthwise and two-feet across, took pride of place with its gleaming black granite finish.

Someone had laid a bottle of oil and a black blindfold out on the table. The faint sound of soulful music coming from unseen speakers added another touch to the room. The instructions he had received earlier had been clear and precise.

He moved towards the table and swiftly took off his t-shirt, shoes, jeans, and underwear. He folded them away and laid them on the table; tardiness wasn't allowed.

He picked up the oil and opened the bottle, closing his eyes as he breathed in the cocoa butter, chocolate, and vanilla fragrance. There was a fourth scent, floral and light, bubbling through the other three that he didn't recognize. He poured some oil onto his palm, rubbed his hands together, and slowly and sensually massaged the oil all over his body. He imagined someone else's soft hands massaging him as he paid close attention to his wrist and ankles. The instructions had stipulated to leave his dick untouched.

The black velvet blindfold felt soft and warm to his touch. He placed it over his eyes and took his position near the door. The blindfold had been created in such a way that the person wearing it could not cheat once it was on. It fit the face snugly.

He assumed the position; blindfolded, upright, kneeling with his hands on his back resting on his arse.

The soft breeze on his torso, alerted him to the subtle change in temperature and made him aware of the opening door. He heard the soft click of the door shutting behind the person who had just walked into the room.

He cocked his ear as his senses were heightened.

There was someone else in the room. He could feel their presence, but he could not hear any footsteps. The gentle but firm twist of fingers on his nipple got him kneeling straight and upright. He had been slouching.

Whoosh! A jolt of excitement went through him, in anticipation of what was coming. He stilled his body as the rope went around his wrists and ankles.

His nipple was twisted again, as he tried to adjust to the bonds, sending a jolt of desire to his dick as it hardened in response.

"I want your knees wider apart," the voice said. He felt the whip between his legs forcing them wider.

His heart beat faster and his balls felt heavier.

The sound of a zip being pulled and the soft murmur of clothes hitting the floor sent his heart racing in trepidation.

Chapter 1

Remi wiped the sweat off his brow while decreasing the incline on the treadmill. He struggled with his breathing as he tried to keep up with the pace being demanded by the machine. He breathed in heavy, quick short bursts, as even more sweat poured down his face.

He hated cardio.

He had read in Men's Health magazine that HIIT was the way to go to get fit and lose weight. So here he was, running as fast as he could for sixty seconds and walking at a leisurely pace for thirty seconds. The sixty seconds part of it had never felt so long and uncomfortable, making him realize just how unfit he was.

Pressing a button, he lowered the incline further and adjusted the pace on the treadmill to a gentle stroll while he caught his breath. He took a sip of water from his water bottle as he looked around the gym taking in the brand-new cardio machines that had just been installed since the gym's recent refit.

There were running machines, elliptical machines, cross trainers, skiing machines, you name it. They had squeezed all of them into the space they had. There were a few machines he had never seen before either.

Two women were walking and talking on the treadmills, and at least five men. The men looked out of breath as they strolled on the treadmill. However, most of them still found the time to look at their phones rather than concentrate on their workout and break out into a proper sweat.

No wonder no one ever lost any weight or looked any different, Remi thought. Social media had taken over people's lives.

They should ban phones from the gym, he thought.

The vibration on the handle of the treadmill alerted him to a notification on his own phone that took his attention away from running as fast as he could. He hit the pause button and looked at the screen of his phone.

Instagram and Twitter had pushed through notifications.

Socialite Janet Akinwunmi has announced her engagement to Peter Akinbode, Twitter announced. The bloggers repeated the same headline on Instagram.

Hmm, interesting, Remi thought.

It hadn't taken his ex-girlfriend that long to get hitched to her so-called 'friend'. He had always suspected that something was going on between them, but she had always insisted that they were just friends.

Peter always turned up to their events with whoever his girlfriend was at the time in tow, and they had always kept up the facade of a happy couple.

He hadn't heard anywhere that Peter and Toyin, Peter's latest girlfriend had broken up either. Maybe he had missed that tidbit of information.

Good luck to them.

Remi put his phone back into the holder on the treadmill and looked up just as a young woman walked past the cardio machines and headed towards the free weights area.

Remi gave her a cursory look. She wasn't his type - dark-skinned, short, and petite. Her boobs weren't anything to write home about either, only a handful at the most. But what she lacked on the top part, she more than compensated for with her arse. The two globes were more than a handful.

Ooh la la. Yep, the arse was something. It was round and he could just imagine cupping them in his hands as he tried to feel just how firm the cheeks were.

A tall, statuesque, light-skinned lady took away his attention, as she stepped onto a treadmill a couple of feet away from him. He immediately forgot the dark skinned girl, as he looked over at his new eye candy. However, she was busy staring at her phone and did not notice his gaze on her.

Remi's phone beeped again, rattling the treadmill and forcing his eyes away from the lady on the treadmill he had been admiring. This time a WhatsApp notification came through from Bayo, his best friend since forever.

He went to lower the incline on the machine again and realized that it was flat. He changed the intensity to a very slow stroll.

Bayo: Old boy, what are you up to this evening?

Remi: Not much my friend, at the gym. I was about to chat up a girl on the treadmill next to me. What do you have in mind?

Remi looked over to the girl on the treadmill.

ding

Remi looked back down at his phone.

Bayo: You never stop chasing, smh. I have a guest pass for my club tonight and I wanted to know if you would be interested in coming along with me.

Remi: Well, I am single. Club? A nightclub?

Remi knew Bayo was a very private person; he had to be, he was gay. He hadn't been able to tell his family or any of his other friends. Bayo had never really told Remi, but they both knew Remi knew, and it hadn't put a strain on their relationship. For better or for worse they had each other's backs.

Bayo was the only person who had really understood his misgivings and reluctance when Remi had said he wasn't ready to propose to Janet.

Bayo: It's a very, very private member's club in Lekki. It's taken five months for them to do all the background checks on me. I have been there a few times. It's a nice discreet place. I think you will like it.

Remi: Have I heard of the club?

Bayo: I doubt that you would know the place, it's unusual.

Remi looked up from his phone and looked around the gym. The girl he had dismissed earlier was in the free weights area. She was currently squatting and from what he could see it was some serious stuff. She had looked so delicate walking through the gym. She intrigued him.

The light-skinned lady had finished on the treadmill and was now sitting on a sofa busy on her phone.

Remi: Can you pick me up and we go in your car? If so, what time?

Chapter 2

Remi looked at the stats on the machine, hoping that he had burned off a few pounds.

The display congratulated him on burning 72 calories. No wonder he lost no weight. He had done all that work for only 72 measly calories.

His phone pinged again and he saw another WhatsApp message from Bayo.

Bayo: Be ready for 9. It's not too far away from u. Note, u can't take ur phone into the club with u.

Remi: Why not?

Remi stared at his phone and laughed. No one could ban phones.

Bayo: Rules of the club and you also need to sign an NDA since I am vouching for you.

Remi looked up from his phone confused, NDA?

Remi: Old boy, where are we going? Are we going for a secret service meeting?

Bayo: I am serious. It is not the kind of club you have been to before. Well, I don't know if you have been to such a place. You can be a dark horse sometimes.

Remi: Me? Look who's talking! I'm not the one going to a club that does not allow phones and patrons must sign NDA's. Are we going there to be entertained or work?

He typed into his phone, waiting for Bayo to respond. He was curious.

Bayo: Look at it as leisurely work. There is a lot to learn if you are that way inclined and want to know more. They even run workshops to teach people how to do stuff.

Remi stared at the last message Bayo sent. It intrigued him.

What kind of club was Bayo taking him to?

Putting his phone in his pocket, he stepped off the treadmill and walked towards the reception area. The dark booty girl was at the front desk, talking to the receptionist.

"I am just following up on my query regarding getting more weights. The plates that go on the barbell?" she asked.

Gifty, the girl manning the reception desk looked up at her. "They got delivered a few days ago, aren't they there? Can't you see them?" Gifty asked, the implication of being blind left unspoken.

Remi shook his head. Gifty was the rudest receptionist he had ever met. How she held onto the job was a mystery to him. Well, not so much of a mystery, as he knew why.

"There are just two new 5kg and 10kg plates that don't add up to much," she sighed. "That's a measly 30kg," the dark girl continued, "it's a free weights area. There's hardly any heavy weights there."

Gifty's eyebrows went up. "That is a lot. We don't really have a lot of people using that area." She stated, putting a hand on her forehead.

"Are you trying to become incredible hulk? You're a girl. What are you doing with that heavy stuff anyway? Why don't you use the machines like the other girls who come here? Mitchew." Gifty gestured to the gleaming machines behind her.

"Even the men who come here don't use that area. The ones that do are *happy* with what *we* have," Gifty continued, putting her hand on her half naked cleavage.

"That's because you don't have enough plates to get *the real men* to use that part of the gym," the nice arsed girl responded placing her hand on her hip.

"Can I put in a request that the club gets more plates please?" she asked, picking up a pen from the counter.

"Okay," Gifty said, drumming her fingers on the counter. "I will pass on the request to the manager and get him to email you."

"Thank you," the girl said with a genuine smile on her face.

Very polite girl, Remi thought, as he stared at her arse again.

Mmm, yes very nice.

~ 18 ~

Remi watched her backside as she walked towards the exit.

Good thing Gifty didn't work for him. He would have sacked her on the spot for speaking to paying customers like that.

"Hi Remi," Gifty smiled as her voice softened. She reserved the hard-dismissive tones for women she viewed as rivals.

"Hi Gifty," Remi started. "What was all that about?"

"Oh, that one? She has been hassling Oga to buy more stuff for the weight area, but we don't have many people using it," she sighed.

No wonder, Remi thought. If he owned the place he would have sent Gifty packing ages ago, but it wasn't his call to make.

"He bought some plates just to keep her quiet, but she said that is what she uses to warm up." Gifty let out an indignant laugh. "Can you believe that? To 'warm up'."

She repeated shaking her head. "Can't she warm up like everyone else and use the machines?" she said, rolling her eyes.

"She should just use the machines like everyone else." Gifty repeated as if trying to prove something to herself.

Then she asked, "How was *your* workout Remi?" gazing at him intently. Her gaze worked its way down his wet t-shirt, towards his training shorts and beyond.

"Not as intense as I wanted it to be," Remi replied.

Gifty arched her brow and leaned over towards him, her cleavage visible as she rested her arms on the counter. "Really?" she prodded. "Were you after an intense workout?" she asked, staring at him.

Remi took a step back and ignored the suggestive glance and innuendo. "I spent too much time on the phone, unfortunately. See you," he said, as he made a swift exit towards the door.

He looked at his phone and typed a reply to Bayo.

Remi: Okay, I am looking forward to it. See you later.

Phew, that was close he thought. Gifty had made it clear a few times that she was interested in him. But he wasn't interested in dipping his wick into the community candle; most men at the club he knew had slept with her. There was a lot of information you could pick up in the men's changing room.

Remi got into the car and had the gear in reverse when his phone rang.

Mum flashed up on the display screen.

He had been glued to his phone today, he smiled.

Remi switched off the engine and pressed accept. "Hi Mum," he said.

"Remi, how are you? I called to see how you are?"

"I am fine Mum, I was just leaving the gym," he replied.

"I saw the news on Twitter and Instagram, are you OK?" she asked, her concern radiating over the phone.

Jokingly he said, "Mum, what are you doing on Twitter and Instagram? It's not for the likes of you."

"Silly boy, you guys think you invented social media."

"You should know better than that. On a more serious note are you OK?" his mum asked.

"Mum, I am fine. I broke it off with her. I can't begrudge her finding happiness elsewhere," he replied.

"Ok, my baby. You never really went into why you guys broke up. It's a good thing I hadn't commissioned any aso ebi."

His mum went on, "Well to be honest we got tired of waiting for you to pop the question. But you never did."

She paused, hoping for Remi to say something.

She continued, "Your father warned me not to hassle you about when you were going to get married. For once I let him tell me what to do and stood by it," she sighed, over the phone.

Remi chuckled, yes it must have been hard for his mum not to say a word.

"But I hope you find what you are looking for. Just remember that sometimes masterpieces don't always show up as priceless until you start chipping away at the surface. Then you realize that underneath all the grime you have a true treasure."

Remi cleared his throat. "Thanks Mum, for the support. But I am not going back to Janet," he said.

His mum sighed over the phone, "I wasn't referring to Janet, somehow I just couldn't see the two of you marrying to be honest. But you are not getting any younger Remi."

That was news to him; his mother had always welcomed Janet into her home and had always been very nice to her.

"Why do you say that Mum?" he asked.

"Well there just wasn't any chemistry between the two of you, I mean sexual chemistry," she chuckled.

"Unless there was, and I wasn't seeing it."

"Janet always came off as being cold and aloof, even towards you Remi."

"Mum!!!"

"It's true, if it doesn't exist now after the number of years you have been going out, what do you think will happen when you have kids and the drudgery of domesticity kicks in?" she asked.

Wow, he thought his mother was a very astute woman. He was shocked by what she said but comforted that she understood him completely.

Remi should have known, he had seen the way his father looked at her when he thought no one was watching. He had always wanted that for himself, but he hadn't met the one who would understand his needs.

Who he could trust enough to tell and would not think he was a freak.

"You are your father's son," she said enigmatically.

What does that mean? Remi thought.

"You will find her, that special woman, hopefully soon. We want to be grandparents while we can still run around."

A big sigh came over the phone. "Anyway, since you sound ok, I will love you and leave you babes. Are you coming on Sunday?"

Chuckling, Remi said, "Yes Mum, see you on Sunday. Love you too babes."

Remi switched the engine back on, finally moving the car into reverse to go home and get ready for his mysterious evening with Bayo.

Chapter 3

Sam stared out of the window of her office overlooking the main hall area of the club. She stood there lost in thought, knotting and untying the soft piece of rope she held in her hands while she watched the staff below go about their duties getting the club ready for the evening.

TLC – The Lekki Club, was a private member's only club, open to members in the evenings from Thursday – Sunday. It had existed for over two years and it was going from strength to strength.

The club was very profitable with each member being charged more than $70,000/annum for the privilege of privacy and discretion. This ensured that only a certain class of people came through their doors.

Money alone did not guarantee you entry into TLC. Background checks were also done on prospective members. If anything untoward was found, like charges regarding domestic violence or assault for example, they were not granted membership.

Even with the high level of vetting, this did not stop the waiting list from growing.

The rope was helping calm her nerves for the evening ahead and it also helped soothe her melancholy. She turned around and stared at the Arsenal t-shirt hanging on her wall before her eyes moved and settled on the framed picture on her desk.

The owner of the t-shirt and herself smiling in Japan.

Sam sighed. She walked back to her desk where a medium-sized brown box had been all afternoon, waiting for her to open and claim her prize.

Sam finally opened the box. The smell that assailed her nostrils was like the scent of freshly cut grass on a warm summer's day.

There was something about the smell and feel of new rope that made you want to touch it sensually; stroking it ever so gently like a lover caressing a secret spot.

She stroked the rope softly in its packaging and took it out of the box. Admiring the stitching, Sam was happy that it had arrived in time for her show. She had placed the order a week ago, and she hadn't been sure that it would turn up on time.

Sam would give another class in bondage tonight. When she did this, she normally liked to use new rope. It felt better on a new subject. Rope was an art to her and her art demanded new rope, so she got it.

She sat down at her desk and sighed again. She had given in to the demands and requests from their members and rather than create a YouTube video, that might have breached someone in the world's moral code, she had decided on a live performance. This meant that the club would be busy; they would be packed to the rafters.

For the few live sessions she ran, a male subject would have been preferable. However, Sam had never found a male subject that was ready, willing, and brave enough to come forward. So she had always been forced to use female subjects.

Most of the men would not come near her or refused to come on stage even if she pointed at them. They would never admit in public those true desires they thought she could fulfill. Which is why she always had a female subject as backup, ironically that interested them more.

If it brought in the punters and that was their preference, who was she to complain?

She would just have to keep on looking for her own elusive male subject. That was the disadvantage of living in a very male dominated country. Anything that went against that patriarchy was frowned upon. If such things did happen, they were meant to be well hidden.

Even the non-heterosexual members of the club were careful not to flaunt their preferences. They still tried to keep up the expected heterosexual facade.

It would be nice if just for once she could find a nice, confident, virile, young man who would not be too ashamed to come on stage for her, just for a lark.

Women Dommes were something no one was ready to deal with, other than as entertainment.

Her mind briefly went back to the man she had seen checking her out earlier that day in the gym. He had potential. Now if he turned up, ...mmmm that would be juicy pussy dripping territory. *Ah, but a girl can dream*, she sighed while stroking the rope.

She would make do with a female subject. She had nothing against her, she just wasn't into women that way. Plus, most of the girls who worked at the club were not into anything kinky. They only exhibited kinkiness due to the incentives offered by some of the patrons.

Most of the patrons were not kinky either. They were only there because of the cachet of the club, and the membership fees being extremely steep was something they could brag about.

Funnily enough, the real kinky people were the married couples that frequented the club. Human beings never ceased to amaze her.

Sam sighed as her mind went back to the task at hand. It was always best when there was chemistry. She promised herself that she would make it work, no matter what. A true performer always performed to the best of their ability with the tools they had.

A knock on her door took Sam away from her musings.

Yomi, the head of security at the club stuck his head through her door to check if she was busy. He proceeded to walk in.

Tall, dark, and very handsome, he looked like a model from bodybuilding.com. He had appeared a few times on their Instagram feed years ago. Most of the girls in the club were in lust with him. Some of the men too, but they were not so open about it, of course.

Sam and Yomi went way back and were also friends away from work.

"Hi Sam," he said, plonking himself on the chair in front of her desk.

"Hi Yomi, what's up?" she replied, looking up at him as he sat down.

Yomi brushed off some lint on his jacket. "Are we all set for tonight?" he asked.

He did not wait for an answer as he continued. Grinning he said, "We are going to be packed. Word has got out that you will be delivering another live performance on bondage."

"Oh really?" Sam replied rolling her eyes, "you don't say."

"Of course," he said.

Yomi picked up a sweet from the bowl on her desk. "All the men out there will be hoping that the mysterious lady on the stage with the rope will choose them."

Sam laughed and rolled her eyes. "If that were truly the case Yomi, why do they always refuse to come onto the stage then?" she asked him.

Yomi winked at her. "That's because they are all scared of you Sam."

Sam grinned back at him, her hands making intricate patterns on the piece of rope in her hands.

Stretching his arms. "Most of the men out there will never admit to their friends or themselves that having a woman dominate them sexually is their ultimate fantasy."

Yomi tapped his fingers on her desk. "Admitting that female sexual dominance turns them on is hard for them

Sam. It goes against the African alpha male stereotype," he sighed. "I can just hear them. *Heaven forbid, a woman dominating me sexually? Never! She must know her place even in the bedroom,*" he laughed.

Stretching his arms behind his back. "Just to buttress my point, I read on a blog this morning about a guy who said his girlfriend was disrespecting him," he started. "Do you know why Sam? Because his girlfriend liked being on top during sex." Yomi shook his head in amazement.

Sam burst out laughing. "For real?" She followed suit, shaking her head in amazement.

"They just won't admit to liking it Sam."

Yomi grinned, "Plus, you also have a very limited pool of prime male specimens to choose from that would look erotic and tasteful after being tied up by you."

What he said was true, most of the men were middle-aged who had decided that carrying the extra pounds in front of them was the best look possible. Fitness or muscles was not something that bothered them. They knew as long as they had money, getting women to sleep with them was not a problem.

Sam sighed, "Well, maybe for once lady luck will send someone my way who I can use."

Yomi held up two crossed fingers. "I will keep my fingers crossed for you Sam." He said, stretching his legs further under her table.

"Maybe we have set our sights too high. The young muscle-bound guys you are after might find our fees prohibitive." He continued.

"No, I don't think so Yomi. Have you forgotten that we have a whole new set of the so-called young ones who all came in on the back of the singer Baxid?"

"They are just not going to admit to enjoying female sexual dominance while they are out there with their friends," she continued.

"I know they all prefer to see me tie up a woman. Most men like seeing a woman being dominated and submitting. In addition to the female on female sexual dynamic that most men think and fantasize about. It's a shame I am not into women," she laughed mischievously. "I would have a lot to choose from." They both laughed at her joke.

"Alright, if you say so. Anyway, back to the business at hand," she remembered. Sam had a concerned look on her face. "We are going to need extra security to get our guests through the door as quickly as possible." She started walking to the window in her office. "With this show, a lot of patrons might try to sneak in people who are not on the pre-vetted list," she continued. "Yomi, do you think we are going to be busier than usual?"

Yomi leaned over her desk. "I have got it under control Sam. I have drafted in a few more people from that security firm we have used in the past. They are very trustworthy and discreet," he reminded her.

Yomi winked at her. "Shame you're not interested in them. They have more muscles than Arnie." She rolled her eyes and threw the rope she had been holding at him.

"Is Joanne the Caterer aware of the extra food and snacks she needs to prepare and provide tonight?" he asked.

Yomi had every reason to be concerned about the food.

Sighing deeply, he said, "I don't want us to get caught out of food like we did the last time you gave a demo."

They had been so busy the food had run out ninety minutes into the evening. They had been forced to improvise and had quickly slapped up some snacks in the kitchen to keep the patrons happy.

"Our servers crashed the day with enquiries for membership after your last performance. We also had a few members asking if you ran one-on-one training courses." he said with a smirk on his face. "There must have been a lot of chemistry between you and your subject after all." as he winked at her.

Sam grinned. "Well it's helped raise our profile and send the right customers our way." If things continued they would have to close off the waiting list, as it was growing at a very steady rate.

Sam logged into her personal email to check if she had any responses to her ad for a male submissive.

The unintelligible responses she saw in her inbox made her wonder just how they had passed the vetting of the club. She hoped that they were from the club. That was something she might also have to consider.

She had to be careful. There were a lot of strange people out there.

Sam placed a call to the front desk to round up the staff for a quick chat before The Lekki Club opened that evening.

Most of the waiting staff who worked at the club were university students with a splattering of recent graduates who were seeking jobs, but were at TLC as a stop gap. The pay was quite reasonable. The club made enough money from its patrons not to have to bother dipping into the staff's tip box. All tips at the end of the night were divided equally amongst all staff, irrespective of rank.

They also got the opportunity to mix with some of the most influential people in the country, who put a very high price on their privacy. It was one of the reasons the club's waiting list was so long. TLC was a discreet member's only BDSM club. It was so discreet that unless you were introduced to it by someone personally, from the website you would not know what goes on behind the closed doors dotted around the premises.

Sam also realized that quite a few hookups took place between the patrons and the staff. As long as the job got done, she wasn't too bothered by that. The staff had all signed Non-Disclosure Agreements as part of their contract of employment. The few that had decided to blab had experienced the long arm of the law and had promptly learnt from their mistakes the hard way.

The members of staff started filing into her office. Yomi was still sprawled on her chair, busy on his phone, a faint smile hovering on his lips.

Must be a text from his lover, she thought amusingly.

Sam stood up to address the faces of people in front of her. "As you all are aware, we are going to be very busy tonight, due to the show we are putting on."

"I want everyone on top form; putting new bottles of drinks on members tables before they ask for it." Sam said, staring at the head waiter.

"Joanne's food is exquisite, so push it too," she said, looking around the room. "You know the drill; if you hear any strange or uncomfortable remarks from the patrons, get one of Yomi's people on it ASAP." She pointed to Yomi who was still busy on his phone.

"Ok, that's it guys. Enjoy the evening."

"Can you three stay behind please?" she asked, as she pointed to two ladies and a man from the group walking out of the room.

Chapter 4

Remi splashed on some aftershave and studied his profile in the mirror. He was wearing black jeans and a plain white t-shirt. He looked at himself critically. The once loose t-shirt was now tight across the middle. He was packing on the kilograms and he wasn't too pleased about it. His midriff wasn't as flat as he wanted it to be. He turned in the mirror. He was way too young to be sporting a pot belly.

Note to self, he sighed, *leave the phone in the locker when you are in the gym.*

A beep on his phone notified him of Bayo's arrival outside. He picked up his wallet and his house keys, and walked downstairs towards his front door. He looked around one more time, set the alarm, and walked out towards Bayo's car.

"Hey, man," he said, as he got into the car.

"You're looking cool dude," Bayo replied, as he switched gears and moved forward.

"So, where and what is this mysterious club we are going to Bayo?" Remi asked getting to the point.

"It sounds all cloak and dagger. Is it a secret society club?" Remi asked.

Remi looked over to Bayo with an arched brow. "I have heard there are a lot of those around now. Mostly made up of politicians, the rich, and famous."

Remi paused and laughed, "Sorry for the deluge of questions, I will keep quiet now."

He noticed Bayo take a deep breath before he responded. "We are going to a BDSM club," he stated in a neutral voice. Concentrating on his driving, Bayo said, "If you're uncomfortable with going to such a place, we can go somewhere else tonight."

"Oh," Remi paused. "...interesting.' After a while of silence, he burst out laughing.

"Why would I be uncomfortable Bayo?" Remi asked, as he turned towards Bayo. "I didn't know there were such places in this country. I mean to the extent they would open their club to outsiders?"

"Without incurring the wrath of the religious police?" Remi asked his friend.

Remi wasn't surprised though. Things had changed radically; anything was possible. The explosion of social media had made people aware of things, and with that awareness, people's attitudes had also changed.

Eyes focused on his driving, Bayo asked, "Oh, have you been to one before?"

"Yes, I have my friend. I used to go a lot when I was living in New York. It's the home of the kinky alternative lifestyle," Remi replied. "Bayo, no one over there would view you like a freak because you have certain kinks that differ from the norm."

Bayo burst out laughing, "Wow. Remi the dark horse. I would never have known or thought you would go to such places," he said winking at him. "I should start saying *'hello Remi Grey,'*" Bayo joked.

Bayo continued laughing at his own joke. "Remi Grey, making submissives obey his commands since 2000."

If only you knew the truth, Remi thought wistfully. He was looking for a Ms. Grey; he wasn't Mr. Grey not by a long shot.

"Look who is talking," Remi replied, shaking away the wistful thoughts. He stared into the darkness through the car window.

The route Bayo had taken to the club did not look familiar to Remi. Even though he had been living in the area for a while, he had never ventured this way before.

Bayo made a sharp left and then they were at a gate. A dark-skinned man with a shaved head and a beard put a hand up indicating for them to stop. He was at least 6'4 with broad shoulders. The black t-shirt emphasized his rippling biceps and torso muscles, as he stood sentry at the gate. He wasn't your average Nigerian gateman. He had an earpiece in one ear, a walkie talkie and a tablet in his hand, and some very serious attitude.

He gestured Bayo to wind the window down.

"Good evening Sirs, name and IDs please." He instructed, peering into the car with his flashlight.

Bayo and Remi took out their driver licenses and Bayo produced the guest pass he had been given for Remi.

The guard checked the photos while the glare of his torch shined on their faces as he compared features.

Remi wandered what he had gotten himself into. Was all this necessary to get into a club?

The guard handed back the IDs. "Thank you, you may go through. Please remember phones are not allowed on the premises. Have a nice evening." He pressed something on the tablet and the gates opened.

"This no phone policy is real," Remi spoke.

"You thought I was joking? If you try to sneak a phone in, they will know," Bayo replied.

They got out of the car and put their phones in the glove compartment before walking toward the main door of a huge house.

The security guard at the main door was a clone of the gateman. The door opened into a hallway that was tastefully furnished with black leather sofas and chairs dotted discreetly around and away from each other on wooden floors. The subtle scent of sandalwood, cedar, and vanilla filled the air. The pictures on the walls softened the masculine setup. There were hand drawn pieces of art they were tastefully erotic, as opposed to pornographic pictures of men and women in various poses of intimacy. The artist was talented. Remi made a mental note of their Instagram handle @deetonz.

The guard asked them for their names and IDs. He studied them and their faces, before consulting his tablet to ensure that they were on his list.

Returning their ID the guard asked, "Do you have any phones or electrical gadgets on you?"

Bayo put his hands up. "Nothing other than my car keys," he replied.

The guard ran his eyes over Bayo. "Please go through that door," he said, pointing to a door down the corridor.

Chapter 5

Remi and Bayo walked towards the door the security guard had indicated. Standing in front of them at the door was a portly man wearing a white top with baggy black trousers.

They slowed down their pace to allow the portly man to go through the door first. As the portly man put his hand on the door handle, a piercing red light started flashing from the door.

Bayo and Remi looked at each other puzzled, wondering what was going on and kept back.

Another clone of the guard at the gate and door materialized from the shadows. He had the mandatory ear piece, rippling muscles, and mean face, only this time he didn't have a tablet. His biceps, the span of the average Victoria Secret Angel's waist and would put the fear of God in anyone.

The guard put his hand on the portly man's shoulder. "Excuse me sir," he said, biceps bulging.

"Can you step aside, please?" the guard asked, moving him away from the door.

The guard held up his hand for Bayo and Remi to hold on.

"Why?" the portly man responded. "You are delaying me here with all this talk," the man continued arrogantly.

The guard looked frustrated. "Sir, as you are aware, the club rule states no phones." He paused. "You have your phone on you and that means you can't enter the club tonight. Can you step aside, please?" Guiding him away from the door.

Pointing a finger at the guard. "What do you mean, I can't go in? I need my phone and shall take it in. Don't you know who I am?" the portly man said.

Exasperated at the portly man, the guard said, "Sir, we are very busy tonight and you are holding up the rule abiding members. Can you step aside please for us to deal with this?"

Bayo whispered, "You thought I was joking earlier."

"To be honest, I did. I wondered why you were so ready to adhere to the rules," Remi said.

The security guard eventually nodded at Remi and Bayo to go through the door.

This door opened into a large room which was the size of a banquet hall. There was a stage dominating the wall towards the back of the room. Enormous tropical plants were dotted around creating an indoor garden ambience. The faint sound of a waterfall completed the picture. The dimmed lights also added to the ambience of the room. The smell of cooked food permeated the air.

The pictures on the walls in here were a mixture of stills of rope knots and rope tied on the different subjects; both male and female. The other stills were mesmerizing; various poses of men and women in various stages of undress. They were not pornographic; they were tastefully erotic. A professional photographer must have taken the pictures because they all looked like works of art.

Eroticism seemed to be the central theme of the club.

Remi looked around. The photographer responsible for this display had an exceptional eye for detail. It captured the essence of what the couples were trying to portray, Domination & submission. He wandered over to the far corner of the wall taking in the images as he walked along.

The lighting at the end of this part of the room was dimmer than the rest of the hall.

One picture caught his eye. It was that of a man on his knees tied up with rope with his hands behind his back and his knees shoulder width apart.

The rope had been skillfully and artfully wound around the ankles and wrists of the subject. The intricacy of the knots hinting at the passion the Dom had for rope. It was breathtaking and beautiful.

The model's muscle-bound body glistened. Remi touched the picture absent-mindedly.

Was it sweat due to the exertion of trying to keep upright and still? Was it the oil used to prevent rope burns? Or was it sweat due to the self-control required to stop him from cumming?

Yes, Remi was aware of a lot more reasons. He smiled wistfully.

The model did not look uncomfortable. On the contrary, the look on his face was one of pure surrender and hunger.

Sexual hunger. He looked off camera to the face of the lady whose hand was resting on his shoulder.

The lady's face was hidden from view. He assumed it was a lady from the nail polish on the tips of her fingers which was a deep shade of red. There was a hint of a bare leg in the picture. Could he be staring at her face begging or the place between his Domme's legs hoping to get a taste?

The ache and the need he had kept hidden and buried suddenly returned. Remi wished at that moment he was the man kneeling in the picture; understanding how the man in the picture felt, submitting himself fully, mind, body, and soul, totally to his Domme.

Remi's sexual musings retreated when he felt someone's gaze on him. Looking around, he noticed a small, petite, dark woman in a mask staring at him from across the room. He watched warily as she walked over to where he was standing. Scanning the room for Bayo, he had disappeared and was nowhere to be seen.

The masked lady turned towards the picture. "It's a nice picture; very powerful imagery if you really understand what is going on." Sensually tracing her fingers over the man's torso in the picture, she whispered, "The man looks blissfully happy, don't you think?" she asked.

Remi's eyes were mesmerized as they followed the red tips of her nails raking over the picture. The voice low, mysterious, but firm as he turned to look at her. The accent tagged her as having spent a long time in America.

The masked lady turned and stared up at him. Remi felt his face grow hot under her knowing, direct gaze. The mask covered most of her face. The only thing it did not cover was her chin, her lips, and her eyes. She was dark-skinned; the rich color of coffee beans. The mask which was fashioned in various shades of green and bronze made her look even more mysterious. Her skin looked so smooth, silky, and inviting. Her lips were full and red; as vibrant as her nails.

For Remi, he couldn't stop staring at her. Everything about her screamed danger and mystery. He had to force himself to look away from those knowing eyes. They were boring into his soul, taking and playing with the secret desires they both knew he had kept hidden from everyone else for so long.

Whispering, she said, "That is the look of pure surrender, want, and need." The words were like a caress on his skin.

"He wants what he needs, and he needs what he wants."

"You do know what is going on and it's something you yearn for isn't it?" she asked.

Remi felt himself harden, followed by a deep ache in his balls in response to the question. He shifted slightly. His jeans suddenly felt tight.

Yes, it was something he yearned for but he wasn't about to confess to the strange woman standing next to him. Remi suddenly felt very hot and uncomfortable. He needed and wanted to get away from this mysterious lady.

"What do you think he wants right there? His Mistress's pussy? Her hard clit on his tongue or her whip on his hard-throbbing dick?" she asked him, as her eyes travelled down his torso staring at the bulge in his jeans.

Moving closer to him, whispering she continued, "Which one would you choose?" she asked in those soft hypnotic tones. Her eyes coming back to his face watching him squirm under her scrutiny. The difference in height did nothing to minimize the impact of her words on him. Her closeness was also distracting the hell out of him.

Remi swallowed. He needed and wanted to get away from the picture and this mysterious all-knowing woman. He was thinking of how to respond to her questions when he realized that she was no longer at his side.

Damn, he thought.

Instead, Remi saw Bayo approaching him with two bottles of cold beer in his hands. Looking around the room he noticed that there were three women wearing the same mask and clothes as the mystery woman he had been listening to.

He had been too tongue-tied to speak to her.

Remi then noticed that all the women in the masks had the same build and skin color.

Damn. How was he going to find the lady who had talked to him briefly but had touched him so profoundly? His dick was still hard from her scrutiny. *Fuck*, he thought.

Whoever she was, she had seen through all his walls immediately. He moved away from the picture and decided to walk over to another. This time a safer picture with a female subject.

Remi heard someone laugh. When he looked over to where the sound was coming from, he noticed that it was the woman with the mask. She shook her head at him. She knew why he had moved away from the other picture.

Then he watched her walk out of the room. She was gone.

Looking towards Bayo he asked, "Who is the woman in the mask?"

Bayo looked around. "Women, you mean? There are at least three of them tonight, other times it's five."

"Oh," Remi said.

Remi studied his surroundings. There were sofas dotted around the huge space; a bar dominated the left-hand side of the room. Soft muted lighting added to the ambience, and a few tables and chairs had been placed directly in front of the stage. He could see four large speakers and a DJ deck had been placed near the stage.

Waiters and waitresses flittered around the room taking orders from the club members. He counted three women and a man wearing the same full-face masks as the mystery woman.

Remi asked, "What's with the masks Bayo?" as he eyed one of the ladies walking towards them.

"I actually don't know. It's always been that way whenever I have been here," Bayo replied.

"More so when there is a live show," he added.

"Let's take our drinks and get our front row seats for this performance," Bayo said.

Chapter 6

Sam stood in front of the mirror in her office and practiced her power pose, putting her hands on her hips and looking upwards. She called it her superhero pose and she needed to feel like a superhero tonight.

Her nerves gnawing away at her, she never took things for granted. All kinds of things could go wrong.

The breathing and voice exercises she did helped get her into character; that of an alpha Domme Mistress.

The faint scent of sandalwood assaulted her senses as she picked up the mirror on her desk and checked her makeup especially around her eyes. She opened her drawer, got out her makeup brushes and expertly touched up her eyes. When she felt she was ready, she walked out of her office to perform for the night.

Sam locked the door and was heading for the bar when she noticed a tall dark man staring at her favorite picture; a man on his knees, tied up and looking up at his Domme.

Most men found the picture uncomfortable and walked straight past it, but here was someone engrossed and in awe of it. His stance in front of the picture was open. He wanted it. He knew and understood what was going on.

Probably has submitted to a Domme before, interesting, she thought.

Sam looked towards the bar where chaos reigned. The waitresses and waiters who were waiting for their drink orders would just have to wait a bit longer.

Instead, she made a quick detour towards the pictures and the mystery man. She wanted to find out whether her observations were correct.

Chapter 7

Remi was about to take his phone out of his pocket to check his messages when he remembered that he had left it in the car. He took a sip of his beer and looked around the room as the lights dimmed and a spotlight lit up the stage.

One of the ladies wearing the mask walked onto the stage to a round of applause.

The spotlight then moved to a spot on the stage away from her, keeping her silhouette in the shadows.

"Good evening ladies and gentlemen," she said in her Brooklyn accent creating another fission of excitement down Remi's spine.

"Thank you for attending this event."

"Tonight, we are going to talk bondage. This can be a very erotic experience for both parties," she paused and looked around at her rapt audience.

"In the past, I have used females for this demonstration. I will be looking for a male volunteer this evening," she said, as she looked around the room, her eyes settling briefly on Remi.

Remi heard most of the men around him snigger. He looked around. There was a group of middle-aged men that looked unfazed as they knew they would not fit her mold of a subject. There wasn't an ounce of defined muscle between them.

There was also a group of youngish fit looking guys a couple of tables away from them and they started strutting and puffing out their chests. Daring each other to take up the challenge of being a volunteer.

Remi wondered if she was the lady who had spoken to him earlier. He moved his eyes back to the stage, and he felt her eyes on him. Looking away he concentrated on his bottle, anything to take his eyes away from that knowing gaze.

"Playing with rope can be an enjoyable experience for the person being tied up and the person performing the binding. It allows the Dom unrestricted play time with their subject or submissive."

"Just imagine all the things you could do to turn them on; they are at your mercy."

"Under your control, either dripping wet or rock hard and still dripping." Remi heard laughter from the other people in the audience.

The woman paused and looked around the room. "The submissive person is surrendering all control to the other person at that moment. It is a special gift, as the person bound is saying I trust you," she said.

"As a responsible Dom, you should never abuse that trust," she paused.

"Maintaining eye contact with your submissive is very important. It lets them know that it is okay to feel uncomfortable initially. Make sure you both agree on a safe word. Make sure you respect that safe word; it's vital." She said.

Remi watched as her eyes swept over the floor and came back to rest on him.

"Is there anyone who would like to volunteer to be my subject tonight?" she asked. The question was met with silence.

Remi studiously kept his eyes on his bottle. He swore he could feel her gaze on him again.

"Seems we will be starting with a female subject tonight," he heard her say.

He breathed out a sigh of relief.

There was a roar of approval from all the guys. This is what they wanted to see. A woman tied up made better viewing than a male subject, especially if she was half dressed.

The audience all watched in awe and fascination as the mysterious woman tied up her female volunteer.

Remi turned to Bayo and whispered. "Who is she?"

"Does she work here or is she a member like you?"

Bayo shrugged his shoulders. "I really don't know. I can never tell the ladies in the masks apart, they all look alike to me," he said.

The lights dimmed and the curtain went down on the stage for five minutes.

Then the lights got brighter and the female volunteer was hanging from a hook in the ceiling. Her legs and arms tied in intricate knots, she looked spectacular. There was a round of applause as fevered chatter broke out on the tables around the stage.

The tap on his shoulder took Remi's attention away from the hanging lady. A waiter was standing next to him with two tumblers of what looked like brandy.

"Good evening sirs, some brandy for you," he said.

The waiter put one glass in front of Bayo and one in front of Remi. He also handed over a small envelope to Remi, titled 'Open' and walked away.

Remi looked at Bayo, pointing to the drinks. "Did you order more drinks? It should have been my round," Remi said.

Bayo shook his head. "Nope not me, but it looks like you have an admirer," he said, eyes bulging and curious to see what was in the envelope.

Remi opened the envelope. Written in red pen was the message: *Be in Room 3 in 30 minutes, Mistress Eve.*

Bayo leaned over and peered at the note and winked at him. "You have definitely caught someone's attention," he said, rubbing his hands together.

Remi read the note again. He could only assume that the lady who had been on the stage and who had spoken to him earlier were one and the same person. He wasn't sure if he wanted to go and see the woman in question.

She had made him feel vulnerable, uncomfortable, and exposed. It had put him off kilter and it was a strange feeling.

Remi enjoyed being in control, and for once he wasn't.

Bayo noticed Remi's hesitation. "Remi, what have you got to lose?" he asked.

Bayo winked. "Worst case scenario you don't like her, best case you might actually score," he said with a knowing look on his face. Bayo continued, "Go and talk or do whatever you two might get up to. Emphasis on the up please," he said, raising his eyebrows in the process.

"If she proves too much for you Remi, I am sure you can always give your excuses and make a swift exit."

Remi rolled his eyes and shook his head. Sometimes he really wondered about Bayo. He acted so juvenile at times. Yet, this was a man who was the head of one of the top companies in the country.

He tried to talk himself out of it. She wasn't his type. He had never been attracted to dark-skinned girls. If it had been a Beyonce look alike, he would have been out of his chair before he even finished reading the note.

Remi looked at the note again. Twenty-five minutes had already passed since the note had been delivered to him.

Remi looked over to Bayo and he suggested, "I can't leave you here on your own Bayo." Even to his own ears, his excuse sounded pathetic.

Bayo looked at him and laughed. "I am a big boy Remi. I do think I can manage being on my own while you go and answer that summons," he said, as he winked at him. "There are some boys over there who were drooling about your masked lady. I am sure they will willingly trade places with you immediately."

The boys in question were buff, muscular, and would give the Kupe boys a run for their money and they knew it. They made Remi feel fat and middle-aged.

No, they would not trade places with him. Remi hated competition. With that thought in his head, he got up and walked towards the opposite side of the room in search of Room 3. There was a code on the card which was meant to unlock the door.

It was now forty minutes since the waiter had delivered the note to his table.

Chapter 8

Remi tapped in the code for the door. He looked around the main room thinking everyone was watching him. He turned and noticed no one was paying any attention. Going into the rooms seemed normal on a night like this.

Walking in, the door locked softly behind him. Someone had dimmed the lighting, but it was bright enough for him to see that the room was set up as a living room of sorts. There was a sofa to the right, with various cushions and throws over it. Little baskets were dotted around the room, full of condoms. Man-sized cushions were scattered on the floor next to the sofa. Opposite, taking pride of place was a black table, roughly six-feet-long and three-feet-wide. The granite top gleamed in the gloominess of the room.

Remi did not want to think what the table was used for.

The plants scattered around the room took his thoughts away from the table. They were huge, tall, lush, and green; dotted close together around the room to give the illusion and feel of a garden. The plants looked so real, Remi could see droplets of water on the leaves. Looking up towards the ceiling he saw the stars. The ceiling was made of glass.

The setup reminded him of being in the Rainforest Café, but this was not a restaurant for food. This was a place for other hungers to be fed and savoured.

He cocked his ear. Somewhere in the background he could hear a waterfall. The only thing missing from this tropical tableau were the sounds of the animals that roamed the forest at night. On cue, he heard the croaking sound of frogs calling out to their mates to come out and play.

Towards the end of the living room was a door that led to what he assumed was a bedroom and bathroom.

The motif for the rest of the room was green. The walls were painted green, with drawing of trees of various forms adorning the walls. Emphasising the forest theme, making you feel you were in a mysterious place. There was a breeze coming from somewhere, the leaves on the plants were swaying gently in the background. A lot of thought had gone into decorating this room.

Remi wondered what it would look like during the day, with the sun shining through the glass ceiling.

Scented candles were dotted around the room, the scents of cocoa butter and chocolate were warm and inviting.

His eyes swept over the room once again that's when he saw her. The green leaf design of her clothing blended in so well with the surroundings he had missed her silhouette next to one of the huge plants, the first time he had scanned the room.

The masked lady was standing on top of a wooden ledge, next to one of the plants.

"You're late," her accent playing havoc on his senses. "You kept me waiting, that's a huge infraction," she said, as she kept her back to him.

Uncertain of what to say. "I wasn't sure," the words came out of his mouth before he could articulate a proper sentence.

Turning around, her mask glittered in the gloom of the room, eyes on him, staring at him.

"Sure about what?" she asked.

Remi kept quiet, staring at her, she was wearing a top that criss-crossed her taut torso; the straps crossed over each breast leaving her muscular torso bare, from which a red rose appeared. The stem adorned with sharp thorns, started above her navel with the flowers blooming from the cleft of her breasts.

The vibrancy and intricacy of the tattoo, made him wonder how much time and pain had gone into it. He did not like tattoos on women; it was a turn-off for him. The tattoo looked spectacular on her; adding to the aura of her being a Domme. However, he would be willing to make concessions for her.

Her shorts were the same green ankara design as her top, they stopped mid-thigh, and rested low on her hips. There were various pieces of rope and a whip looped around the belt holes of her shorts.

Her legs looked strong and lean, she reminded him of a mysterious forest nymph, standing outside her lair luring men in with the promise of food and a warm bed.

"Sure about what?" she asked again.

Remi was spellbound, and for once he was tongue-tied in front of a woman.

Confident, cocky Remi was lost for words. The masked lady was sexy as fuck, the voice, her attitude, and the room added to his nervousness.

Staring at him she asked. "Sure about what you are looking for? About what you know you need? What exactly aren't you sure about?"

Whoosh, the sound startled him.

Remi looked around to see where the sound was coming from, something went around his ankle. Looking down, a piece of thick rope was now tightly wound around his ankle.

The masked lady pulled the rope ever so slightly and used it to drag him towards her.

He didn't resist the tug as she dragged him, half walking, half limping towards her. Even though he was at least three inches taller than her, she still conveyed her authority.

Pulling him slightly she asked, "Tell me, have you been with a female Domme before?"

"You stared at that picture too intently for you not to have understood the dynamics of what was going on," she said.

Remi looked away and answered softly, "yes," as relief swept through him.

Finally, he had found someone who understood him.

"Where was that?"

"It was while I was living in America," he said.

"Your name?" the mysterious woman asked, moving closer to him, her eyes raking over his body.

All Remi could do was stare at her breasts, they were hardly kept in place by the thing she wore that was meant to be a top. From what he could see her breasts were firm, dark, smooth, and inviting; he could not take his eyes off them.

Remi licked his lips, he wanted to bite into them like a piece of chocolate, and feel the nipples harden on his tongue. The thought of running his tongue over the crease where the breast rested on her torso played on his mind as he stared at her. He was certain she wasn't wearing a bra, he could see the outline of her taut nipples underneath her flimsy top.

The masked woman, moved slightly. "Take your t-shirt off."

Remi swallowed nervously and stared at her.

"You are used to taking instructions, aren't you?"

"What's your name?" she repeated.

The woman sighed exasperated. "You kept me waiting, I give you an order, and you stare at me."

"Take your t-shirt off," she repeated.

Remi was frozen in shock.

Her eyes glittered with displeasure, she flicked her wrist, causing him to trip over the rope and he ended up on his knees, in front of her his face inches away from the v of her shorts.

Shock momentarily forgotten, Remi realized if he moved ever so slightly he could breathe in her scent.

Imagination wandering, he closed his eyes; he wanted to touch her there, use his tongue and lips to show her how well he could serve her and make her scream out in ecstasy.

The masked woman took a step back. "I don't think you will move any closer," she said. Pulling something out from her belt hole. "Take your t-shirt off or I will rip it off you and you will end up going home without a top."

The whip came out of thin air and she used it against the hard outline straining his jeans.

Shit, Remi thought as sensations long forgotten tingled and awakened around his body.

"What's your name?" she asked him again.

"For someone who has been a submissive, you are no good at taking orders are you?"

"Either you can't take orders, or you can't talk, which one is it?"

The masked lady shook her head. The sound of whoosh and the sting on his arse helped open his mouth immediately. The radiating heat felt so good as the blood rushed to his dick.

Remi hesitated for a second. "It's Adam," he said, as he pulled up his t-shirt.

The laugh was strange, it was so unexpected. "Adam mmm...," she repeated softly.

Remi took it off, folded the t-shirt and placed it on the floor between them. The cool air playing havoc on his body.

She moved closer into him, taunting him with her body. The smell of cocoa butter and chocolate assailed his senses, god he wanted to eat and taste her.

Remi was under her spell and he did not want to break it. Watching her, as she raked her eyes over his body again, now he understood what it meant to be objectified. Remi suddenly felt self-conscious, he needed to do more at the gym, what if she found him wanting?

Remi watched as she pulled another whip from her belt, this time it had a soft feathery tip. Using it to trace patterns on his torso, then she pinched his nipple sharply.

Not hard enough to cause pain, but enough to send a jolt of desire straight down to his dick and make him so hard, he thought it would rip through his jeans.

Oh, My Fucking God, he thought, *who was this witch* as he stared at her.

"I don't think your previous Dommes knew what they were doing, your eyes are meant to be on the floor." The sting of the whip on his dick helped enforce the message.

"You can only look at me when I say so."

"Do you understand?" she asked.

Remi looked down. "Yes Mistress," he said, his hard on getting harder by the minute.

"Well, at least you got that right," she said.

But looking down took his eyes past the thorns of her tattoo and to her pussy, he could still feel the heat coming from there.

His imagination ran wild with thoughts of whether or not she was shaved. Would she allow him to serve her that way by shaving her pussy? Remi found it a very sensual experience, but most women he had been with found it invasive.

Whoa hang on, he thought, she wasn't even his type and here he was thinking of what he wanted to do to serve her.

Remi's dick and balls on the other hand, firmly and heavily reminded him he was deceiving himself. If this woman asked him to lick her, he would jump before she finished the sentence. He tore his gaze away from her pussy and worked his gaze down to her legs.

They were strong and lithe, encased in green sandals with string straps stopping mid-thigh. Remi imagined those legs straddling his shoulders while he buried his face between them, sucking, and nibbling her hard-swollen clit.

The whip being wrapped around his dick, brought him back to reality. This time around he really thought he would rip open his boxers.

Damn it, this witch was good.

Suddenly without warning, she moved back and pulled away leaving him on his knees as she retreated into the shadows of the room she had appeared from.

Remi adjusted his gaze, she was now sitting on a chair hewn from wood, she beckoned him over.

The masked lady stared at him, "Take your jeans off and come over here," she said, as she sat back on the chair and placed her legs on a stool made from the same piece of wood.

Remi quickly obeyed her command and was out of his jeans in seconds. His dick jutting forward in his boxers as he walked over to where she was sitting.

The sight stopped Remi in his tracks. The mystery woman in the mask, had taken her top off, he could not tear his eyes away from her breasts and the magnificent tattoo. Her nipples had areolas nearly the same circumference of her breasts, her taut nipples the size of erasers he remembered from his primary school days.

They were hard, taut, dark, and long.

The only thing he could do was to stare in awe, he licked his lips, he wanted those nipples hardening in his mouth, while he used his fingers to tap her clit.

Picking up a bottle of oil, she said, "Take my shoes off and give me a leg massage," as she handed over a bottle of oil to him.

The label on the bottle read "lania.naturals". Remi moved closer to where she was seated.

Whip in hand, she said, "You are not meant to go past the hem of my shorts."

Playing with the end of her whip she looked at him. "Let's see if you know how to give a good massage," she said.

Remi bent down and unlaced her sandals, took them off and put them to one side. Her feet were tiny, a size four or five, her toenails the same red as her fingers.

Remi rubbed the oil into his hands, placed his hands on her legs and gently kneaded her calves, her skin felt soft and smooth. The higher he went on her leg the softer the massages became, he wanted to go under the hem of her shorts.

Would she count a happy ending as a good massage as his massaging got softer and lighter?

She sighed softly. "Don't forget my feet," she said, as she relaxed into the chair, her eyes closed.

"Massage each toe," he heard her say, as she made herself comfortable on the chair.

Remi ensured he pulled and gently twisted each toe, as he let the oils work its magic on her feet. Taking her other leg, he performed the same routine; Remi wandered what would happen if he gave her a happy ending.

Instead he said, "I have finished the leg massage Mistress."

There was a slight pause as he waited for an acknowledgement of a job well done.

Opening her eyes, she sat up and stared at him. "That was ok," she said finally.

Was that it was great, or it could have been better, Remi wondered briefly. For an American, her response had sounded very English.

"Is there any oil left in the bottle?" she asked. Her eyes were now closed.

Remi picked up the bottle. "Yes," he said.

The masked lady opened her eyes. "Good, stand up, remove your boxers and rub the rest of the oil on your dick," she said, as she watched him.

Remi looked at her shocked. WTF!!

"Stand up straight, with your feet apart and move closer to me," she commanded.

"No point wasting such good oil, it helps keep your skin smooth, firm, moisturized, and elastic," she said. "It's been specially blended for me, by one of the best aromatherapists. Iania is the best oil mixer around."

He hesitated briefly, but got up to obey her command, wriggling out of his boxers he poured some oil onto his hands as he watched what she was doing.

Remi was stunned. The masked lady took some of the oil and rubbed it onto her breasts, not sensually but practically, like putting on suntan lotion when hurrying out on a hot sunny day.

He massaged the oil on his dick; it hardened under his touch, he took his mind away from there and watched the masked lady.

For Remi, watching her as she pulled on her nipples and rubbed oil on them was witchcraft. The more he watched her, the more he imagined those hard nipples in his mouth, the more he drowned into the bewitching sexual atmosphere she was drawing him into.

"Do you like these nipples Adam?" she asked, her voice soft, and caressing, as she stared at him while tweaking the tips of her nipples.

"You're meant to softly and sensually rub the oil on your dick Adam," she said, as she stared at him, while continuing to massage her nipples.

Remi slowed the pace he was using to massage his dick as he fell under the spell of her low seductive voice. Imagining her hands around his dick, his tongue biting into those taut nipples, his dick pulsed in his hand. The spell was broken when he realized he had gone beyond the point of no return, he felt the tightening in his balls and before he knew it he came all over her legs.

Hot gushing spurts of cum.

He gasped, as he tried to stem the flow of cum seeping out of his dick, but he couldn't. The oil, the visual prop, her voice had been too much, as the last drop of cum spilled on to her leg.

There was silence, deafening silence.

Shit, Remi thought embarrassed.

There was a sharp intake of breath. "Adam, you have no self-control. I told you to massage oil softly on your body and you mess up my floor and waste my oil?" she asked.

Remi thought to correct her, the word body was very misleading. She had specifically stated his dick.

Damn, he thought.

Shaking her head in disappointment, her eyes glittering in her mask. She threw a hand towel at him. "Clean up my floor."

Remi thought she looked fucking magnificent, taut nipples, firm breasts, rose tattoo, and his cum all over her legs. *What more could a man ask for*, he chuckled inwardly.

The masked lady stood up and walked towards a door that led away from where they were.

Remi looked at her bereft, damn it.

Who was this fucking witch of a woman?

What had he done wrong? Cumming on her leg couldn't be considered a crime could it? She hadn't complained about that, she had only complained about him messing up her floor.

The masked lady said, "You can put your t-shirt back on, when you're done cleaning," she turned away, "then see yourself out."

With that she disappeared into the door and slammed it shut. What the fuck had just happened, had she been disappointed?

Suddenly Remi, wanted and needed to win back the favor of this mysterious woman. He scrambled up, feeling adrift, his anchor snatched away.

Her dismissal had been sudden and abrupt, Remi wanted to know why.

You can't rub oil on full taut nipples and breasts like that, and not expect a red-blooded man to respond, he thought.

Even a monk would have found it difficult; just remembering the visuals got him hard again.

Remi looked around the room, he wanted her, he had noticed that there were other men in the club that night who might pique her interest.

There was a writing table next to the sofa, he picked his t-shirt off the floor, and pulled it over his head. Deep in thought as he picked up and pulled on his jeans, determined to get serious about his fitness regime.

There was a pen and paper on the table, he wrote down his phone number and email on the off chance that she might want to see him again.

Remi sincerely hoped she did, otherwise he was going to look for her himself.

Chapter 9

Sam made some final notes on her case files and logged out of her computer. Clearing up her desk after a long day in the office; the session with her last patient had been draining.

The girl, aged 13, had been a survivor of great trauma, she was treating her pro-bono, and it was rewarding to see the young girl flourish after her harrowing ordeal.

Locking her office, she had a quick chat with her receptionist to go over her diary for the next day and headed out to drive to the gym. The traffic was light which pleased her. Sam's mind was on other things as she changed into her gym gear, three quarter leggings and a sleeveless scoop neck crop top that left her torso bare.

The gym was empty save for a few men on the cycling machines, going slower than the average 5-year-old on bikes with stabilizers.

Most of the men were all busy on their phones, typing, staring at messages or talking. Sam walked over to the weights area, where as usual was peaceful, quiet and empty. *It would be nice to have someone spot for her occasionally*, she thought wistfully.

Or just to appreciate seeing the muscle-bound guys pumping away with their dumbbells. She was onto her third set on the bench press when she noticed a man hovering near her.

The person was Adam, the man she had met at the club the weekend before.

This will be interesting, she thought. Her heart was pounding, she modulated her breathing to help control her voice. Slipping up wasn't an option here.

Sam got up from the bench, left the weights on the bar and moved to go over to the squat rack.

Adam pointed to the bench. "Erm, Hi, have you finished on there?" he asked.

Lowering the volume on her headphones. "Sorry, I wasn't listening," she said, pointing to the phone.

"I asked if you are finished on there?" he asked.

"Not really," she replied. "Do you want to use it?" she asked him.

Smiling at her. "Yes please, but I can wait until you are finished with it."

"It's not a problem, just take off the weights you don't need, and we can alternate," she said.

Sam went back under the bar to do her next set of squats, music blasting through her headphones. Watching in the mirror, as he got under the bench to lift the bar, he stalled.

Grimacing, he stopped when he realized he couldn't lift the bar. Staring at her back with a what she liked to call a 'what the fuck' face. Smiling at her reflection, she bent down and did a slow deep pause squat.

Shortly after watching the squat, he got up and took the weights off the bar.

Sam smiled as she watched him, it would not be nice to laugh out too loudly. *You're a tease*, laughing inwardly. After finishing her third set of squats she went back to the bench.

Adam was still on the bench press, but this time he was using the empty bar, he got up and looked over at her.

Shaking his head in amusement. "How can a small framed girl like you lift that much, and yet you don't even look muscly?" he said.

"It's clean food, clean living and I practice a lot," Sam said, nearly choking on the clean living, but covered it up as she waited for him to finish with the bar.

Sitting up from the bench. "I think I need to do that too," he said, as he rubbed his sore muscles.

"You just need to practice," she said. "No steroids and find your own version of clean living."

Adam got up. "Let me help you put the weights back on the bar. I am Remi by the way," he said, as he put the weights back on the bar for her.

"Nice to meet you Remi, my name is Sam," she replied.

Looking at her. "Any advice on how I can improve my weight lifting regime?" he asked.

"I need to lose this," he pointed to his torso, "and I want to be a bit more muscular," he continued. There was quiet determination in the words.

"Practice, practice, and try to lift more every so often. But you need to get your technique right first, otherwise you will injure yourself," she told him.

"Which could keep you out of practice, while you recover," Sam continued. Which she did not want, she needed this specimen in tip-top shape.

Sam ended up spending the next twenty minutes explaining and showing him the various techniques and sites he would find useful.

She watched him pack up his gym gear and walk over to a light-skinned lady on the treadmill; they had a chat and Sam watched as they left the gym together.

Hmm, she decided to compose the email and send it later, texting was just a bit too immediate.

Let's see how keen he really is, she thought.

Lost in thought, she wandered to the mat area to do her stretches. She liked rope and wished she had someone to practice her art on, it was erotic and scintillating for her.

It was times like this that she missed him, he had been taken away too soon.

Chapter 10

Remi put the dumbbells down and wiped the sweat off his brow, he felt pumped. He had been to the gym four times that week, the minute he got back home last week he had decided that he would get fitter.

The rejection from the lady at the club had rankled him, it was a feeling he wasn't used to. Remi was used to women throwing themselves at him.

The encounter with the mystery lady had made him so horny that after he left the club that evening he had invited a girl he had met online via @Joroolumofin's weekend hookups to his place.

He had fucked the girl's brains out, but for once he felt unfulfilled. The hookup had been all he wanted, tall and light-skinned, but he kept on seeing that masked face, with chocolate-colored skin, and it was that face that had made him erupt furiously into the girl.

The hookup in question, he could not even remember her name. Must have thought all her prayers were going to be answered, a single rich man who could also fuck well.

Instead, Remi had sent her home in an Uber and said he would call her. He wasn't going to, even though he had not promised her anything, he was sure his behavior would be gracing one of the renowned love doctor's pages sometime soon.

The first day after the club, he had gone to the gym and bumped into the dark-skinned lady he had been staring at the week before. She had been on the bench press and one thing led to another and they had started talking.

For Remi, watching her squat while he had tried to lift the bar off the bench had been a real distraction, her arse was loaded. *Yes, he had a predilection for arses, nothing wrong with that,* he thought. Imagining cupping her arse cheeks in his hands while...... an image flashed through his mind.

Remi shook his head to dispel the image if she wasn't so dark he would have made a play for her.

The dark-skinned girl's name was Sam, he didn't know much else about her other than she came to the gym a lot and they talked about fitness in general. He had been surprised at what she was lifting; she had shown him how to improve his techniques on the squat, deadlift, the bench, and somehow, they had been at the gym the same time the days he had come in.

Today he had his eye on the light-skinned girl he had exchanged numbers with the week before. She was on the treadmill and most probably checking out her likes on Instagram. Why did such people come to the gym he wondered?

Remi was taking her out for a meal, and he would be looking forward to fucking her later. He needed to empty his balls; that witch on Saturday had made him as horny as hell.

All he could think about was sex, he kept on hearing her voice in his head, he also noticed that his libido had increased. The weight lifting had pumped up all his muscles, including his dick. If he could not have the masked witch, someone else would have to help.

Yes, he knew his life was complicated, but it was just sex. He made sure he told his hookups that from the get-go, he wasn't interested in anything else. Which was why he rotated his hookups, fuck once and move on, there was no place for drama in his life.

Remi was about to go into the shower when a beep came through on his phone, from an email address ME_001@TLC.com he did not recognize. The title was 'Instructions'; he was intrigued. Clicking on the email to read the body of the message, he was being summoned to the club on Friday night, his dick hardened involuntarily in anticipation.

Yes, he pumped the air, pleased with himself for leaving his email address in Room 3.

Remi immediately sent a message to Bayo to see if he was going to the club, asking if he could tag along with him.

There were more detailed instructions making his eyebrows rise, which would not pose a problem for him.

His dick hardened, it was time to get that girl off the treadmill.

The weekend and the witch in Room 3 was a long time away. He had a hard on that needed seeing to.

Chapter 11

Remi thanked the shop assistant and walked out of the shop. Scratching his chin against the thick bristles on his jawline, shaving was out of the picture, the instructions received had stipulated no shaving, so he had left it and it itched like hell. But he felt a secret satisfaction and excitement of doing something she wanted and had ordered him to do.

Would he get the chance to fuck her that weekend? That's all he had been thinking about all week. The thought of having those legs on his shoulders turned him on, shaking his head as he wandered into the perfume shop to pick up his favorite aftershave.

Bayo arrived at 8.00pm as promised, the evening was warm and humid. Remi welcomed the cool air in the car as Bayo drove them to the club.

"Bayo, come on, spill the beans. Who is that lady? You must know something about her?"

Bayo looked over at him. "Remi, I go there to chill, unwind, and meet the movers and the shakers. I get to finish a lot of business deals, that is why I go there," Bayo said.

Bayo shrugged. "But I can ask around for you and find out who she is. But why don't you ask her yourself?" Bayo asked and winked. "You are seeing her tonight right?"

Remi answered, "Um I think so," and looked away.

Bayo laughed out loud. "Old boy just enjoy your time o, we are all consenting adults."

Bayo pulled up into a space in the carpark. "However, I heard through the club grapevine that there will be an impromptu show. Let's see what she is up to tonight," he said.

Remi's heart tripped, was he going to be part of that impromptu show?

After going through the checks, they entered the club, tonight there was a big table fully occupied by ladies. A few men occupied the other tables, *where were all the men tonight*, he thought.

The light dimmed, and the spotlight was on the stage.

Mistress Eve came on stage, the tattoo magnificent as the last time he saw it.

"Good evening ladies and gentlemen, as promised, I have a male subject for all you ladies out there."

Remi froze in his seat, he felt a sickening feeling in the bottom of his stomach.

Mistress Eve's glance fleetingly settled on him. The glance she had put his way had been like the cool harmattan breeze on a hot night, going down to his toes and the other sensual bits of his anatomy. The look was full of promises and secrets; he had to look away. Shakespeare was right, *the eyes were the windows of the soul.*

Those eyes transported him back to the room he had been in with her the previous week as the vision of her breasts appeared unaided.

Tonight, her lips were red and full, her arms bare. The mask combined with the pattern of her Ankara dress reminded him of the forest temptress that had enchanted him the week before.

Bayo's elbow on his ribs pulled him out of his breast reverie. "She wants you on the stage, my friend," Bayo said.

Remi looked around and at the stage, she was beckoning to him; he hesitated.

"Your day don come my friend, just don't cum in your boxers," Bayo said.

I hope not, Remi thought. The experience of the week before rankling him, he wasn't a teenager who couldn't control his urges.

But he had failed at controlling them the week before.

Remi looked towards the stage. "Me?" he asked, hand to his chest, as he raised his eyebrows at her.

Mistress Eve stared back at him. "Yes you, are you going to obey me or am I going to come over and drag you onto the stage?"

The table with the women cheered, even the men burst into laughter.

Remi could hear other men saying take me if he isn't able to handle you. Feet feeling like lead he stood up and walked towards the stage.

The walk to the stage felt like an eternity, then he was standing next to her, her scent assailing his nostrils, cocoa butter, chocolate, and this time he also sensed vanilla, a contradiction to the events that were certainly about to unfold. The curtains came down, and she beckoned him to follow her.

There was a comfortable sofa in the corner of the room, she sat down and stretched her legs.

Mistress Eve's dress rode up her thighs as she stretched, giving him a glimpse of her athletic thighs. The smooth, dark sheen of her skin was so inviting. It gleamed like silk, calling to him to run his fingers over the surface.

Bringing back the memory of the touch of her skin against his hands as he had given her a leg massage the week before.

"Sit down," she said.

Remi perched himself on the edge of the sofa she was sprawled on.

"I take it you got my instructions young man, otherwise you would not be at the club tonight."

Young man, indeed, he thought, bristling with annoyance.

There was no way this slip of a girl was older than him, she was just saying that to get to him.

Mistress Eve started sensually massaging her thighs, soft, gentle, lingering touches near the crease of her legs. "You don't like me calling you young man?"

Remi stared at what she was doing, mesmerized. The crotch of his trousers suddenly felt uncomfortable as his dick hardened at the sight.

Mistress Eve sighed, her tone changed. "I asked you a question. I could call you boy, if young man annoys you?" she asked, staring at him, as she stopped massaging her thighs.

"Why do you find it so difficult to answer the questions I put to you?" as her hands kneaded her thigh again.

Remi took his eyes away from her thighs. "Young man is fine," he replied.

Mistress Eve asked. "So, Adam tell me, has anyone tied you up before?" her eyes daring him to lie.

Remi whispered. "Yes," his eyes staring at the floor, at her feet. Today they were enclosed in what girls called fuck me shoes.

Only he couldn't control the fucking in this scene, she had all the control. Which wasn't a problem, he would let her fuck him anytime, anyway, any day.

"Look at me," she said.

Leaning in closer to him she asked. "Did you like it?"

Before he could answer, the rope came out from nowhere and he was on his knees again; she used the rope to drag him towards her. This witch was crazy, there was no doubt about it.

Remi was fascinated by her, as he watched the muscles ripple in her arms. He stared at them in wonder, then remembered to stare at the floor.

Remi whispered, "yes," as a slither of shame washed over him.

Mistress Eve knew what he was; she had somehow known.

Touching his shoulder gently. "Nothing to be ashamed about, Adam." Her voice was low, "We humans are complex beings, especially when it comes to sex."

Remi looked up suddenly, there was a deep understanding in her gaze as he quickly looked down again. She had maneuvered him he was on his knees in front of her in between her legs.

Because of the difference in height he could not see what was between her legs, he wished he could.

"I see you have been hitting the gym since the last time I saw you." Eyes lingering on his chest as she touched his arm and squeezed firmly on his biceps.

Pushing him gently away from her. "Lose the t-shirt and trousers," she said.

"Let's see if the gym has made improvements elsewhere."

The words were like water to a thirsty man, this is what he craved. Getting up from his kneeling position, Remi did not wait for her to repeat the command. Watching the rise and fall of the rose tattoo between her breasts as she breathed, the scent of cocoa and vanilla filling the space between the two of them.

"I want to see what I will be working with today," she said.

Mistress Eve stared at him. "Last week you were too busy cumming on my floor, I didn't get a good look at the rest of you."

Damn those eyes they were mesmerizing, Remi thought.

Mistress Eve oozed mystery and sex appeal. His dick agreed, making its presence known, his balls felt full, heavy and ready to drop.

Remi slowly took off the t-shirt, *damn* he thought *I really need to work more on my pecs.* Thank goodness he had started working out, the t-shirt was now looser on him than it had been the week before when he had been standing in front of her.

"I bet your dick is rock hard," she whispered. "I wonder what will happen if I were to touch it right now," she said, as she watched him.

Her voice was not helping, Remi was trying to control the blood flow that was giving life to his dick. There was a wry smile on her face as she watched him, she nodded slightly when he hesitated on his belt buckle.

"Today please Adam, our audience awaits," she said, with one hand on her waist, as she stood up.

Mistress Eve laughed. "What's with the sudden shyness Adam, you came all over my floor last week, spectacularly I must say."

"You were pumping your dick so hard, I bet you imagined it elsewhere. Somewhere hot, moist, and tight. Feeling those warm walls rubbing against your dick. The juices running down your thigh as you thrust up, deep, and hard hoping to hit that spot," she whispered, as she stared at his dick pulsing at her words in his boxers.

She hasn't even touched me, and I am ready to explode, Remi thought.

"What is your safe word?" she asked suddenly.

Her voice softer, she asked, "You do know about safe words, don't you?"

Remi whispered, "I do," while staring at the floor, trying to control the sensations in his body. As he imagined her on top of him.

Remi said, "Cassava." It was the first thing that came to his mind as his trousers came off.

There was a hint of amusement in her voice. "Cassava!" she repeated, as she stared at him in his boxers.

Mistress Eve leaned in closer and touched his chin, the stubble scratchy and brittle to her touch.

That slight caress, so unexpected only made him harder, gosh, this was hard. Chuckling to himself as he realized the pun.

She walked around him, her gaze was more appraising than sexual.

"Not bad, Adam. I hope you would know how to use it to pleasure your Mistress."

"Do you?" she asked, as she grabbed hold of his dick.

Jerking at her touch. "I can show you, if you give me the chance." Remi groaned, the words out of his mouth before he could stop them.

Remi's dick hardened at those words, *shit* he thought.

"Really?" she asked, as she put her hand in his boxers, her fingers grazing the tip of his dick.

Gasping, he lifted his eyes and stared at her. "Yes, I do," short of breath. "Let me show you. I'm outstanding, you will never find a lover like me," he groaned, as she squeezed his dick tight he felt the pre-cum drip onto her fingers. Watching as she took her hands out of his boxers and licked her finger.

Mistress Eve shook her head. "We shall see about that."

Remi swiftly put his eyes back towards the floor.

She handed over a bottle of oil to him. "Put this on your torso and your arms."

Remi opened the bottle, it was a mixture of lavender, vanilla and something else he didn't recognize, but it was a familiar smell. Following her orders, he put a generous amount on his arms and torso and handed the bottle back to her.

"You can put your trousers back on but leave the belt off," she said.

He chuckled to himself; she had wanted to see his equipment he really hoped it met her exacting standards.

"Right, come on show time. Let's show them how to tie rope."

Chapter 12

Later that week, Remi got back home late from the gym, weary and tired. Luckily his mum had sent him home on Sunday with enough food to last for a week. Checking his emails as he put a plastic container of jollof rice in the microwave.

Work had been a killer day, an executive management board meeting that had gone on forever and decisions he had hoped would be ratified hadn't.

No one wanted to say yes to certain projects, no one wanted to be accountable if the projects failed. However, the fact that they were needed was glaringly obvious. Oh well, things could be worse, he thought.

The lack of sex was also making him cranky as he desperately needed to get laid. Saturday night at TLC, had been TLC with no happy ending for him. That fucking forest temptress had taken him to the edge so many times that evening while being tied up that he had been a hair's breadth away from cumming in his boxers. The pre-cum had soaked his boxers so much that she had told him to remove them and go home without them.

Yes, he had obeyed her command and had been commando thinking of her while Bayo drove him home. The soaked boxers folded into his pocket.

Mistress Eve had been so skillful with her ropes and that light feather whip of hers.

It had felt exquisite, with blood rushing to all his extremities. Mistress Eve had turned on every single blood vessel in his body with her rope. The need to fuck her had been so great, he did not know where his self-control had come from. Remi had left the club that night unfulfilled in the fucking department and without his boxers.

She had managed to get under his skin, all he wanted to do was to kneel between those toned legs and listen to her telling him how to please her.

No, he wanted to hear her scream his name, while he was on his knees licking her swollen clit, while he put his fingers up that pussy of hers. Damn it, as he felt himself harden in his sweatpants, rice forgotten.

Mistress Eve, that name really suited her.

The irony wasn't lost on him; she wasn't the type of woman he normally went for; he never went for dark girls.

However, none of the women he had gone for understood his kinky side. He knew deep down it was the reason most of his relationships hadn't lasted.

It must have been the mask he thought and sighed, bringing his attention back to the microwave.

Wandering into his living room, he sent a message to Mercy his 'Friend with Benefits' to see if he could wangle an invitation for the next night. Remi needed to have sex and masturbating wasn't doing it for him at the moment.

Remi got a text message five minutes later, the answer was yes, *she must need an itch scratched too*, he thought.

Mercy had made it known a few times that she wasn't looking for anything serious, so it suited him fine, they both knew how to scratch each other.

His email notification pinged, it was from Mistress Eve. This would be the third time he was being summoned, he wanted to know who the woman was behind that goddamn mask.

Chapter 13

Sam woke up to a faint light shining in her face, originating from the far-right corner of the bedroom, she turned over, the bedside clock read 02.05am. Somebody was in her room she could feel it, her heart pounding in fear. Sitting at the foot of the bed was Michael. He was smiling at her as his favorite scent, sandalwood assaulted her senses.

She had figured out ages ago that when she smelt sandalwood that meant he was close.

The scent had been his favorite aftershave when he was alive and used it to communicate with her when he died.

It did not surprise her, Sam had felt his presence at the club when she did the demo. Michael knew what her nerves were like when performing to crowds.

"Michael," she whispered, this was the only time she had ever seen him since he died.

Michael smiled, the light behind him getting brighter.

"Sam you need to let go of me baby, you are going to be ok. You don't need me anymore," he said, pride and understanding in his eyes.

"Michael, please don't go," she cried.

"Sam, you're still a perverse masochist," he chuckled, smiling at her.

"It's not your fault I died, but you're hurting and punishing yourself by holding on to that thought," he said, staring at her.

Michael's eyes were wet. "My gravestone says beloved husband, because of you Sam. You sacrificed a lot for me, and I will be eternally grateful."

The light got brighter. "Know that you have your own guardian angel looking out for you. Call me and you will hear me," he said.

Michael got up, blew her a kiss, walked towards the light and he was gone.

Sam felt the tears on her cheeks, her heart still pounding. As she put her hand to her face to brush away the tears.

Sam woke up suddenly, disorientated, and sat up in her bed, her head felt both heavy and light-headed at the same time. The back of her head felt as if something was trying to pop out. Heart beating erratically in her chest, she took a deep breath to calm her nerves.

Michael was here she thought, there was a faint lingering scent of sandalwood in the room.

Sam turned to her bedside clock; it read 02.05am.

Sam packed her gym bag and put her work clothes in another bag, she would go to work from the gym that morning.

The only way she knew of letting off steam, was punching a bag or lifting some very heavy metal. The hope and dream of having the gym to herself was shattered, when she found Remi doing chest presses with dumbbells on one of the benches.

Watching him as she walked over to the free weights area, Sam noticed that his technique sucked. If he carried on the way he was, he would end up injuring himself. It would deprive her of using his body and watching him jerk off for her. *Yes, she enjoyed watching and talking to them while they jerked off for her;* she acknowledged to herself. It was the closest thing to having sex with a man, without doing the deed with him.

Sam sighed, getting injured would not happen; by the time she was finished with his bodybuilding routine, Remi would give the Kupe boys a run for their money. In the meantime, she had to look after her property. Sam shook her head as she walked over to where he was. The guy had lots of potential and if she broke her vow of celibacy with anyone, he would be in the running.

Standing over him. "Hi Remi, shift down the bench and move your back down slightly," she said.

"Hi Sam," placing the dumbbells on the floor beside him.

Sitting up. "What are you doing here, so early?" he asked, wiping sweat off his face.

"I couldn't sleep, thought I would come to the gym and lift some iron instead," Sam said, with a wry smile.

"Do you work around here?" he asked.

Sam hesitated for a couple of seconds. "Uhm, yes. You?" she asked.

Looking down at the dumbbells, he said, "yes, I work at the Union & General Bank. Have a busy day ahead and thought I would get a workout before work."

Remi smiled. "Thanks for all the help you have given me, I have taken up a lot of your time."

"No problem, did you get my email with the workouts?" Sam asked him. She had devised a workout plan that would help build muscle and lose fat in all the right places. She couldn't wait to assess the results while he was kneeling in front of her or better still tied up groaning and begging her to cum. Yes, the possibilities were endless, as she smiled back at him.

"Yes, thank you so much," he replied.

"If you have five minutes to spare this morning, can you show me how to use the squat rack?" he asked.

"Mmm sure, no problem," she said. "But I think I should show you how to do hip thrusts first. Thrusts help activate the glutes before doing squats."

It will also help you thrust deeper while I am on top of you, Sam thought.

"Squats can be hard on your back if you have bad form," Sam said, pointing to the bench. "I always tell newbies to activate their glutes first like this."

Sam got on the bench and demonstrated the hip thrust, he was watching her pubic area with interest.

The morning had taken an interesting turn, she thought as she watched him practice hip thrusts with the empty bar. *Thrust power was a high priority skill on her list for a suitable submissive*, she thought. Training him to thrust her body weight would be fun as her pussy contracted at the thought.

Sam felt the burn of his eyes on her backside as she showed him the right technique for squatting.

Doesn't he realize that I am watching him in the mirror, she chuckled to herself.

After correcting his form, they took turns on the rack discussing the pros and cons of Buhari's austerity program.

Before she knew it, the timer went off, checking her watch, she needed to scoot. Watching Remi squat and thrust had made her hot and horny, she needed at least thirty minutes to shower, cool down, and change for work.

Picking up her water bottle Sam said, "I have to leave you to your workout I'm afraid Remi," as she looked at her watch again.

"Thanks for your time Sam, it's really appreciated," he said.

"Can I buy you dinner tonight?" he asked.

Chapter 14

Remi had found it very hard to concentrate when Sam had been showing him how to hip thrust; whoever had invented the exercise didn't like men. As all he could do was imagine her pussy thrusting up to meet his dick. The squats had made it worse fuck. *Boy oh boy that girl pack some serious arse o. He wanted to grab her from behind, handle the two melons in each hand and ram*, he thought. Yep Kanye West and Co were correct, a G-string would get lost in there.

Remi talk a deep breath and willed his erection to go down, luckily Sam had shown no interest in him at all, so hopefully she wouldn't notice his erection. For all he knew she might not be into men.

Having women falling over themselves to get his attention was the norm for Remi. The catty looks other women sent Sam's way while helping him out at the gym, was what he was used to.

Two voluptuous, light-skinned ladies had given him their numbers when they found out he and Sam were just friends, not that it would have stopped them if there had been something going on.

"Thanks for the invite, unfortunately I can't," Sam said, as she packed up.

Remi was undeterred. "You have given me a lot of your time and expertise, and I wanted to show my appreciation," he said, with a smile. His dick was also nodding in appreciation after that arse show it refused to go down.

"You don't have to Remi, I am working tonight," she said.

Remi looked up. "Oh, where do you work?" he asked, with interest. *Was she a woman of the night?* he thought. He had come across a lot of runs girls in his time. But none had come out to say they worked at night.

"At a hospital, I…," she stuttered.

"…So, you're a nurse?" Remi asked.

"That must be very grueling for you, I know you guys have to work all kinds of funny shifts," he continued.

Sam picked up her bag. "Don't forget to stretch before you leave," she said, as he watched her move towards the exit.

Mmm, I would like to grab that arse, he thought watching her walk away.

Unlocking his phone Remi went on to WhatsApp, he wanted to know if Bayo was going to the club that weekend.

Remi typed into his phone.

Remi: Hey, Bayo, are you going to your club this weekend?

Walking over to a mat to do his stretches. *ding* A few seconds later Bayo responded.

Bayo: Yes o, you wan go see your Madam again.

Remi: yes, but na she tell me to come on Saturday.

Bayo: cum or come

Remi burst out laughing at Bayo's message, resulting in a few disapproving looks from the other people in the gym.

Scrolling through his contact list he decided to text one of the girls from the gym who had given him her number. Getting laid was a high priority for him that night.

There was no point in letting a stiff go to waste.

Chapter 15

Remi had spent the last few days going around the shops looking for tight black jeans. Truth be told they were not that easy to come by for a man. However, every pair of jeans he had touched had created a fission of excitement and the promise of something mysterious to come.

Would Mistress Eve approve?

Who the fuck was she and what did she look like? He wondered what she did as a day job; the questions were always there whenever he thought about Mistress Eve.

Who was she? Where did she work? What did she really look like during the day? She liked her lists and instructions for goodness sake.

Remi needed to see her; she had appeared in a few of his dreams since that first night at the club. The need to fuck her and get her out of his system dominated his mind.

For goodness sake, how was it possible he had seen her boobs, yet he had never seen her face. If he told any of his friends that, they would laugh at him. Identifying her by those smooth muscular legs he had massaged wasn't an option either.

Damn it, one could hardly go around town, see a dark girl and say, "Can I look at your legs, please?"

He would be on someone's blog before he could even say sorry, not to talk about the police.

Remi had found shaving down there weird, he had previously read about men who shaved down there on the internet but had scoffed at the idea. Yet here he was looking for the best way to shave without leaving bumps because Mistress Eve had decreed it.

Nairaland, his trusted place for inane and sublime pieces of information had advised against using a blade down there. One had to look after the crown jewels after all.

Fortunately, while stocking up on his favorite aftershave he had stumbled across NAIR for men.

His pubic bone was now as smooth as a girl's bottom. The no underwear decree made him very aware of his dick.

There was nothing to shield it from his jeans, a good thing he had shaved, otherwise he would have caught his hair in the zipper of the jeans.

Whenever he moved and thought of what might happen tonight, he hardened involuntarily.

The lady in the mask had seen all of him, in his hard and flaccid glory, now she would see him hairless.

Later that evening, Remi stared at his reflection in the mirror as he put on a snug black t-shirt, his biceps looked pumped helping create the illusion of increased muscle along his pecs. He noticed that he was now standing straighter and taller.

Yep, he had to say he was looking buff.

Sam had also advised him on his diet, he had changed things around, he was not eating carbs late at night. His stomach was now looking flatter. In the right light he could even see a hint of a four-pack coming through.

He wondered what her story was; she had made no advances on him and she had shown no interest in him either, other than helping him with his workouts. The time he spent with her, had made him realize just how beautiful she was. Remi had noticed the way a lot of the men in the gym stared at her.

That wasn't surprising; she had a killer body, but she was not the most approachable person, Sam was aloof most of the time. Being ignored or not being hit on by women, was something Remi was not used to, he found Sam's lack of interest in him odd.

Bayo's message that he was outside took him away from his musings. He wondered how Bayo had even found out or who had invited him to the BDSM club. There was a lot about his friend he didn't know about.

"Do you know who Mistress Eve is?" Remi asked, staring out of the car window, as they drove away from his place.

"Not really, no one knows," Bayo replied. "I never really had any reason to find out who she was," Bayo continued.

They drove in companionable silence for a few minutes.

Staring at Bayo. "She told me to go to Room 3 again. What is special about room 3?" Remi asked.

Bayo shrugged. "All that I know is that there are quite a few rooms for couples to use. Each equipped with enough stuff to fulfill any type of sexual fantasy."

Bayo laughed. "Well, most kinds."

Remi stared at Bayo intrigued.

"There are actually quite a few married couples who come to the club you know," Bayo said.

Remi's head snapped back to Bayo. "Really?"

"How do you know that?" Remi asked.

Bayo tapped his nose. "Haha, I just know."

They pulled into the club just as Remi was going to ask him how he had found out about the club in the first place.

They parted ways as Remi headed to Room 3.

For the first time since he had been coming into the room, the wall to his right had opened and revealed a rack that held a multitude of accoutrements, some of which he had never seen before. Bayo's words came back to him.

When he had gone to the clubs in New York, most of the things on the wall came with the territory. The sight of them here filled him with a nervous excitement and dread.

How far would this mysterious woman push him tonight? He was going to find out who she was and unmask her. Was she married, single, or attached, he wondered.

He was going to do his best to win her over if she wasn't married. Remi would marry her first and get to know her after, he knew he might never meet such a woman like this again. He would even pay four times her bride price, just to show how much he would cherish her.

Remi walked over to the table and ran his fingers over the granite. The sound of running water reached his ears he turned around, she had entered the room.

Mistress Eve stood there watching him intently, the mask was on her face, the same one she wore the first day he had met her.

Today she was wearing black leggings, black laced high-heeled boots, with a black sequined crop tank top.

She had something about showing off that magnificent tattoo, she never covered it up. The clothes molded to her body like a second skin; she looked phenomenal, the muscles in her stomach rippled as she moved towards him.

"Good evening, Mistress Eve," he said, as he lowered his eyes, involuntarily lingering on the v between her thighs.

She stared at him as she walked towards the wall, her hand lingering on a whip which she picked up as she moved closer to him.

The scent of cocoa butter assaulted his nostrils, he just wanted to take away every piece of her clothing, taste her and revel in that cocoa scent.

The sting of the whip on his balls brought his attention back to her.

"My instructions were t-shirt off and to lie on the table," she said. "Why aren't you?" she asked, as the whip gently wrapped around his balls once again.

This time his dick hardened more, making his balls feel heavy, tight, and full.

Moving closer to him she used the tip of the whip to trace the hardness pressing painfully against his jeans. Her scent intoxicated him as he watched her use the whip to tease him mercilessly.

Mistress Eve stared at his hard dick. "Remember you can always say cassava if it gets too much for you."

Running her fingers over the outline. "Very impressive... Adam," staring at him, tightening her grip on his girth. She loosened her grip and gently caressed the ridge of his dick through the fabric of his jeans.

Remi groaned, his jeans were too tight at the crotch, it was too much to bear, Remi put his hand over hers, and looked up into her eyes.

Mistress Eve paused, staring at him. "Do you want me to stop making your dick hard for me?" she asked, as she squeezed him hard.

He took a deep breath and shook his head, lowering his eyes down once again. Remi was sweating as the urge to cum consumed him, he didn't want to.

She whispered softly. "Do you know how to use it Adam?" she asked, staring at him. Caressing his hard-on through his jeans. "Do you know how to fuck Adam?" she asked, this time squeezing his dick hard.

The whip came out of nowhere once again grabbing his balls in a vice grip. She must have been a cowgirl in a previous life he thought as he felt the grip on his balls once again.

Remi looked up at her, she was staring at him hands on her hips.

"I want that t-shirt off and you on that table before I count to three."

Looking towards the wall, most probably searching for another implement to torture him with.

Remi quickly pulled his t-shirt over his head.

Chapter 16

"Why did you come back here Adam?" she asked, suddenly turning away from the implements of his impending torture.

Remi hesitated; he had been taking his t-shirt off as per her instructions.

This lady knew how to ask questions, they were some he couldn't answer. The truth was, he had been looking for a strong, kinky, dominant woman for a long time.

Forever he would say, once he had opened that veritable pandora's box of kinks, he had been looking for the right woman who would know how to press those buttons.

It had been serendipitous to find one right here on his doorstep.

Hence, this was one opportunity he would follow through and see where it led. Taking risks was what he did for a living and this was one he wasn't averse to.

Remi grinned. "You summoned me to come here and I could not say no. I am here to serve you Mistress," as he lowered his eyes, trying not to focus on the rose between her breasts.

"That's not a real answer Adam, I could grab one guy out there and he would tell me the same thing."

"Why?" she asked again.

"Maybe I am wasting my time, I believe this is a game to you."

"I have been looking for a Mistress to serve. I want you to be my Mistress," he whispered.

"I am asking you again Adam, why?"

Mistress Eve moved closer. "You haven't answered the question."

"You have given me a bullshit answer someone else might buy. You still haven't answered the real question Adam."

Picking up the whip. "Why are you here?" staring at him. Sighing as she moved away.

Remi noticed the imperceptible change in her body language, she was about to walk out. Panicking, he did not want her to leave the room.

Mistress Eve put the whip down. "I might as well summon one of the guys out there, I know they will give me a real answer."

Remi couldn't bear that thought, no.

Remi whispered. "I enjoy being dominated sexually by a woman," his cheeks burning with the admission.

Remi hoped that she had picked up on the preference, he thought wryly. He had limits. This was the first time he had ever vocalized his submissiveness in front of anyone, the admission made him feel wary.

Mistress Eve sighed. "Now we are getting somewhere."

"Was that so hard to admit?" she asked.

Remi looked up and nodded, he could not meet her gaze.

"Have you been with a Mistress or female Domme before?" she asked. Moving closer to him, her scent was intoxicating, he really wanted her.

"And..." her eyes glaring.

"Yes, I have been with quite a few Dommes, most of our encounters were for one scene. I did not build a connection with most of them." Remi whispered. "Apart from one mistress that was for three scenes, but I didn't feel comfortable with her," he said, as he looked down. Not wanting to meet her eyes.

The masked lady moved closer. "Why?" she asked.

Mistress Eve still hadn't picked up the whip, her nearness was affecting him.

Remi looked up briefly. "She was a sadist masquerading as a Domme, enjoyed inflicting real pain and some scenes made me very uncomfortable." His eyes were back staring at the floor.

"She also liked to stress the racial differences between us during play. It stopped me from connecting with her," Remi said, his eyes still not meeting hers.

Remi was finding the conversation difficult, baring his sexual soul to a woman he hardly knew.

Mistress Eve placed a hand on his shoulder. "Is that why you were seething when I called you boy the other day?" she asked.

Remi felt a wave of gratitude come over him; she had noticed, she had known. He nodded.

"What are your hard limits?" she asked.

Remi paused, he wasn't expecting anything dangerous from her. "Erm, none," he responded.

Mistress Eve stared at him. "Are you sure Adam? Everyone has a limit, a line they will not cross."

Remi wondered what kind of job she did in the real world. Mistress Eve sure knew how to probe.

"I am sure," he replied.

Taking her hand off his shoulder. "Did your scenes involve sex?" she asked.

Remi paused for a minute, what kind of question was that?

"Always," he replied, remembering scenes he had been in. He had always enjoyed the sex after that was the whole aim wasn't it? Hot sex after all the fun and games.

"Did your Domme share you with anyone else?"

Remi paused again, he did not want to answer that question.

Remi wondered if she had been the off screen Domme in that picture he had been so fascinated with, on that first day at the club.

Mistress Eve was intuitive, inquisitive, but she was still a mysterious witch.

Making his confession to her had made him feel vulnerable and it was a good thing the mask hid her face.

Mistress Eve was sexy, dominant, and from what he could tell Nigerian. Making him more determined than ever to make this woman his Mistress, he was going to find out who she was and worship at her temple.

But first he had to unmask her.

Chapter 17

Remi watched as she walked back to the wall of torture, stopped by the table and opened a drawer placing a bottle of oil on the surface.

Mistress Eve's eyes glittered behind the mask. "You still have your t-shirt on Adam."

"For that infraction, I want everything off," she turned to him, hands on hips.

Throwing the bottle of oil at him. "Rub that all over your body," she said, walking back to the wall.

The oil was the same he had massaged into her legs, used to cum on her floor, and the night she had used him as a subject for her ropes. Vanilla, lavender, and the other scent he still couldn't place.

Taking your clothes off in the throes of passion was one thing, being told when to take them off and being watched critically was something else.

Especially when the woman watching you was her, the mysterious queen of Room 3, appraising a prime male specimen for her pleasure.

However, undressing and being scrutinized by her was a lesson in sensuality it made him hard.

Remi decided he would put on a show for her, a striptease. Starting with his t-shirt, he tried to think of the moves Kevin Hart had made in Think Like a Man 2. That foray into stripping had ended in disaster in the film, reminding himself, chuckling silently.

Remi massaged the oil on his chest and arms slowly and sensually, the crotch of his trousers was getting so tight it was now uncomfortable.

His arousal was obvious to see.

"You didn't answer my earlier question," she said.

Remi felt reluctant to answer that last question, he wasn't willing to give her an answer, he knew she might punish him for the omission.

Bending down, he slipped off his loafers, stood up again, rubbed more oil on his stomach and moved his hand towards the buckle of his belt, as he imagined her nails, raking a path down his pelvic bone.

His trousers came off in one fluid movement. Woody, his nickname for his dick, stood proud, erect, and ready for action.

"Do that last," she said, she was now sitting on a sofa next to the open wall of torture.

"Considering what has happened in the past."

Mistress Eve stretched her legs wide apart in front of her, his eyes were drawn to the valley between her legs.

Remi massaged the oil on his thighs and legs, each sensual stroke heightening his arousal, a drop of pre-cum dripped onto the floor.

"Oh, dear Adam, not again," she said, shaking her head.

She had seen it, his cheeks burned.

"Massage the oil on your dick, do it slowly and sensually, such tasks are not meant to be rushed. Keep at it for… mmm…," she paused. A finger on her lips as she stared at him intently.

Taking her finger away. "Three minutes, you must not cum Adam," she said. "You need to learn self-control."

"I am sure you can manage that Adam."

Chapter 18

"Oh my God," Remi thought. Staring as she widened her legs on the sofa, her hands caressing her thighs.

"Adam making you put oil on your body while I sit here doing nothing, may not do much for you," she said.

Caressing her thighs and asking him to massage oil slowly on this dick was doing a fucking lot, he thought.

Mistress Eve was a witch and a tease. His mind momentarily wondered if he would see those magnificent breasts again tonight.

"Men aren't complicated when it comes to sexual stimulation. Create an erotic image for a woman, by the written word or a sexy voice and she will become wet."

"Men however, need visuals," she said, as the hand caressing her thigh moved up near the spot he had been dreaming of touching, near the crease of her thighs.

Remi watched as she put one hand into the band of her leggings. "Are you imagining your hands here Adam?" she asked, as he watched her move her fingers in her leggings. "Or better still, are you wanting to kneel in front of your Mistress with your tongue on her hard-throbbing clit, as her juices run onto your lips?"

"Which one do you want Adam, or which one do you need?" she asked, as she took her finger out of her leggings and put a finger in her mouth. Sucking the juices off her finger.

Remi wondered if she was trying to keep his mind occupied to stop him from prematurely ejaculating if so, she was wrong.

Woody had jerked at the word visuals and more so at her questions.

Shit…it was doing a heck of a lot of jerking.

Remembering that first night watching her, as she had spread oil all over her magnificent breasts, as if it had been nothing.

Woody pulsed as if someone had passed an electric current through it. His balls felt heavy, tight, and were ready to drop at any moment.

What kind of woman was this? She was a witch. He needed to give her another name, The Witch.

A mysterious seductress ready to suck the life source out of him. *Wrong turn of phrase*, he thought ruefully.

I can do it, all I must do is think of something else, to take my mind off the task at hand.

Shit, it was in his hand as Woody got harder.

Damn, it was getting harder for him to control the sensations running through him.

Remi should have looked away from the couch to help keep his mind focused. The wall, the instruments, anything to take his mind away from the scene she was playing out in front of him. But he made a mistake, he watched her as she caressed her thigh with one hand and the other hand back in the crotch of her leggings, the whole time she was staring at him intently.

It should be his hands inside those leggings, his tongue on what he knew would be a hard-throbbing clit. His dick pumping into that pussy fucking her so hard that she would feel it in her throat, their juices cuming together.

Not wasted and seeping in his hand instead. "Shit." He had broken her rule, carried away by the visuals she had so skillfully laid out.

Damn. He hadn't lasted two minutes, his legs felt weak.

What punishment would he get for this infraction?

Chapter 19

Remi cursed softly under his breath as he looked at the mess in his hands and on the floor. Her laugh travelled over to Remi as she watched him cringe in embarrassment.

Shaking her head, she said, "You have messed up my floor Adam, yet again." Pulling a box from underneath the sofa she was sitting on.

The masked lady threw over a warm hand towel to him. "Clean yourself up, your mess, and put the towel over there," she said, pointing to a wooden box next to the table.

Remi caught the towel and wiped himself down.

Mistress Eve stared at the ceiling, the mask glittering in the gloom. "Then get yourself on that table." Looking at the hook dangling above the table. "I want you on your knees," she said.

Oh no, Remi thought.

What the fuck is she going to do with that hook, walking over to the table, watching her. His heart rate increased in fear.

Mistress Eve said, "I hope you got a good amount of the oil on to your body. Since you used most of it there instead," pointing to Woody.

That was all the attention it needed, coming back alive again.

"So, did you?" she asked.

"Hmm, yes I did," Remi said, staring back, getting bolder.

"I hope you did, otherwise you will be in a lot of pain tomorrow from chaffing," she said.

Remi was feeling wary and nervous, the way she had looked at the hook hanging from the ceiling made his heart skip a beat. Cuming all over his hands for her made Remi bold. "So how do you want me on the table?" his tone playful.

Mistress Eve stared at him. "I want you kneeling down, with your wrists behind you on your back and your arse in the air."

Remi stared at her, afraid of what she was about to do to him. Yepa!!

Opening a drawer, she pulled out a blindfold and deftly covered his eyes. Cheating was out of the picture, whoever had designed the blindfold knew what they were doing. It was as black as night.

"Keep still."

Remi felt something warm on his back, it must have been the oil as she massaged his back. Her hands were soft, soothing, and relaxing, until she massaged his arse, then her touch became firmer. He felt himself harden as she massaged, then stopped.

"Are you afraid of heights Adam?" she asked, concern coming through her voice.

Remi tried to figure out where her voice was coming from. "Umm no, don't think so," he replied.

Whoosh, by the time Remi had processed what the sound was, there was a sharp sting on his arse.

Remi gasped, took a deep breath, and flinched, the sting wasn't painful it was unexpected. He had gone from having a soothing arse massage to a spank, the rush of blood and the tingling on the surface made him jerk forward.

With each lash of the whip, she softly caressed his arse, and with each caress the agony of his hard-on increased.

"Adam you have such a delectable arse, next time you're told to be naked, make sure you are," she said. "I really like spanking this arse it's very responsive and firm," she whispered.

Mistress Eve suddenly grabbed hold of his dick while using the whip, on the area where the arse and thigh met.

The feeling was pleasurable sexual torture; she knew just how much force to use. The pain was bearable, each lash awakening several nerves he never knew existed, all he could think about was pumping into her pussy, with the force of need running through him.

The pressure was rising in his dick as her hand went around, pulling, and milking him. Just as he was about to give in, she suddenly stopped.

Remi was sweating profusely struggling to maintain his position on the table. *Maybe cardio wasn't so bad after all*, chuckling to himself. As his mind went back to the picture in the hall, the guy must have been trying to control himself from cumming. If what he was being put through was anything to go by.

Remi took a deep breath, thankful for the short break. A pair of headphones went over his ears, the dulcet tones of Barry White started crooning about 'The Secret Garden'

With his sight temporarily compromised, his hearing over compensated, listening and visualizing what Usher and Co who had collaborated with Barry White were singing about.

It was at Akon and Snoop Dog's explicit version of 'I Wanna Love You', that he stopped trying to get Woody to behave, when he felt the first piece of rope wrap around him.

This mysterious woman either had a PhD in male sensuality or she was just plain barking mad, every song on the playlist had him visualizing exactly what he wanted to do to her.

Mistress Eve was wrong, men in the right circumstances got turned on by words, most especially if you had a jet-black blindfold on.

Remi could feel her, smell her, sense her, as she wound the ropes around him. His skin was super-sensitized and stimulated, the lack of sight heightened his arousal as his brain and imagination went into sexual overdrive.

This was sensual torture, the kind that if he were to be released would have him bellowing like an animal as he came into her. His balls were going to explode; he could feel the pre-cum seeping out again.

The witch brushed against him, at the exact moment the lady in LL Cool J's song 'Doing it again', started screaming in ecstasy.

"Very impressive Adam, your dick is responding all on its own to those lyrics," she whispered. But she did not touch Woody. "Do you want me to touch and feel how hard you are?" she asked.

"Please," he whispered.

Mistress Eve asked, "Please what Adam?" the voice coming from somewhere behind him.

"I need to cum," he whispered.

He moved his knees. "Do you want me to lick you?" he asked, groaning.

"Please Mistress Eve or let me show you how good I can fuck your pussy," he growled, in frustration.

She sighed into his ear. "Adam, where is your self-control. It's not all about fucking you know," she whispered, tickling his balls.

Suddenly he felt a pull on his wrists, he was being pulled up. The need to cum was temporarily forgotten.

Remi panicked, *his arms were going to come off* he thought. But miraculously they didn't, instead the pulling motion enhanced the feeling of lightness and sensuality.

The mysterious woman had him bound in such a way, that the ropes stimulated his pressure points, it felt like he was being given a full body sensual massage.

Mistress Eve pulled the headphones off as he was drifting away to another song.

"Wow, Adam you look sensational," she said.

Remi could pick up on the nuances in her voice, she was excited.

Mistress Eve stroked his torso sensually. "I am going to take off your blindfold and I want you to look in the mirror in front of you."

Chapter 20

Remi had to blink a few times to help his eyes get accustomed to the gloom of the room.

He *was* dangling in the air by the hook all right, oh my fucking god. A temporary wave of panic engulfed him, it was very disconcerting. Remi was perfectly balanced in the air; the hook was looped through a knot that intersected between his hands and feet.

Remi took a deep breath to calm his nerves. *God no go help you here,* his inner voice responded.

But chai, this woman was crazily brilliant or brilliantly crazy, he thought staring at his reflection.

The image staring back at Remi, reminded him of the human art pieces seen in galleries and city centers. He had to say it himself; he looked sensational even if he felt strange and disorientated. *If only he could take a selfie*, chuckling to himself.

Remi realized at that moment he was dealing with a woman who really was passionate about rope. The masked lady was a genius, the right photographer would win awards using her work. The intricate designs and knots showed someone who knew and loved their art. *Scrap that*, he thought, *this woman knew and understood the mystic art of tying rope, it was beautiful, erotic, and sensual.*

She had balanced the knots in such a way that his body was balanced perfectly as it gently swayed from the hook.

Remi made a mental note, he was going on Google to research on her and rope. Every slight movement he made felt like someone was giving him a soothing, gentle massage.

However, Woody jutted out obscenely, making his presence known and felt in the whole sensual proceedings.

Or maybe it was because it had noticed first, before his eyes did, that she had changed out of the black leggings and top.

The masked lady was wearing a flowing dress instead; the sweat was still pouring off her. It must have taken a lot of strength to tie and pull him up on her own.

This mysterious woman was kinky as hell, and strong, he thought, a very deadly combination.

They stared at each other for one minute before Remi lowered his gaze, her eyes too knowing and penetrating for him to bear in his bound state.

She touched his shoulder. "I have saved the rest of your punishment for next time."

Arching her brow. "You did not answer that question. Did your Domme share you with anyone else?" she asked, taking her hand off his shoulder.

Yes, there will be a next time he thought, Woody was bobbing in agreement. Remi had been hoping that he could show her tonight how good he was as a lover to ensure there would be a next time.

Mistress Eve moved closer to him, her breasts raising the petals of the rose with each breath she took.

"I am going to let you down now Adam," she said, as she lowered him onto the table.

She put a hand on his shoulder. "Just relax as I untie you."

Mistress Eve unwound the rope off his skin, as it came off and exposed the skin to the air his skin screamed for a touch, a caress.

Remi's skin was on fire, for her, for something. But she didn't touch him.

"Lie down Adam," she said, as she took the last piece of rope off him.

"Get up and hold on to me, you are going to feel very weak."

The masked lady was right, Remi's legs felt weak his dick on the other hand didn't. Bobbing happily away like a third appendage as he held onto her as they walked to a door leading into a bathroom.

The bath was full; the lavender scented white bubbles promising relief for his aching muscles.

Pointing to the bath. "Get in," she said.

Remi watched as the mysterious lady took a washcloth and wiped him down, avoiding the lower section of his body.

Grabbing hold of her hand. "Join me," he whispered, desire and need racing through his blood.

A playful smile on his face. "Let me show you my appreciation, for not meting out my punishment," he said.

"You are very cheeky Adam," she replied, pulling her hand away. Mistress Eve asked, "How will you show me appreciation Adam?" her tone serious, eyes glittering in the mask.

Lowering his eyes. "Let me taste you Mistress," he said, trying to see through her dress. "Let me show you how good I am at making you cum."

Laughing, she said, "You're very confident Adam, I must say."

Remi watched her as she got up and placed clean towels on the toilet seat.

Mistress Eve stared at him in the bath. "Adam, I don't sleep with my submissive, my scenes don't involve sex with me."

The masked lady got up and walked towards the door.

With her hand on the handle. "Take as long as you want to relax and close the door behind you."

Then she was gone.

Chapter 21

Sam laid on her back relaxing in the sauna as she tried to soothe her body and mind after her gym session that Sunday afternoon.

The previous night at the club had been exhausting, physically and mentally. Watching Remi perform his strip tease had been a herculean battle in self-control which she had lost.

Watching him massage oil onto his dick had been sensual torture. She was sure that he had spent his sweet time doing that massage just to tease her.

Remi had been right she had been mesmerized, it wasn't every day that a nice, hunky, sexy man jerked off for you, while you watched intently as your knickers got progressively wetter.

Sam had found it very difficult to sit still watching him, which was why she had gone into the whole visual bullshit thing between men and women. It hadn't helped in the end, as she couldn't tell who had cum first, either she or him.

Sam chuckled, yet she had berated the poor guy about lack of self-control. She was going to have a great time helping Remi hone that skill she thought.

Sam had orchestrated all her moves to tease him and for him to lose self-control. He hadn't even noticed that she had used the movement of her legs to hide her reaction.

Phew, it had been hot to watch.

But she had snapped out of it, when she got up she had been as cool as a cucumber. Miss Evans, her old drama teacher, would have been proud of her. She had gone back into her character with ease, grace, and supreme-control.

Sam's trousers had become too hot and tight after that display, which was why she had changed into a dress, her body needed to breathe. It surprised her that he hadn't smelt her arousal in the air.

Her reaction to his visual display wasn't surprising, considering she hadn't done the dirty with anyone for over two years. Two years of inflicting pain on herself, Michael knew what he was talking about when he had said his goodbyes.

But she wasn't willing to soil his memory for a quick tumble, it wasn't her style. At this rate she would end up with no style at all if she continued along this path, she thought ruefully.

Or was it what she never wanted to admit, she was scared shitless of being with another man. For someone so dominant and full of vigor, most people didn't realize how insecure she could feel sometimes.

Sam sighed, hey ho, in the meantime she could visualize and enjoy the show. Mr. Remi Adonis was the perfect specimen to help any red-blooded woman get back on the bike.

She had been tempted to self-service herself last night but had decided against it. There was nothing like the real thing, she thought, when you could take your fingernails down their back.

Mmm, she closed her eyes as she continued basking in the memories of the night before, next time she needed to think about what she was going to do to that cute arse of his. There were some new implements in Room 3 that would be nice to try. She laughed softly.

The workout plans she had written for him was bearing fruit. Remi was looking hot in his gym clothes, the longing glances from the other girls in the gym hadn't gone unnoticed by Sam. They were all the same type of girls she knew he went for, tall, fair, and voluptuous.

The door of the sauna opened, and the object of her thoughts walked in.

Chapter 22

Remi walked into the sauna deep in thought. Gosh, he ached all over rubbing his shoulder.

The original plan on the journey home from the club the night before had been to question Bayo about the Masked Lady in Room 3. However, sleep's embrace had taken hold of him instead.

Remi had spent the early hours of the morning thinking, aided with his early morning hard-on, of unmasking that witch of a woman and fucking her hard. So hard that in his own submissive way he would leave his mark on her.

The thought of her playing with any other submissive made Remi jealous. He planned on spending the afternoon back on Google, to see what he could find out about the club, the rope, and those knots.

Bayo's excuses were wearing thin and something told him Bayo knew more than he was letting on.

Remi went towards the left-hand side of the sauna and placed his towel on the hot bench. He looked around and noticed a figure lying down in the corner, a woman by the look of the swimwear.

Sighing deeply as he laid down and took himself back to the previous night.

The night had been physically and emotionally draining. When he had been active on the D/s scene in New York he had been with only one Domme whose scenes did not involve sex. That had been because she did not like sleeping with men, only liked torturing them; yep, there were a lot of strange people out there.

The other Dommes once they had seen the size of his manhood, sex had been on the cards. They even brought along female subs for him to play with while they watched. But they had also been into all kinds of other things he had hard limits on.

Although those things had been a hard limit with them, there were some things he would willingly explore with someone else. Yes, someone like Mistress Eve, the witch who was messing with his mind.

His testosterone had been on full charge since last night he needed her badly. The no sex decree had surprised him. Remi had not seen that coming. He respected that, it only made him want her more. Remi needed to know what her story was, he desperately needed to find out who she was.

Remi had been doing research on Google regarding rope, the sight that had welcomed him after the blindfolds came off had been breathtaking.

While online he had stumbled upon an image of a man, like his reflection the day before with the caption Shibari; he had bookmarked it to read later.

It was an unusual pastime for a Nigerian lady; it took a certain kind of mindset to turn that into an art and a sexual pastime. The pictures dotted around the walls of the club must have been the masked ladies subjects. Who had taken the pictures?

Who was the mysterious masked lady? The unanswered questions spurred him on to find out who she was. Bayo was going to have to tell him what he knew.

Remi had also tried Google to find out about the owners of the club that had led to a dead end. He had even googled Mistress Eve that yielded similar results, nothing.

Remi sighed, he had been with her three times and was still a mystery to him. He wanted to unmask her; wanted the opportunity to talk to her face to face in real life and see if they could take it to the next level out of Room 3.

That next level for Remi was out of the club and if he had his way, she would never come back to the club again. As far as Remi was concerned, what happened in the club, now needed to come out of it, into the open and daylight.

Remi wanted to see her in the sunlight, watch her eat, talk, get to know who she was. He needed her and that meant he had to fuck her soon as he was going out of his mind with need for her.

Damn it, as he remembered how she had rubbed oil onto those breasts of hers.

Remi sighed, even though he had quite a few girls he could call upon to help solve that issue. It was the woman in the mask he wanted. Remembering how soft the skin on her legs had felt when he had massaged her legs.

Come to think of it, how did Bayo find out about that place? There was no way in heaven they advertised, TLC was too discreet and too secretive to put up billboards stating that there was a new BDSM club in town.

It was a sex club, why would a couple go there? These thoughts churned through his mind as the heat of the sauna worked its magic.

Remi was curious to see what else was in those other rooms. He sat up and was rubbing his shoulder again when the lady in the far corner stirred and got up to stretch her legs. Giving him a good eyeful of her behind in the dark gloom.

She was about to walk out when Remi thought he recognized her. Was it Sam?

"Sam is that you?" he asked, in surprise.

She looked over her shoulder a look of surprise on her face. "Remi hi, fancy seeing you in here."

"How are you?" Sam said, as she stared at him.

Remi rubbed his shoulder again.

She walked over. "Are you ok, have you pulled a muscle?"

Remi said, "Hmm, no I don't think so," as he sat up and took her in.

Sam was wearing a blue and green one piece, but the designer knew what they were doing. It was sexy, and revealing, molding to her curves in all the right places, it had a low neckline leaving you wondering what the wearer looked like naked. She looked good in it, her skin that was exposed was dark, smooth, inviting, and tattoo free. I bet her skin will feel as soft and silky as it looks Remi thought.

Suddenly, I am being surrounded by dark chocolate beauties; he smiled at the thought.

"Ok, I'm just going for a shower, I will be right back," she said, as he watched her walk out of the sauna.

Remi laid back down on his towel and an unbidden thought entered his mind, Sam and Mistress Eve together with him. *Some threesome that would be*, he thought. Sex deprivation made for some very kinky thoughts, he mused.

He sighed and put a hand on his forehead, too much exposure to the club and being as horny as hell; since last night didn't help matters, he needed to do something.

Remi didn't want to go back to the lady he had met at the club who he had fucked for a night. She had been good with her mouth, but she had asked him for money after. Which had come as a shock to Remi, he had not realized that they were peddling their wares everywhere.

Mercy, his friend with benefits, was also getting too clingy for his liking. He was wary to explore that option. There had been an accident during their last encounter. Mercy knew the rules of their game and he was not ready to change them.

Wiping the sweat off his brow, it must be the similar skin, that kicked off his subconscious sexual musings, he sighed. As he tried to move his mind away from male based needs, wants, and threesomes. *Might as well try his luck with Sam*, he thought, *she had a body to die for. Her breasts looked phenomenal in the swimsuit.*

Remi went back to rubbing his shoulder again when he noticed Sam coming back into the sauna. He sat up as she opened the door.

"Hi, I'm back, can I join you?" she asked, as she sat next to him.

She looked at him, concern in her eyes. "Are you sure you haven't injured yourself Remi?"

"Where does it hurt?" she asked.

Down there Remi nearly sputtered as he caught himself.

Coughing slightly. "Mmm, I think I did too much on the free weights. But I am ok," as he gathered himself together.

He looked back at her, there was an amused glint in her eyes.

Remi put a hand to his chest. "I followed all the instructions you gave me. Like a good boy scout," he said, as he held up two fingers to his chest.

The word *instructions* sent a sudden shiver down his spine.

Sam laughed. "Did you stretch after?" she asked, as she stared at him.

Oh yes, I did. I stretched so much last night, he thought, *I came on the floor.*

Shit, his mind was wondering and finding innuendos where none existed. Plus, she wouldn't understand or know anything about D/s play, she looked too straight-laced for that kind of stuff.

Remi noticed that she was staring at him intently, a good thing this room is dark he thought, otherwise she would see his cheeks and erection. He picked up his towel, wiped his brow and placed it strategically on his lap.

The lethal combination of her swimsuit and physical closeness suddenly made Remi view Sam differently, she was fucking hot.

Remi looked down at her thighs. "Um, yes I did. Unless you can think of any other stretching I can do," he said, as he smiled at her.

Trying and succeeding, he hoped in keeping a very straight face. *Damn it, he should have paid more attention in his drama classes as a kid.*

Sam took hold of his shoulder. "Here, let me show you another stretching exercise."

She manipulated his shoulder by pressing a few pressure points and voila the twinge was gone.

"Wow, thank you Sam."

Remi rubbed his shoulder, and the irritation was gone. "I think I should have you as my personal trainer. A personal trainer who also provides hands on stretching after a grueling workout. What more could a guy ask for," he said, as he winked at her.

Sam giggled. "Are you trying to flirt with me Remi?" she said. "I can show you what you need to do. I only helped now since it looked like you were in pain." A quizzical look on her face.

There was something familiar about the current tableau that he couldn't put his finger on, he put it to the back of his mind, and chalked it up to an unexplained case of déjà vu.

"Can I buy you some lunch today if you're not in a rush?" Remi blurted out.

Shit, Remi thought. Did that sound a bit too obvious?

Sam hesitated for a minute.

"It's only lunch Sam, I promise I won't eat you," he sputtered.

Oh shit. He needed to get out of this room with all the sex innuendoes going on in his head. Remi admonished himself.

Remi hoped Sam hadn't picked up on where his mind had been going. Something in her eyes told him she was considering the offer, phew, she hadn't picked up on the eating part.

Which showed her mind wasn't in the gutter like his.

"Oh, that's kind of you Remi. Where do you have in mind?" Sam asked.

Chapter 23

Remi watched Sam as she walked towards him in the reception area of the gym.

"We can either stay here or go to the Chinese around the corner," he said, when she stopped in front of him.

"Mmm, Chinese sounds good," she replied. "Are you ok walking, instead of taking the car?" she asked.

They agreed to meet back at reception as they went to drop off their bags in their cars. Something was nagging him, but he couldn't put his hand on it.

They walked to the Chinese restaurant talking about the state of the economy, the one conversation on everyone's lips in the country. They had ordered their meals and were waiting for their drinks when Remi's phone beeped.

It was an email from Mistress Eve.

Remi picked up his phone. "Excuse me, it's an email from work," he said, apologizing opening the email. Quickly scanning the message; he would have to reread it later.

Mistress Eve wanted him at the club on Friday and no cumming all week, however he was to take himself to the edge and stop twice a day, preferably morning and night. What the fuck was this woman into? If the request was going to pose difficulties he should email her with reasons why he couldn't restrain and control himself and fulfill her wishes. Feeling his cheeks go warm he put the phone down.

Sam looked at him. "Is everything ok at work, Remi?" she asked, "you look pensive."

"Um, nothing too serious, just the schedule for next weekend's cover," Remi replied distractedly.

Remi had been hoping that if he played his cards right, he might score with Sam tonight, latest tomorrow if he turned on the charm. Women could not resist when he turned on the Remi charm.

"What do you do?" she asked, as he put his phone away.

Remi hesitated, "I am just a boring analyst," he said.

"The word boring always implies hidden depths in a person, that they don't want other people to see," she said, looking at him enigmatically.

Remi squirmed briefly as the words hit home. What she said was true, he presented a well-rehearsed facade, there were hidden depths he hadn't revealed until *she* had turned up, he shook away the ghost of Mistress Eve from his mind.

Then he realized what had been nagging him, the third component of the oil he had used the two times he had been with Mistress Eve.

"What's that scent on you?" he asked, curious.

"The perfume I am wearing? Are you allergic to it?" Sam asked, the concern obvious in her voice.

"No, it's not that, I came across something close to it a few weeks ago and I haven't been able to place it. It has been bugging me ever since," he replied.

"Phew, I thought you were going to go into cardiac arrest or something," she said, as she smiled at him.

"It's jasmine," Sam replied.

Remi nodded his head. "I am sure if I went into cardiac arrest you would be there to save me."

"You're a nurse, right?" he asked.

Smiling at him. "What made you peg me as a nurse?"

"I have noticed your reactions, firstly when I was rubbing my shoulder and just now when you thought I was allergic to your perfume."

"Your concern for my welfare comes on automatically," he continued.

"Ah, that makes sense. I am a psychiatrist and psychologist," Sam said staring at him intently.

Remi was shocked and amused, he had jumped to conclusions. *I hope she isn't analyzing me right now*, he pondered. The appearance of their food saved him from more rumination.

Remi was the Chief Risk Officer at his bank; he was used to thinking about outcomes and taking the long view. That view was always based on probabilities and outcomes; it was never left to chance. For once in his dating life, he didn't want to string a woman along, however, being a man, he still wanted to keep his options open. Just in case down the road option one did not work out.

So, he added the unpredictable variable of chance into the equation.

Here he was on the horns of a dilemma, should he embark on the mission to unmask Mistress Eve or try his chances with Sam?

Remi was torn.

Sam was such a sweet woman, when you got to know her, even if she worked with some weird people.

"What are your plans for the weekend Sam? Can we do this again on Friday?" he asked.

The dice spinning metaphorically in his head where would it land? Heads or tails, in whose favor?

Remi waited for the answer to his fate.

"Unfortunately, I can't do lunch on Friday and I am scheduled to work on Friday night, and I am going away on Sunday for a convention. Saturday will also be busy for me," she replied.

"That's a shame," he sighed, quietly relieved.

"I really enjoy your company and thought we could get to know each other better," he said.

"You are single I hope?" Remi asked.

Sam picked up her fork. "Yep I am single," Sam replied somewhat wryly.

That's it, decision made, he thought. Fate and circumstance was pushing him towards Mistress Eve for that weekend.

Remi decided there and then he would see Mistress Eve on Friday, but he would make it his mission to unmask her.

They parted in the car park of the gym; with Sam telling Remi she would call him when she got back from the Far East.

Remi got into his car and swiped away the push notifications he didn't want.

Isis was making its usual threats to the people in the East and West. There was also more analysis about the Trump administration as he settled down to read the message from Mistress Eve.

From Mistress Eve,

You will make yourself available to me at the club on Friday. You will be there and in Room 3 by 9.30pm.

You will be naked, hard, and lying on the table waiting for me.

You are not allowed to cum before I see you on Friday. However, I want you to masturbate twice a day without cumming, in the morning and evening. I will know if you have and the ramifications will be severe if you disobey.

If this is difficult for you or you can't make Friday let me know.

Mistress Eve.

Chapter 24

It had been a cranky week for Remi; he had taken Mistress Eve up on her challenge.

Remi was curious and wanted to see if he could abstain for a week, he was competitive by nature and never enjoyed being challenged. Survive he did, but boy oh boy, he needed something from her tonight. The whole exercise had made him more aware of his dick than ever before, his balls had never felt heavier.

Bayo had promised he would pick him up that Friday, fortunately his guest pass guaranteed him one more entry into TLC.

Remi thought he would have to ask Mistress Eve how he would get into the club if they were to see each other again. Would she be able to help him with a guest pass or would he have to go through Bayo? Remi wanted to ensure that they saw each other again.

Because of what he had learnt, he decided to keep things between him and Sam friendly and non-sexual for now. She was too sweet a person to toy with her feelings in a haphazard fashion and use as an object of sexual release. Plus, the fact she was a shrink would enable her to smell his bullshit a yard away.

They continued to train together during the week at the gym. The improvements in his physique was all due to her expert knowledge on training and nutrition. The longing looks he got from the ladies at the gym and work spurred him on to continue.

Remi still did not know a lot about Sam as she mainly listened to him and never volunteered much about herself.

His phone beeped alerting him to the fact that Bayo was outside.

After the usual pleasantries, Remi came out with his questions.

"So Bayo, how did you hear about this club?" he asked, as he stared at his friend intently.

There was a perceptible pause.

"Um, Yomi mentioned it and invited me as a guest," Bayo said, concentrating on the road.

Yomi was a casual friend he had met through Bayo, whenever or wherever they went or were, Yomi always appeared with a bevy of girls. A player with a capital P and a very charming one as well; how he escaped all the drama from the women surprised him.

Compared to Yomi, Remi was a player with a tiny p. Remi could never keep up with whom Yomi was going out with, as the main girl changed every month. *Maybe he was secretly married*, Remi thought.

"Ah, ok," he said.

Still not satisfied, Remi turned towards Bayo. "Do you know who Mistress Eve is?" he asked, as he stared out of the window as they pulled into the car park.

"I don't know her Remi; I could walk past her in the street and not know her. I see these masked ladies in the club and unfortunately I don't keep a tab on who might be wearing one or not," he replied apologetically as they drove into the car bay.

Remi sighed. "Bayo I need to know who she is, she has been playing with my head."

"Not in a bad way if you know what I mean. I just can't stop thinking about her," Remi said. "I want to take her out of the club. I want to see her in the daylight, you know, do normal things," Remi sighed as he stared out of the car window.

Bayo laughed. "Shit Remi, someone finally got under your skin."

Bayo looked at him sympathetically. "That lady has got you all tied in knots, my friend."

Bayo stared at him. "You need to figure out how to unravel them."

They parted ways as Remi headed towards Room 3.

Chapter 25

Remi took his clothes off and folded them over the chair and went to lie on the table. The granite top felt cool against his skin as his mind wandered. The anticipation of what might transpire tonight had kept him on tenterhooks all week. If he didn't have her today he was going to ask for her mask in return.

In your dreams, he thought.

Mistress Eve looked like the type who would reveal the mystery of her identity in her own time and on her own terms.

The day dream about what he was going to do ended when he heard the door click, and the next thing he knew she was standing next to him.

The rose was as brilliant as ever, she must have had that tattoo done by the same tattoo artist Cheryl Cole had used. They both had used the rose motif. However, up-close Mistress Eve's was mesmerizing.

Her voice and accent never stopped bewitching him. Where had she stayed in America, he wondered and how had she ended up in Nigeria?

"Adam, nice to see you made it," as she moved towards the wall of torture.

Today she was wearing a green Ankara dress that clung to her in all the right places, with a deep v neckline, when she turned towards him briefly it gave a full view of what lay beneath. Remi was shocked to see a glint of a chain on one of her nipples; the chain was keeping her nipples stiff as they pushed against the dress.

Shit, she had clamps on her boobs, this woman was teasing him, Remi thought.

The sides of the dress were slit to just below the hips; showcasing her athletic thighs to perfection, they were on display for him to feast his eyes on.

The mask which always covered most of her face, added an edge of dark sexual excitement to the proceedings, his fantasy at that moment was to take that damn mask off her face.

"You were very impudent last week now's time to pay for that recklessness Adam," as she moved towards the torture wall.

Mistress Eve came back holding a harness that struck the fear of God into Remi.

Remi had seen such contraptions before when he had played at various clubs, he had never gone that far to allow any Mistress to put one on him. Never, that had been one of his many hard limits, where his safe word had come into play.

"So, tell me Adam, why did you come here today, here to the club I mean. Not the cumming you will be doing for me later," the amusement obvious in her voice.

Remi thought through the question, how could he answer? How could he tell her she had him tied up in knots since that first night he had met her? That he couldn't sleep without her appearing in his dreams that he jerked off to the memory of her face. *No*, Remi thought, he couldn't say that.

"I want you to kneel with your feet at least 3 feet apart and your hands laced together on the back of your head. No slouching either, breathe in, and chest out," Mistress Eve said, as she stared at him.

Mistress Eve looked down between his legs. "Remember, if I do anything that is out of your comfort zone you have your safe word."

"Mother nature has blessed you with a superb piece of equipment Adam."

Remi looked at the woman and shook his head in amusement, she was quirky. The way she had delivered the last sentence made him chuckle.

Mistress Eve stared at him, wondering what was funny.

"You haven't answered my question Adam, why did you come here today?" she asked again.

Remi watched as she pressed a button on the table; the button activated a pulley in the table and it lowered slightly, lowering him to her height and bringing his dick in line with her hands. She lifted and pulled his dick, making him catch his breath. The cool touch causing his dick to come to life as a drop of pre-cum dripped onto her wrist as she clicked the harness into place. The harness encased the whole length stopping short of his tip, it hurt just enough to take his mind away from cumming.

The harder he got the tighter and heavier it felt, but it also felt pleasurable bizarrely, making him very aware of his dick. Adding in the fact that he had been pushing himself to the edge every day, it was surprising he did not blow.

Mistress Eve stared at him as she licked off the drop of pre-cum deposited, from her wrist. That simple erotic action made him harder. Remi wondered what her lips would feel like around his dick. Warm, moist, and welcoming.

Mistress Eve moved towards him. "Today is all about control Adam, can you control yourself from cumming and can you cum for me when I tell you to?" her nipples taut, and teasing, through the fabric of her dress, the chain glittering brightly in the lights.

This woman was a witch, she had cast a spell over him and now realized he had fallen hard under that spell. Dick, mind, and body, he was seeing her in his sleep for God's sake. Remi wanted her to make him hers, he did not want her doing this on anyone else.

Remi wanted, no he needed to know who she was. He cleared his head; he was going to try to obey or misbehave by cumming, he thought chuckling to himself.

Staring at him. "What's funny Adam?" she asked.

Remi looked down and shook his head.

Mistress Eve used a whip to push his legs wider apart, causing the harness on him to lift and separate his balls. The whole time keeping her neckline in his sight of vision.

Remi was as hard as steel and getting harder by the minute. The music playing softly in the background helped keep his mind focused solely on sex. The songs were all about sex, orgasms, and how many ways to make their partners climax.

Focusing his mind on the music with the contraption on, only made him harder, as he watched her bend down. Her dress shifted up on her legs, he watched mesmerized as he looked and searched for her panty line.

Mistress Eve looked up and caught him watching her.

Whispering softly. "What's going through your mind right now Adam, tell me," as she brushed her hand against the top of her dress.

His arms and legs were aching, and his dick was so hard he could not think if it had ever been this way before. Scratch that, it had never been this hard before, he would have done something about it.

I want to fuck you so hard, he thought, *and make you scream.*

Mistress Eve asked, "Cat got your tongue Adam? Or should I show you what you want to do?" she watched him, as she slowly lifted her dress. Stopping just before she showed him her crown jewels.

Damn it, Remi thought. He had never seen the area between her legs as his mind went into overdrive thinking about it.

"What's going through your mind Adam?" she asked, repeating the question.

Remi knelt up straighter and stared boldly at her. "I want to see your face, I want to see the real you outside of this room," he blurted out without thinking. He knew the dynamics were different in this room, she held the power and control. Mistress Eve would decide if she wanted to see him, but Remi needed to help her decide in his favor.

The real answer he had wanted to say in his mind had been different. He had wanted to tell her '*I want you to allow me to give you pleasure, please don't let me waste this. When I could be serving you anyway you want,*' as the sweat poured off him, trying to control his hardness. Things had gone beyond games for Remi, he wanted the woman behind the mask.

It wasn't the answer she had been expecting; she went still.

Mistress Eve looked at him, her eyes appraising and something else he could not fathom. Her hand went to the base of her neck.

"Well, well, Adam, let's see how you serve my needs tonight and then maybe you might have yourself a deal," she said.

"If you do well tonight, you will meet me at the bar of this club in nine days' time next Sunday, at 7.30pm."

Pausing briefly. "I would advise you to get your harem sorted out during that time."

Mistress Eve ran her hands down his torso. "Then I will decide if I want your dick, mind, and soul," she whispered. "I didn't add body as that comes without saying."

Squeezing his dick hard and tight. "Think about this carefully Adam before I see you next week. **I don't share**, do you understand?" she said, letting go of his dick abruptly.

Remi winced in pain and stared at her, did she know him? He did not know her, he would have noticed her. He was going to make sure he helped in her decision making, nothing was going to be left to chance.

Remi would ensure she spent the next nine days thinking about him and only him. The same way he would be thinking about her. Damn, as a mental countdown went off in his brain.

Mistress Eve moved her whip between his legs, making him widen his legs and blindfolded him. She tied his hands behind his head and his ankles together and sensually massaged his back and torso. Remi relaxed a bit as he got used to his position as she played with his nipples incessantly, each pinch making him incredibly hard.

Remi was getting used to the knots he was kneeling in when she abruptly stopped the massage. Then he felt it, he jumped as her hands that were massaging him moved down to his back, her finger scraping at the opening between his legs. She steadied him gently with her hands.

Remi went still as her finger massaged his opening. *Oh my god, no,* he thought. Panicking, pulling roughly against his bonds.

"Relax Adam," she whispered, as she nibbled his earlobe.

"I won't hurt you. This is all for you."

"Relax." Her voice hypnotic and soothing.

Remi felt her other hand on his tip as she gently caressed the pre-cum dripping from his dick, she then moved down to caress his balls.

Just as her finger went in, the urge to cum came over him so bad he thought he would explode.

Remi jerked forward as he tried to move away from the caresses she was giving him. His balls, his taint, then his prostate, he growled.

"Please," he muttered, scared of the way his body was responding to her touches, her caresses. Every nerve ending in his body came together, joined up, and created a feeling so intense he could not describe. The need to cum was insane, alien and all-consuming, he no longer controlled his body. She was playing him like a violin.

Mistress Eve whispered, "How does it feel Adam?"

Remi felt as if his body was about to explode, the feeling was alien to him, how could he explain that to her.

Whispering into his ear. "Are you hungry Adam?" she asked.

The urge to cum temporarily forgotten as he tried to understand her question. The sweat poured off him as he tried to control the tsunami building up within him.

"No," he whispered, as she continued her torment. He was getting used to her finger when he felt a vibration.

The harness tightened, his urge to cum increased as she kept up the pressure, finger in, out, vibration, and the slight squeeze on his balls.

The harness was doing the job on his dick, she suddenly twisted his nipple harder this time. It was too much, he couldn't control himself and jerked as a massive orgasm ripped through his body. A thousand stars exploded behind the blindfold, he felt disconnected from his body, as wave after wave of pleasure washed through him.

It took Remi a few seconds to realize that the bellowing he could hear was coming from his throat.

My fucking God he thought, he had never experienced an orgasm so intense in his life.

Then she stopped; the vibration stopped as he felt her pull out; he fell backwards, her strong arms caught him, and she released the rope on his hands and feet.

Mistress Eve unbuckled the harness off his dick as he collapsed into her arms. Holding and caressing him, and he held onto her as he caught his breath and came down from the most intense orgasm he ever had. He felt exposed and vulnerable.

Now he understood how druggies felt trying to chase or recreate the highs they had. This experience blew him out of the water, the feeling scared him, she had stripped away all his fears and walls and had laid him bare in front of her. He had experienced the elusive subspace bottoms talked about, his fears were gone, the pain of hiding, and not being able to say what he was, gone. He felt euphoria, and an intense plethora of feelings.

Mistress Eve had made him her submissive.

But who was she?

Remi was sweating profusely, his legs and arms ached from trying to keep still while the witch had played with him.

This mysterious woman knew all about male sensuality, all the things she had done so far had never been to hurt, but to give him pleasure.

And there lay the real crux of D/s relationships, when a submissive met a true giving Dom, the pleasure was always for the sub.

Mistress Eve removed the blindfold he gazed at her, she gazed back at him, her eyes were glittering in the mask. Remi felt so open and vulnerable, but he also felt at ease with her. It was a hard emotion to describe.

Helping him up she led him onto a chair in the bathroom. "Sit down Adam, you will be feeling very weak." As she went to the sink, coming back with a warm cloth and a bowl of warm soapy water. "Close your eyes," she said.

Mistress Eve wiped down his brow, his hands, and ankles before proceeding to wipe his dick. Her hands soft and soothing, when she finished she applied her oil to his wrists, feet, and shoulders.

"Are you hurting anywhere?" she asked him.

Remi opened his eyes and stared at her, really stared, as he went through a range of confusing and strange emotions.

"I need to put oil on here," she said, taking his dick in her hands.

"Don't worry, just relax. This will help prevent bruises from the harness," as she rubbed the oil in.

In all the time Remi had dabbled into D/s play no one had bothered about his welfare after the scene, even when there had been sex involved.

Remi felt a deep bond to a mysterious masked woman whose face he was yet to see and who he hadn't even fucked.

It was all very strange as he closed his eyes again. She had given him the most sensual mind-blowing experience of his life and here she was cleaning him up; it was too much for him to comprehend.

Her closeness, her nipples brushing against him, and her scent soon sent his dick into an orbit of desire.

This wasn't the cocoa butter, this was her musky scent drawing Remi in, and it was driving him crazy.

Mistress Eve turned and was about to put the washcloth in the sink, when Remi suddenly fell to his knees, trapped her into the corner and put his head between her legs and breathed in her scent.

"Please Mistress," he whispered, as he rubbed his stubble against her thighs.

Remi heard her quick intake of breath. *Was that shock or desire* he thought?

Mistress Eve did not push him away, she wasn't wearing any panties, there was a fine sheen of moisture running down her legs.

Remi used his tongue, to lap up the juices on her thigh till he got to his prize. She was shaved bare but had a small landing strip on her pubic bone.

"Please mistress let me give you pleasure," he said, as he breathed into her pussy as he gently maneuvered her between the wall and the hand basin.

Remi used his hands ever so gently to move her feet apart. As he put one leg onto his shoulder, rubbing his stubble on her thigh as he did so.

Noticing that there was more moisture now coating the other thigh. Remi moved his head and stopped still as he breathed on to her pussy, making it warm, making it wait. He heard her whimper, his tongue went over her now swollen clit, her body tensed as she responded to his tongue.

The leg on his shoulder pulled him in, her hands went on his head as she moved his head slightly so that his stubble could graze her thigh again.

Her breathing was ragged, as Remi alternated between using his teeth on her swollen, hard, clit and his lips on her pussy. He lapped up her juices with his tongue and put a finger in her pussy while biting softly on her clit. Her pussy felt hot, tight, and moist against his finger as he moved it in and out.

Mistress Eve was buckling against his mouth. He could tell that she was close, she squeezed his finger tight, her muscles refusing to let him go.

Damn, his dick hardened at the thought of what would happen when it got into her pussy. Remi put another finger in, and her breathing changed further, she was close.

Remi moved his fingers in her, to the angle. "Please cum for me Mistress," he said.

Her nails dug deeply into his shoulders as he felt the contractions against his fingers. She pushed his head further into her pussy as if she wanted all of him in there.

Remi felt the contractions against his finger, as she arched her back, jerked over him and screamed, as the liquid ran down her thighs and into his mouth. Mistress Eve finally relaxed her hold and slumped, he held her as she came down from what he hoped was a powerful orgasm, her breathing was now ragged and shallow.

For Remi it had been beautiful to watch even though his head and shoulder was probably full of scratches. She had sunk her nails deep into his shoulder. He wasn't complaining he would bear those scars with pride.

Mistress Eve's eyes were closed behind the mask, her breathing was now steady. It felt so good carrying her in his arms.

In this relaxed state she looked so small and delicate. How could someone like this have him tied up in so many knots?

Remi did not know what to do, he wanted her comfort. Carrying her out of the bathroom he headed towards the other door he had seen, he wanted her now more than ever.

Shit..

He was rock hard, and the woman of his dreams was in his arms, the chain on her nipple was still hanging on even after all the thrashing she had done.

"That was very brave of you," she said, her eyes were now open, appraising him.

Remi looked at her he wanted to kiss her, he realized in that moment they had never kissed before.

"Put me down," she said, as she got to her feet.

They were now in the big room, near the sofa, the throws and cushions were on the floor. There were also little baskets holding condoms near the throws on the floor. *The owners of the club had thought of everything*, he thought.

Mistress Eve walked over to the wall and came back with a feather, very innocuous looking. Holding the feather in her hands, stroking it softly. "I like riding horses Adam," she said, slipping out of her dress and stood naked in front of him.

Throwing over a chocolate-flavored condom. "Lie down on those throws and put this on," she said.

Remi stared at her, this was the first time he had seen her fully naked. The rose tattoo was as vibrant as the first time he had seen it, the stem full of thorns till they gave way to the red rose petals on her breasts, one of them adorned with a gold chain. Was she going to sting him with her thorns before he got to the rose petals?

Mistress Eve was magnificent, he lowered his eyes and went to lie down. His dick hard, and at attention as he waited for further instructions.

Why had she mentioned horses, was she a cowgirl? Her rope throwing skills were phenomenal as he remembered how she had used it to pull him in.

Mistress Eve stood over him and straddled him. "Let's see how good you are," she said, twisting one of his nipples.

She stopped, gasping as she adjusted herself to his girth, the mask glittering in the gloom of the room.

"I am about to fuck you Adam, let's see if you can cope."

Damn. Remi thought, this woman was sexy. *Fuck me anytime* he thought.

"Don't you dare cum before I tell you to," Mistress Eve said.

Remi gasped, she was squeezing him so tight with her pussy muscles he thought he would snap in two.

"Open your eyes and look at me as I fuck you Adam."

Her eyes glittered behind the mask, her nipples swaying across her breasts, with the chain on her nipple.

Her nails scraped a path down his torso as he concentrated on matching her thrust for thrust. The witch was squeezing him rhythmically while teasing his balls, squeezing his nipples, and using the feather down his torso. It was all too much for Remi; he tried to get up and tried to dislodge her, but her thighs were made of steel, they did not move.

"No, Adam you stay there." Mistress Eve growled.

Damn, Remi thought, *he had found a tiger no doubt.*

"Look at me," she repeated.

Remi felt a heaviness in his balls, she was so fucking sexy; she squeezed on his dick again and twisted his nipple ever so slightly.

Mistress Eve's gaze on him was too much for him to bear, Remi growled as he felt the orgasm grab him and take hold of his body, the vice grip released as he felt her pussy pulsating against his dick inside her.

The juices ran down his leg, without thinking Remi pulled her into his arms and kissed her. The kiss awakened desire in him again as he touched her breasts and felt her nipples harden under his touch.

Mistress Eve's eyes were open as Remi laid kisses against her collarbone.

"Please let me see your face," he said, as his hands went up to the mask.

"No," she murmured, panic in her voice.

The panic in her voice was mirrored in her eyes, for a brief second. Getting up suddenly off the bed Mistress Eve picked up her dress.

Looking over her shoulder. "See yourself out," and she was gone.

Lying on the floor where she had been standing was her nipple chain. Remi was confused; was she disfigured, was that why she had been afraid to show her face? Who the fuck was she?

Mistress Eve had done things to him in one night that he had never experienced since he had become sexually active. He needed this woman scar or no scar, he wanted her.

Fuck he needed her, he wanted to be her submissive.

Chapter 26

Sam zipped up her suitcase and looked around her room to check she had left nothing behind.

The arsenal t-shirt was on the chair in her room, she stared at it and sighed.

Her mind wandered back to Friday night, she had not expected things to go that far, with Remi.

Sam had not been with anyone for over two years, and the idea of looking for anyone else had scared her. The thought of physically being with another man had also alarmed her.

Everyone around her had tried in one way or the other to set her up with someone, but she had always dropped out at the last moment. Mostly she had used work as an excuse, being on-call.

Her adopted brother had done all he could, he had said she was wasting away and would dry out if she did not have sex. He had gone as far as showing her an article online about a woman whose vagina had closed up due to a lack of sex.

That brother of hers was crazy as she laughed out loud thinking of him.

But who would want to go out with her?

Sam knew that in some parts of the country going out with a widow was perceived to be bad luck. So, she had resigned herself to being single. Using the pain of Michael's death as a shield, to keep people away and even Michael had come back from the dead, to tell her to let go.

Plus, her non-vanilla tendencies would scare most men off, she sighed.

Her pussy contracted every time she thought back to her night with Remi. *OMG!! No, add F into that.*

From having no sex in 2 years to that, had been fucking amazing. She had cum so many times she had spent the day after just drinking water.

Her brow felt hot, sure that someone on Google would say over-cumming did cause dehydration, or maybe it was because she got hot and flustered thinking about the night before.

Remi was sexy as hell, a sexual submissive and she had found him right on her doorstep. Well doorsteps to be honest, she had seen him for the first time at the gym. Then he had mysteriously appeared at the club. When she got back she needed to dig through the guest passes to see who had invited him.

Sam still had her doubts about the whole thing. Remi in his vanilla world did not go out with girls like her, she had seen the women that graced his arm and noticed the ladies he had something going on with at the gym.

Remi came from a very rich, prominent Yoruba family; the family money came from medicine. From what she knew about her background she was Igbo. The tribal feud between the Yoruba's and the Igbo's was still waxing strong, even in her generation. Remi's face always graced one blog, financial magazine or the other. He was a young whiz kid in the international financial world, according to reports he had left his job at a hedge-fund company in England, to join a start-up in Lagos. A lot of people had been surprised when he had decided to work in Nigeria.

Sam picked up her bible and opened it to the book of Psalms and picked up the dog-eared picture. Where did she come from? It was a question she silently asked the woman in the picture. Tracing her fingers round the woman's face, putting the picture back in the bible and back on her bed stand.

Sam picked up the arsenal t-shirt and unzipped her suitcase and put it on top of the rest of her things.

She sent a text message to Yomi that she was ready for him to take her to the airport.

Chapter 27

The incessant ringing of his phone pulled Remi out of a dream where he was fucking Mistress Eve hard and wild.

This time he had been on top, he had been about to cum into her when he realized it was a dream. Remi was drenched in sweat and when he looked down, Woody didn't think it was a dream either.

As a habit Remi always put his personal phone on vibrate, but his work phone was always on, especially at night.

That was the phone ringing, he opened his eyes and picked up the wrong phone in the gloom, there were 27 missed calls. He quickly picked up the other one.

It was Bayo's number on the screen.

Bayo?

It had to be serious for him to be calling on his work phone; he thought as he hit the answer button on the phone.

Remi put the phone to his ear. "Hello Bayo, are you OK?" he asked, half asleep.

He heard sniffling come through the phone, a sudden unease made the sleep vanish from his eyes.

Something was wrong. What could it be? A knot of dread grew in his stomach.

"Bayo, what's wrong, why are you crying?" he asked alarmed.

The silence was deafening, eventually there was more sniffling on the phone.

"Bayo, what's wrong? Please tell me?" he pleaded, alarm bells were going off in his head.

Had something happened to his parents, had something happened to Bayo.

More silence. "Have you seen the news Remi?" Bayo asked.

Remi once in bed never bothered with the internet, he had a routine of bed and a real book, to put him to sleep. Having read somewhere that the light from the phones disturbed sleep, so he had stopped it.

Most of the news sites he followed were news feeds that pushed notifications onto his phone. Had Boko Haram finally moved down south?

What the hell was going on?

Bayo sniffed. "Remi, you need to come to the club right away; there has been a terrorist attack in Japan," he choked, the tears were more evident in his voice.

An alarm went off somewhere in the back of Remi's mind; something was trying to come to the surface. He couldn't put his finger on it yet, but his heart was filling with dread.

"Remi, Mistress Eve is missing, please come to the club as soon as you can," Bayo said, as he ended the call.

Hold on, he thought, *how did Bayo know her*?

All the questions were put on hold as Remi got to the club in ten minutes flat, for once the gods were on his side as there were no police checkpoints, a good thing Nigeria did not have speed limits, as questions churned through his mind.

Remi had tuned into the BBC World service, while quickly changing and brushing his teeth, and heard at least 500 people were known to be dead and scores were missing. In the worst terrorist attack Japan had experienced in recent times. His heart filled with dread, he knew he was in for some bad news.

Men don't cry.

He had wondered why there would be such a big gap till his next meet with Mistress Eve. For the past three weeks they had seen each other every week. She had done things to him that night that even thinking about it now made his cheeks red and warm.

Remi was let through the main gates of the club, this time without all the checks he usually had to go through with Bayo when he went to the club.

Remi was locking the car, when it hit him, what he had been trying to remember. Sam was also in the Far East. He hoped it wasn't Japan, he would text her later to see if she was ok.

How could two women he knew, be in the same part of the world, London or America he could understand, but not an obscure place like the Far East.

Was she connected to Mistress Eve? Impossible, he thought, it's just a coincidence.

Bayo met him at the front door and they went into an office where Yomi was talking to someone on the phone. Remi could tell by Yomi's stance and voice that he was invested in the situation unfolding.

Remi was confused, someone needed to explain to him what the hell was going on.

How did Yomi fit into this whole situation that was unfolding? Yomi was walking around the room they were in with the ease of familiarity and authority.

Remi looked around the office they were in, it was furnished in browns and black; it was a very masculine office. There was a bank of CCTVs on one wall that covered every inch of the premises.

Were the rooms also being monitored? He hoped not, his cheeks suddenly feeling warm.

The snippets of the conversation and authority in Yomi's voice made him realize that there was a lot going on that he wasn't aware of.

Bayo had hugged him when he came for him at the front desk, the security at the gate hadn't even bothered with checking ID, they had waved him through.

The guard at the gate had looked solemn, his face bearing witness to the bad news they were dealing with.

Bayo, he looked disheveled; his eyes were red from tears and despair. He walked as if the weight of the world were on his shoulders.

"I will let you know if we need your help to get us a visa after our meeting. Thank you, Sir," Yomi said, as he ended the call to the person on the other end of the phone.

Remi noticed that Yomi's eyes were also red and from the way he looked, he had been crying too.

Remi banged the table. "Ok, can somebody tell me what the hell is going on here?" he asked, looking from Bayo to Yomi.

Bayo and Yomi looked at each other. Bayo nodded at Yomi before Yomi took the lead and talked; and jove talk they did.

Yomi cleared his throat and sat down on the sofa in the office. "Bayo decided to play cupid and thought it would be a good idea to introduce you and Sam aka Mistress Eve to each other. Bayo and I have been trying to get Sam back on the dating scene, but she either flatly refused or never turned up at the events we invited her to."

Yomi scratched and shook his head. "However, fate also tried to play matchmaker, you and Sam met randomly in the real world at the gym," he said.

Yomi continued the story staring at Remi. "Sam thought you loved the attention from women and she also thought you were a player. However, Sam still said she liked the 'you' of the real world," Yomi paused.

"Mistress Eve was ready to tie you in knots forever."

That statement warmed Remi's heart for an instant. Did that mean they knew what went on between them?

Well, they were in a sex club, they must have seen worse.

Hang on, Yomi was confusing him.

"Hold on," Remi put a hand up, his heart pumping harder in his chest.

"If I am getting this, you are telling me that Sam is Mistress Eve?" he asked, staring at them.

Yomi paused, looked at Bayo, and ignored Remi's question and continued his story.

Yomi looked sheepish and looked down at his hands. "Sam is the 50% owner of the club along with Bayo and I. Sam inherited her husband's share when he died."

"What!!" Remi shouted, "I can't believe this."

Remi banged a fist on the table. "Bayo I asked you so many times if you knew her," he shouted, as frustration tore through him.

"You always said no," Remi said, quietly.

Remi turned to Bayo. "I even asked you how you got into the club, you said Yomi."

Remi was livid, angry could not describe the way he felt.

Bayo looked at him. "Technically it was true," shrugging his shoulders.

Sam had inherited her late husband's share. Sam had been married? The words echoed in Remi's brain.

Married? It made sense now, Remi thought, as she never wanted to talk about herself.

Her husband?

Intense jealousy ripped through Remi's mind, she was married? Then he remembered the phrase late husband.

Mistress Eve was a widow?

Remi threw Bayo a murderous glance at that moment; he had asked so many times if he knew who she was!!

Bayo continued with the story, his voice quieter. "Sam was an orphan who had been raised by Yomi's parents. She had been fostered by his family at one point or the other in her troubled life after Sam's mother had dumped her at Yomi's mother's office as a toddler."

Bayo paused, "Michael's mother was best friends with Yomi's mum, so they had all practically grown up together. Everybody had predicted that Sam and Michael would marry each other way back then and they did."

"Anyway, Sam got through her rough start in life and became a renowned doctor in the States. She is brilliant, she got a scholarship to study in America. The hospital where she worked in New York was sad to see her go when she came back to Nigeria," Bayo said, as he put his head in his hands.

Bayo looked over to Yomi, his eyes were red. Yomi nodded and continued the story.

Yomi rubbed his hand over his face. "Michael's illness cut that stay short, as she helped Michael fulfill his wish of dying near his family in Nigeria, during that time they had set up the club."

"Sam and Michael invited Bayo and I, over for dinner one evening and the four of us decided to open the club. We had noticed there was a gap in the market and we had all gone for it."

"Sam/Mistress Eve is into the mystic art of shibari rope tying and went to a retreat in Japan once a year, every year without fail. The retreat was so important to her they had gone there as part of their honeymoon," Yomi said. "Sam is a very complex individual; the rope has helped her overcome some issues of her childhood," as he raked his hands through his knotted afro.

No kidding, Remi thought.

Poor Sam, being dumped like, like.. he could not bring his mind to say the words and associate them with Sam.

No wonder she liked being in control, it made sense.

Remi briefly sent a silent thank you to his parents and his upbringing, he had been lucky and spoilt.

A woman who could change her appearance and voice was more than a complex woman. When he was with Mistress Eve, he was speaking to a woman from New York, even her linguistics backed that up.

When he was speaking to Sam on the other hand he was speaking to someone from Nigeria, he had never been able to place where, but she spoke like a Nigerian.

No, substitute complexity for genius, he thought

But that was not the issue at hand, Remi muttered, bringing himself back to what was unravelling in the room.

Yomi looked over to Remi. "Michael had been her first and only boyfriend and then her husband," Yomi said, as he glared at Remi.

The message there was unmissable, mess with her and…

Remi sighed and slumped into a chair, he was in shock. It was a hell of a lot to take in at 3am in the morning. He felt that his one true chance at finding the woman of his dreams was slipping away.

Remi had decided after the last time they had met that he was going to waste no time in asking her to be his when she got back from her trip. No matter what scar was on her face, he would treasure her and make her feel beautiful.

Remi had been and was ready to forsake all the hookups and casual dates, for her. He would have to as he would not like to think what Mistress Eve would do if she ever caught him cheating. She would flog him so hard, most probably he wouldn't be able to sit for a week.

Fear ripped through him, he really did not want to lose her, the thing he had been searching for, for a long time had finally fallen into his lap.

How could he have been so blind; all the signs had been there. The scent, that same elusive jasmine. The way her belly muscles contracted; he had noticed, but just thought it was a coincidence.

"Hold on guys, Sam and Mistress Eve can't be the same person I have seen Sam in her swimming costume, she does not have a tattoo," he said.

Bayo and Yomi simultaneously rolled their eyes at him.

Remi stared at them. "It's not a tattoo?" he asked.

Duh, really, the look they gave him said it all.

Bayo continued from where Yomi left off as Yomi's voice was cracking with emotion.

The room was charged with raw grief, Remi could feel it.

Bayo cleared his throat. "Sam and Yomi are very close, as far as Sam is concerned, Yomi is her big brother, she tells him everything. Yomi and Michael had been best friends from childhood."

"Yomi was the best man at Sam and Michael's wedding, while Yomi's dad had given Sam away," Bayo said, as he looked at Remi squarely in the eye.

Remi finally realized that everything that had happened between him Sam/Mistress Eve was known to his two friends.

His cheeks burned momentarily. He did not know whether to cringe or walk out of the room.

Remi noticed the verb Bayo used he had used the present tense while describing her relationship with Yomi; they were not giving up hope on her yet.

As far as they were concerned Sam/Mistress Eve was still alive. *Thank God*, he thought.

The vanilla alpha protector in Remi rose to the surface. He was going out there to find her; he would bring his Mistress back home.

Bayo continued. "Before Sam left for Japan, she told Yomi that she was going to come clean with you to see if you could take your relationship out of the club. Since you had met Sam, she hoped that it would help," Bayo said.

It now made sense to Remi what she had said before they had parted ways. Sort out your harem.

Remi was floored; Sam and Mistress Eve were the one and same person.

A wave of emotions came over Remi as he realized he might not get to see her ever again, the realization brought tears to his eyes.

For the first time in a long time Remi prayed and made a promise to God.

Chapter 28

Men being men, the reality of the situation they faced forced them to work as a team, the role of the leader inevitably and naturally fell to Yomi.

Remi was still in shock and was of no use to anyone. The shock of discovery regarding the identity of Mistress Eve, paired with the news unravelling before their eyes on TV made grim listening for all concerned.

The updated death toll on the TV forced Remi out of his stupor. "I am going out there to look for her," as he stood up and paced back and forth.

Remi put his hand on the table. "I am not asking," he said, as he turned to Yomi who was on the phone and Bayo.

"I am going there," his voice catching.

Remi wiped his face. "I will bring her home," he said, as more tears fell on his cheeks.

Remi remembered the tender way she had cared for him on Friday after their scene, the tears flowed freely, as he put his head in his hands.

The raw display of emotion was hard for Yomi and Bayo to witness.

"Ok guys." Yomi said, as he put the phone down. "This is what we are going to do," as he walked over to a whiteboard in the office.

Yomi picked up a pen. "Remi and I will fly to Japan tonight, or at the latest tomorrow morning. If we look at scheduled flights we are looking at around 33 hour's flight time because of stopovers. I have called in a few favors and hopefully someone will deliver, meaning we might have a private jet at our disposal," looking at Remi and Bayo.

Writing on the board, Yomi said, "Bayo, you will stay here and…" holding up his hand as Bayo objected.

"You will pay the staff, close the club until further notice and fly out and meet us on the next available flight." Yomi's tone put paid to any arguments.

Yomi turned to Remi. "What kind of passport do you have Remi?" Yomi asked, as he wrote notes on the whiteboard.

For a moment, Remi suspected Yomi must have worked in the armed forces or something similar. He was in control, organized, and thought of everything. He was in crisis management mode. Remi was happy Sam had someone like this looking out for her.

Remi pulled himself out of his grim thoughts when he noticed that Yomi was staring at him waiting for an answer.

Remi nodded. "Um, I have a British and a Nigerian Passport," he replied wearily.

Yomi put a tick on the board. "Great, then if someone lends us a private jet we can be out of here in two hours."

"Remi, you can't go on your own, not on a mission like this. We will have to look for her amongst the living and the dead. It's not something either of us should do on our .." Yomi said, as he broke down briefly.

"We will find her," Bayo said, into the pregnant silence.

"We are bringing Sam back home," Bayo whispered, quietly into the room.

The unanswered question no one wanted to address was what state she would be in.

Was Sam still alive?

Remi the eternal optimist asked. "Has anyone tried calling her?"

Yomi looked over to him with compassion and sadness. "Remi, we have, and I have an auto-dialer," pointing to the computer, "that has been calling her number."

"The last count," as he leaned over, "was 300 tries, it all goes to voicemail. The signal of the phone has not moved either," Yomi said into the silent room.

From the initial pictures being shown on the news, there were at least sixty dead bodies on the ground, that had taken the full force of the bomb blast as it had gone off.

They had not shown the bodies caught up in the damage done to the building.

"Whenever Sam travels she always sends me a copy of her passport, travel itinerary and her insurance details," Yomi said, looking at Remi as he went to the computer and hit print. "Each one of us, will have a copy of these documents with us, we will need to show her picture to many people," he continued.

Remi excused himself and went to call his parents. His mum picked it up on the first ring.

"Remi, what's wrong, why are you calling so late."

"Are you ok. Remi!!! What is wrong?" His mum's raised voice came over the phone.

"Oluwaremilekun, talk to me, please," she said.

That's what broke Remi, his full name being called.

"Remi, are you there?"

"Please talk to me."

He heard his dad's voice in the background.

His mother never called him by his full name unless he was in serious trouble.

This was different this was a grave situation.

Silent tears were rolling down his cheeks, he cleared his throat.

"Mum, I need to go to Japan. The woman I hope to marry is missing," his voice catching.

"Oh, oh my baby," her voice changed, the love and concern were getting hard for him.

"Wait o, wasn't there a terrorist attack there a few hours ago?" his mum said, realization dawning in her voice.

"Remi, please be careful, is it safe to go there?"

He heard his father's voice in the background.

"Oh my God!" she cried.

"God will bring you back to me in one piece."

"Remi," she called his name.

"Please be careful, my son."

"Baba Remi, please come and talk to your son."

"Tell me what you want me to do," he heard his father's voice.

"Remi, do you want me to come with you?" he heard his father say in the background.

"No daddy, not now, I am flying out with her brother tonight. I will call you when we land. Love you both," he said, as he ended the call.

Remi paced around the office to regain his composure before he called his boss. His boss granted him immediate emergency leave and promised to check to see if the company's private jet was available.

Composure regained, Remi walked back into the office to see Yomi opening a suitcase and placing all kinds of phones, satnavs and other things he could only imagine what they would be used for, into it.

Yomi looked up when he saw Remi hovering at the entrance. "Wheels up in sixty minutes, we have a plane. We will stop by your place for you to pick up a few things." Yomi said, as he continued to load electronics into his briefcase.

Remi watched as Yomi went over to Bayo, wiped away his tears tenderly, kissed his forehead and hugged him. He whispered a few words in his ear as he held him close.

Tonight, had been a night of revelations all round.

Chapter 29

Sam lay on a sun lounger, the warmth of the sun soothed her as she enjoyed the effect of the sun rays on her body.

This was bliss, she thought covering her eyes with her sunglasses. If anyone could define heaven this was it.

Sam was on an island, just off the mainland. The sand so clean it could only be described as white; sparkling like crystals in the sunshine. Even though sand couldn't really be white, it looked that way as it shimmered luminously in the sunlight. The sand drew you in; luring tourists to bend down and feel the sand to see if it was real.

The air was just right, there was just a slight breeze, helping the leaves of the coconut trees sway gently in the sun.

The sky was so blue she couldn't tell where the sky ended, and the sea began, it was breathtakingly beautiful. She would like to come back to this island, trying to remember the name of the island but couldn't.

This was a killer Instagram view, she thought, looking around for her phone on her lap, she couldn't find it. Sam put her hand under the lounger it wasn't there; she had two phones what had she done with them where were they?

On the horizon, roughly a five-minute leisurely swim away was the mainland, bustling with people, noise, and pollution.

Sam could see the ugly grey smog of the mainland rising on the horizon like the dirty smoke from the old manufacturing plants.

The island where she was, was an oasis of calm, helping soothe her sore muscles. Sam felt so tired and lethargic, her tummy felt like she had glass in her intestines, they were sharp, shooting, intense pains that took her breath away. The pain more intense than the occasional period pains she got, as she rubbed her tummy absent-mindedly, she needed pain-killers.

Three huge dolphins were swimming in the sea, just yards away from her. They jumped in the air showing off their skills whenever they noticed her watching them.

What a lovely sight, she thought, they were beautiful.

The sun felt so good on her skin as she moved to rub more sunscreen on her arms. She couldn't reach her legs it hurt too much, to sit up on the lounger.

I will do my legs later, she thought, as she rubbed more suntan oil on her face.

Bliss, Sam thought settling deeper into the lounger.

A Pina Colada would not go amiss; she chuckled as she realized she was thirsty.

Sam tried to get the attention of the waiters in the distance who were all dressed in white, but they ignored her. She could swear that they were deliberately ignoring her, she would put her hand up, one of them would look over at her, then look away.

Sam was about to get up and look for someone to get her a drink when Michael appeared wearing his Arsenal t-shirt with a huge glass of water in his hand.

"Hey you," she said.

"What are you doing here?" she asked, as she smiled at him.

There was a sad smile on his face. "I am here to give you some water, you are very thirsty," he said.

"I really wanted a Pina Colada," she smiled at him.

Passing the glass to her. "You won't get that here Sam, just water and if you're lucky fruit juice," Michael said.

Chapter 30

Forty-eight hours after the terrorist attack at Tokyo airport, Remi and Yomi landed at a private airstrip on the outskirts of Tokyo without incident.

No group had claimed responsibility for the heinous atrocity; which now saw the confirmed death toll at 560, made up of men, women and children. 100 injured and an unknown number of people missing.

Two American friends of Yomi met them at the airstrip. David Chang 5'8 with a stocky build who to Remi looked to be Japanese-American and Christopher, 6'2, muscular, and lean was an African-American.

Remi didn't even need to ask; these guys were ex-military or security. This made him wonder who Yomi really was and what had brought him to Nigeria in the first place.

They drove in somber silence to their hotel to drop off their bags and formulate a plan of action, how they would tackle the hospitals and the emergency medical centers that had sprung up around the airport.

The scale of the missing was driven home at the contact center outside the airport where people had put up posters, pictures and contact details for their missing loved ones.

Sam's picture now joined the board of the missing and the potentially dead victims of the atrocity.

Social media was agog with theories and conspiracies regarding the group who could be responsible. Most people did their best from their armchairs around the world to set up virtual missing boards.

Every community seemed to have been impacted by the atrocity, from Japan, Africa, India, to the UK and the USA. Everyone had someone's missing person on their timeline.

The world had united in grief on social media. They made the decision amongst them that Yomi and Remi would team up together while David and Christopher would make up the second team. Each team had satellite phones, being out of range would never be an issue. They agreed that they would all touch base in four hours.

They started their search on foot and hence; they started the gruesome task of searching for Sam.

It's funny how you get to grasp the fragility and temporariness of life when presented with the reality, in the aftermath of destruction and seeing death and sorrow around you at every turn. The police had removed the bodies and limbs, but the blood was still visible on the ground.

The heart-rending scenes of listening to parents as they searched for their children, husbands searching for wives, wives searching for their husbands. Little children crying for their parents seeking and looking for the comfort of their embrace that was now lost forever.

By the end of the first four hours on the ground they knew how to say in Japanese.

"Have you seen this black woman?"

Chapter 31

Remi stood by the missing board near the airport, watching as people came to check if there was any news about their missing loved ones.

Some pictures had been taken down a few more had been added. Remi wondered if this was because their loved ones had found them, either alive or dead. Or had the wind blown the pictures away, like dead leaves dropping from a tree.

The one thing they had not and would not discuss was what would happen if it was bad news. The task of going from hospital to hospital, looking through wards, and mortuaries had turned into an emotionally draining but gruesome task.

Saro had arrived in Japan, two days after they landed, hoping that by the time he arrived Sam would have been found.

The news that Sam was missing in the bomb's aftermath had spread like wildfire back home. Dozens of people had left candles, and prayers had been left outside her office on the island for her safe return.

Messages of support kept flooding in on the various social media pages that Remi had set up.

It was through this that Remi realized just how much and how many lives Sam had touched through her work as a mental health doctor.

Chapter 31

Remi stood by the missing board near the airport, watching as people came to check if there was any news about their missing loved ones.

Some pictures had been taken down, a few more had been added. Remi wondered if that was because their loved ones had found them, either alive or dead. Or had the wind blown the pictures away, like dead leaves dropping from a tree.

The one thing they had not and would not discuss was what would happen if it was bad news. The task of going from hospital to hospital looking through wards and mortuaries had turned into an emotionally draining but gruesome task.

Bayo had arrived in Japan, two days after they landed, hoping that by the time he arrived Sam would have been found.

The news that Sam was missing in the bomb's aftermath had spread like wildfire back home. Dozens of people had left candles, and prayers had been left outside her office on the Island for her safe return.

Messages of support kept flooding in on the various social media pages that Bayo had set up.

It was through this that Remi realized just how much and how many lives Sam had touched through her work as a mental health doctor.

Four days had gone into their search for Sam. It was six days since the attack, and they were no closer to finding her.

They had all decided that after seven days, they would regroup and reevaluate their strategy for the search and start all over again.

It was through this emotional turmoil that Remi picked up the phone and called his mum.

Remi needed her voice to tell him that everything was going to be all right.

His mum picked it up on the first ring.

"Remi how are you; I hope you are ok?" she said. "Do you have any news?" she asked.

"No Mum, we have not found her," he said softly.

"You haven't found her *yet* Remi. Yet being the operative word. Are you eating? Please try to eat o," she said. "I know it will be difficult, but you need your strength for when you find her," she continued.

"We are all praying for her here as well, Remi. The women in my group have posted her picture on their Twitter feeds, Instagram pages and Facebook pages."

"You name it, they are trying to reach out to anyone who might help."

"Any kind of social media has Sam's name on it."

"So, by God's Grace and the Grace of God, we will find her soon, Remi," she said, the hope clear in her voice.

"Sam has helped so many people in the past and many people are praying for her safe return," she said, as she started praying over the phone.

Remi closed his eyes as his mum's prayers washed over him.

"Excuse me Mum, you know Sam?" he asked in surprise, as his head got around his mum's rushed speech.

"Yes nau," she said, as she rushed. "She runs a nightclub your dad and I go to once a month."

"Sam also runs a free clinic, a drop-in session for people twice a month, a lot of people have her to thank for the state of their good mental health."

"Depression is killing a lot of people in Nigeria, my dear son. It is the silent killer. That is a story for another day, my child."

"A lot of people are rooting for her o, God will help you find her," she said.

Remi looked at the phone he was holding, as if he had been burnt, were it not for the situation he found himself in he would have burst out laughing.

His mum and dad's clubbing activities were a thought for another day, or no day AT ALL.

No wonder Bayo had mentioned on more than one occasion that married couples came to the club. What other secrets was Bayo keeping from him, he wondered.

Six hours after the call with his mum they got the break they were looking for. Someone called in on one of their phones, to say that a woman matching Sam's description had been brought into a hospital twenty minutes away from their hotel.

Remi was deep in thought as they drove to the hospital, the car was quiet. His hands in his pocket as he touched the chain for comfort and hope.

The group was in silent and somber reflection when they had asked the caller what injuries she had, the person had just said, come to the hospital.

They were pulling up into the car park when Remi felt his personal phone vibrate. He pulled it out of his pocket, it was a text from Mercy.

Hi Remi, hope you are well. Please call me ASAP, I am pregnant.

Remi re-read the message, *this could not be happening*, he thought. As the impact of the message loosened his bowels, he needed the toilet.

Chapter 32

The feel of warmth from the sun on her face made Sam realize she had fallen asleep again on the lounger.

Sam opened her eyes, the sound of the waves hitting the sand repeatedly, *created a calm and hypnotic backdrop, that she could listen to all day, if she was in a place like this*, she thought.

This was bliss, she felt very relaxed, but moving her arm hurt. The sun was still shining, and the sea was still as blue green as ever, why hadn't she come here for a holiday before, she wondered. As she tried to remember the name of the island, how could she have forgotten. It was beautiful, the dolphins were still trying to catch her attention, she would go over and swim with them later she thought.

Sam needed to find her phone, she wanted to take pictures of this island.

The water Michael had given her earlier had helped quench her thirst, but right now she was hungry, if only those talkative waiters would come over.

They studiously avoided her, and it was irritating her.

Very much so, she was about to get up and look for Michael, when she heard a child laughing excitedly near the dolphins.

The little girl was wearing a bright yellow floral dress, she turned and smiled when she noticed Sam looking at her. The smile lit up her face, she was a beautiful child. The girl waved, blew her a kiss and smiled warmly at Sam.

That child is going too close to the water, she thought. Who was she? The way the child had waved at her was with familiarity and love.

Sam was trying to get up, the pain in her tummy sharp and intense, taking a deep breath to steady herself. She needed to ask the girl where her parents were when Michael appeared.

Michael put a hand on her shoulder. "Sam you can't move, you might hurt yourself," he said.

"Michael that child needs help, she is too close to the water."

Michael looked over to where the girl was and looked back at Sam. "Do you regret our decision not to have children Sam?" he asked her, his eyes sad.

"Of course not, Michael, we both knew that our child would be born with life changing defects, we both came to the same conclusion."

"We could have adopted," Sam said.

She paused, she had just said, could have, instead of we can adopt.

"Michael, where am I?" she asked him.

"Where do you think?" he asked, as he looked towards the mainland.

The child's laughter broke into their conversation, she waved at Sam again. Beckoning to her to come into the water with her.

"You were once like that child over there Sam, abandoned, scared and alone. Help that girl get a better earlier start in life than the one you had," he implored.

"It's so peaceful here Michael, I want to sleep and relax," Sam said, as she closed her eyes.

Michael nudged her. "Wake up Sam, you can't fall asleep, it's not meant for you, we are full right now. You and that little girl need to get out of here."

"Remi is a good guy you know. Blind, but he is ok," Michael said, rolling his eyes.

Michael shook his head. "For goodness sake how could he not know it was you!!" smiling at her.

Sam rolled her eyes. "I changed my voice, and I used a visual, that always tricks the layman," she chuckled mischievously.

"She isn't yours," Michael said, as he looked towards the girl.

Michael turned to Sam. "But she is going to rely on and need you. Please help her out, I don't want her here, she belongs to you. For some reason she wants to be with you, she sought you out."

"It might be a difficult decision for you to make, but please try," he said. "It will be very rewarding for you," Michael paused, as he looked over to the child again.

"I am going to make you some fish and then we need to get you and that child out of here Miss," he said as he walked away.

Chapter 33

Dr. Vince Tanaka the Head of the Trauma Unit at Sakakibara Hospital, wished that it was the coffee stand in the canteen he was going to. Instead, he headed to the chart stand and looked over the charts of the patients he needed to attend to.

He was tired, having slept at the hospital for the last two nights in a row. Due to the attack, the hospital had been operating at full capacity.

That meant more staff to supervise and more paperwork that needed signing off, Dr. Vince sighed.

The hospital had been extraordinarily busy, people had been pulled off leave and rostered to do the long shifts needed and expected after such a catastrophic event.

All the incoming victims they had received at the hospital had been identified, apart from two people.

One was now in the morgue and the other one was in a life-threatening coma. The lady in bed 10 had not been identified, even though he had seen a man sitting with her twice, whenever he got to the room to ask the man questions about her, the room had been empty.

Dr. Vince had asked a nurse to keep an eye out and call him the next time the man visited.

The nurse had given him a strange look, no one had been in there to see the woman she told him since she had arrived.

The other nurses also confirmed the same thing, no one had ever been in the room with the lady in bed 10.

Dr. Vince knew what he saw, and he was sure of what he had seen. The same man there twice, the man wore an Arsenal shirt for crying out loud. Sighing, as he ran his hands through his hair.

This was the time he needed his grandmother's sage advice, she had always told him sometimes, some things could not be explained, especially around death. They were currently dealing with a lot of death, sudden unexpected death. Lives had been cut short, horribly and unexpectedly, it was sad. As a result, a lot of lost souls were roaming about, not realizing they were dead.

His grandmother had been a proponent of the belief that just because science didn't believe in it, did not mean it did not exist.

Dr. Vince breathed out, maybe he had seen things, he had been awake for 44 hours in the last 48.

But he was so sure, on one occasion the man had looked up and turned his head towards him, a sad smile on his face. No, he had not been seeing things he told himself. He would go in immediately next time he saw the man.

Dr. Vince took the chart of the lady in bed 10 and went back to her bed, there were two beds in the room, the occupant of the other bed had passed away that morning, due to the extensive brain trauma sustained during the attack.

When he thought about it, this woman was the last surviving victim that had been transferred to his hospital for treatment.

It was sad to see family upon family being given hope that their loved ones were in the hospital, only for them to die from their injuries. It was heart-wrenching to watch.

Dr. Vince really hoped she made it, if only he knew her name. He would be able to talk to her, but all he ever said was "Hello, how are you today Miss?" as he got on with the job of checking her vitals.

Even though she was in a coma, her vitals were good, but her internal injuries were severe. He walked out of the room and moved on to the next patient.

Chapter 34

Remi looked at the text again.

No. No, this could not be happening.

Shit, shit he thought as a wave of fear went through him.

Mercy I am away now; can I call you shortly? He typed into WhatsApp. She wasn't online she would probably get it later, but he also sent her the same message by text.

Remi put his phone away and followed the rest of the group into the hospital, just like the other hospitals they had visited this one was bustling with people.

Yomi walked up to the receptionist and gave her the name of the person who had called to tell them they might have a match to Sam. She checked a list for the name of the person who had called them and directed them to the mortuary.

They all stopped when they heard the word mortuary and looked at each other.

Remi's heart skipped a beat, his hands went clammy, even though it was hot outside a cold wave of dread engulfed him, he could not breathe.

That innocuous statement, the receptionist must have said it so many times in the last couple of days, she did not realize the effect it had on people. Or she had somehow become immune to the trauma and was holding up a professional front.

Remi felt drained, he had received two pieces of potentially life altering news on the same day.

Sam's death and Mercy having his baby. Damn, he remembered the last time he had been with Mercy, and the condom had split. It had happened before, he had dismissed it as one of those things that happened with no lasting consequences.

The other three men were all in quiet contemplation as they walked down the corridor, they stopped in the hallway.

"Guys, please wait here and I will go in," Yomi said, holding up his hand, to discourage any argument.

Remi watched as Yomi opened the door and walked towards a desk, before the door slammed shut behind him.

The minutes passed slowly as they waited for Yomi to identify the body.

Time stood still for everyone, Bayo stood on his own; David and Christopher stood together talking.

Remi was on his own, he wondered how he would feel when Yomi came out, it was one of the longest waits he'd endured. It was also the first time he had dealt with death on such a personal level. He pulled the chain out, drawing strength from it, please he whispered, the tears pricked his eyes. Putting it back in his pocket watching the door, waiting for Yomi to come out.

Fifteen minutes later, the handle on the door moved and Yomi walked out, his face somber.

Yomi slumped against the door as it shut behind him. "It's not her," he said, quietly.

The sigh of relief from all of them was audible in the room. However, there was still one question on the forefront of everyone's mind.

Where was she?

They decided to go back to their hotel room and regroup. As they walked to the lift they were all lost in thought.

The lift door opened, a man in a white coat, a doctor by his badge, looking over charts was the sole occupant, he nodded to them as they got in. *Well, they did look an odd group*, Remi thought. Four big black guys with one Japanese guy amongst them.

They continued talking about the hospitals they should visit next, they would have to go back to all of them again and ask for Sam.

"Hmm, erm, Hi, sorry to intrude. But I wonder if you can help me?" the doctor turned to them.

"Hi, I am Vince Tanaka, I am the head of the Trauma department."

"I don't mean to sound racist or anything, if I do, I apologize in advance," the doctor said. "As you can imagine we have been dealing with a lot of traumas here after the attack."

The doctor looked at them his face apologetic. "Your community here is small and in one way or the other you guys know each other," he said.

The doctor held the charts close. "I bet just like me you have more aunts and uncles than is genetically possible," as he tried to lighten the atmosphere.

Remi cracked a slight smile, he felt sorry for the doctor trying to be politically correct.

"We have a lady here that I have been trying to identify," the doctor looked at them earnestly.

The doctor sighed. "No one has come forward to ask for her, it seems as if no one is looking for her," he said. "She is the only person left referred to us from the attack, who has not been identified and who is still alive."

"Yes, all the other casualties we got died, we lost the last one this morning. I just wish we could have at least one......," the doctor's voice was wistful. The doctor shook his head as if to banish the wistful thoughts.

The doctor sighed. "I have seen a man sitting with her, but anytime I go to ask him her name he's gone, and the nurses say they have never seen him."

"They think I am crazy," the doctor continued.

The lift pinged, the doors opened. The doctor pressed the button to keep the doors open.

"The man stared at me once and even smiled at me."

The doctor looked exhausted, it was possible that he was hallucinating, Remi thought.

It was suddenly obvious to Remi, that Yomi had just gone very still, as if a chill had just entered the lift.

"Can you describe the man to me please?" Yomi said, as the other guys all fell silent.

The doctor looked towards Yomi. "He is very light, compared to you. He had an Arsenal football shirt on," he said. "I am an Arsenal fan, he had it on, on both occasions and he looked tall," the doctor continued.

"Do you know him?" The doctor asked, turning to Yomi.

"Yes," Yomi said, and nothing more.

The doctor was expecting Yomi to say something, but he didn't.

"Uhm ok, let me take you to her," the doctor said.

The doctor rubbed his eyes. "None of the people sent to this hospital made it, which is why I hoped she would, when I saw the man watching over her." Repeating himself.

"Sorry I am repeating myself, it has been an exhausting few days. It looked like he was watching over her."

Remi found the phrase the doctor had used strange, doctors were meant to believe in science not guardian angels.

The excitement amongst them was palpable and evident in the quick long strides they took as they followed the doctor out of the lift.

They walked into the room and they were met with a woman whose head was swathed in bandages. It was obvious from her nose she was black.

Remi had to take the word of the doctor that the person they were looking at was a woman. Other than the color of her nose and arm Remi could not identify who was lying on the bed. Her arms had all kinds of tubes hanging off her.

Yomi went over to her and checked her wrist, he said, "When Sam was younger she opened a can of corned beef the wrong way, she has a scar on her wrist resulting from that incident."

Yomi used a hand to cover his eyes. "It's Sam," he said.

"Let's take... take her home," his voice shaking but controlled.

They had found her, and it was at that precise moment that all hell broke loose on the machines.

Chapter 35

Dr. Tanaka moved swiftly to the machines to see what was going on as he touched Sam's pulse on her wrist.

Even though he wasn't a medical doctor, Remi noticed that Dr. Tanaka looked worried and tense. Please, please don't let Sam follow the same path the others had, Remi thought as he remembered the doctor's words earlier.

"Get me a crash cart in here stat." Dr. Tanaka shouted, as he started compressions on Sam's chest.

One of the nurses came running in through the door, to assist him with monitoring Sam's vitals.

"Page the head of Cardio to get here now," the doctor said checking the monitors as he continued the compressions.

The machines were making warning noises, red lights flashing all over the place.

The second nurse who came in said, "Blood pressure is dropping. Heart rate is dropping."

Watching the monitors, hoping and waiting for something to improve on the numbers she was looking at. Another nurse came in with the crash cart and quickly pulled the defibrillator out of its packaging.

Dr. Tanaka was about to put the defibrillator on Sam when he turned to the nurse.

"Get them out of here now," pointing to the men in the room.

The nurse led them out into the seating area, her eyes were tense and weary. The door had a window on the upper part of the door which enabled Yomi and Remi to see what was going on.

Bayo, couldn't take it and went to sit by himself in the middle of the room.

The atmosphere had gone from hope to despair in the space of one hour; it was tense and the only thing holding all of them together was hope.

Hope. Never had four letters carried such a heavy meaning.

In Sam's room, Dr. Tanaka placed the defibrillator on Sam's chest, passing the current to get her heart beating again, it jerked her up then back down, like a rag doll, the charge rushing through her to bring her heart to life.

"Give me eighty, clear." Dr. Tanaka said.

They could see on the machines the lines were still flat, nothing had moved.

"Give me one hundred clear."

Remi could see the look that passed between the nurse and the doctor from the window. This was real life, not the medical drama shows he watched sporadically when he couldn't sleep at night.

This was someone close to him they were trying to bring back to life. Remi had watched enough of them to know that after two attempts with no response, it wasn't a good sign.

"Give me one hundred and ten, clear," Dr. Tanaka said.

Remi could not take it anymore and moved away from the door and started pacing the room, his eyes were pricking with the tears welling in his eyes. His hand in his pocket, please he prayed.

Yomi stood by the door as if mesmerized, by what was going on in the room.

The head of Cardio arrived and went into the room and told Yomi to move away from the door and the window.

One of the nurses came out to tell Yomi to move away from the door and window, but not before he saw them drop the defibrillator.

Yomi moved and went to sit opposite Bayo, he too wanted to be alone.

Dr. Tanaka had hoped that the defibrillator would have worked. "Come on, Sam," he kept muttering.

"Come on."

"Come on Sam," Dr. Tanaka whispered. "Don't let that man watching over you be for nothing," he pleaded.

Dr. Tanaka threw the defibrillator to the ground and started CPR on her again.

"One, two, three …thirty,"

He tried again until the Head of Cardio told him to stop.

"Vince, please stop. I'm sorry," the Head of Cardio understood.

Sam wasn't coming back.

"Vince, you need to call the time of death," the head of Cardio told him, understanding in her eyes.

Samantha Nkechi Olaofe nee Ojukwu was declared dead at 22.14 Japan time 14.14 Lagos time.

Dr. Tanaka pulled off his gloves and prepared to tell her family that she was gone.

Chapter 36

Dr. Tanaka pulled off his gloves and got ready to inform Sam's family that she hadn't made it.

He made sure that all the wires were taken off her body and ensured she was fully clothed. During CPR they had ripped open her hospital gown to apply pressure to her chest.

Dr. Tanaka placed her hands by her sides and pulled the blanket up to her chest. She looked so peaceful; looking as if she was sleeping rather than waiting to be taken to the morgue.

He had wished and hoped that she would survive, her injuries even though severe and life changing would have been treatable with the right protocol.

Dr. Tanaka had hoped for at least one person who had been sent to his hospital to survive the injuries sustained in the attack. He took one more look at her lying on the bed and went to deliver the news to her family in the waiting area.

Dr. Tanaka walked into the waiting room, and five sets of eyes were gravely staring at him, one of the guys sitting on his own, was staring at him, tears already rolling down his eyes, he was holding a gold chain in his hand.

It was as if he already knew the news he was about to deliver was bad.

"I am sorry, she did not make it," Dr. Tanaka said, looking at Yomi.

"Her heart did not respond, we tried for an extended period, but to no avail."

"I am sorry for your loss," he said, as he walked back into Room ten.

Tears pricked Dr. Tanaka's eyes as he walked back.

Chapter 37

Remi walked out of the room after the doctor delivered the news, in his grief and shock with tears running down his face, he chanced upon a door that led into a small courtyard.

The sobs racked his body, as he thought about how he had dumped and used women in the past, it was ironic the person he had fallen hard for, had been taken away before he had been given the opportunity to declare his love for her.

Why, he cried, as he sobbed, the salty tears fell to his lips. His heart in pain and broken, Remi had prayed that night in Yomi's office that they would find Sam, alive, and he had promised to forsake all women and devote himself to her.

No more messing around, he was ready to settle down. He had learnt a lot about Sam that night, Sam had been through so much, he wanted to make her feel like a princess, look after and cherish her. The intensity of his sobs decreased as he faced the reality of his loss. Sam and Mistress Eve were gone forever, their presence in his life had been fleeting but intense.

The courtyard was dark but serene; he had not initially noticed that another black man was there, sitting towards the end on a long bench in front of a waterfall.

Remi sniffed and tried to compose himself.

The sound of flowing water was soothing and constant, just like the cycle of life.

Remi sighed and sat on the bench putting a lot of space between himself and the other man. He put his hand in his pocket looking for a tissue to dry his tears, instead it touched the chain and the tears fell again, he didn't look at the man he was too absorbed in his grief.

When you spend seven days looking for someone and you see death and destruction around you it makes you realize how fragile life is, Remi thought.

It also made you sit down and think about how temporary life really was. He had learnt a lot about Sam, Bayo, and Yomi in the time they had spent together.

Their friendship would never be the same superficial relationship again. The fabric of their relationship had been ripped and when it came back together, the scars from this experience would remain and bind them together in a deeper kind of relationship.

Remi jumped, he felt a hand on his shoulder, he looked up, the man on the bench had moved closer handing him a tissue. His grief-stricken brain wondered how he had moved so close without being seen, to stand over and tap him on the shoulder.

Remi dried his tears, and heard the man sitting on the bench say, "It feels hard now but believe me it gets better. Life is like a complex piece of fabric, it tears, we sew it back together again," he said, his voice shaking as the words came out.

Silent tears ran down Remi's cheeks, as he listened to the loss obvious in the man's voice.

Remi had never experienced death this close before, looking back at his life now, he realized he had led a very charmed and lucky existence.

The man continued. "Remi, nothing is a coincidence. Everything you're experiencing is meant to happen exactly how it is happening. Embrace the lessons. Be grateful. Trust me you will be fine." The stranger sitting next to him said.

Remi felt the man get up from the bench, he looked up just as a tall man wearing an Arsenal football shirt disappeared around the corner in the courtyard.

Remi wiped his eyes with the tissue, he hoped he would bump into the guy again to thank him for the tissue and the words of encouragement he had given him.

The friendly man must have suffered a loss himself, his words had temporarily soothed Remi's grief.

In one fell swoop, a life had been taken from him and potentially another one had been given to him.

Yes, Remi whispered, he would be grateful and embrace the lessons. How had the man known his name?

Remi brushed himself down and went back into the waiting room, to support his friends who were the closest thing to kin that Sam had.

Bayo and Yomi were crying as Remi walked back into the room. Yomi was trying to pull himself together.

It was obvious to Remi that Bayo was the emotional one between the two of them. It wasn't a criticism; just an observation of the dynamics between the two; that he had previously been blind to.

Yomi took out his phone and started planning on how they were going to take her body home.

"I need to call my parents and Michael's parents to deliver the news," Yomi said.

Remi watched as he walked away and made the calls. He could see tears rolling down Yomi's cheeks as he spoke to them.

Chapter 38

Dr. Vince Tanaka walked out of the waiting area after delivering the news to the men who had been waiting outside for news about Sam.

It had been hard for him to watch the hope fade from their eyes; he sighed.

Sometimes, no matter how long you have been a doctor one patient comes along that touches you for so many unfathomable reasons. For him Sam had been that patient.

Dr. Tanaka went back into Room 10 and stood at the bottom of Sam's bed staring and wishing. Wishing he had saved her.

He wanted to say goodbye. It had been an emotional few days.

Something was nagging him and raising an alarm in his mind as he stared at her.

"Sorry I couldn't help you," he whispered to her serene face. As he put her hands by her sides, the standard protocol they followed in such circumstances.

In such circumstances!! *Hold on a minute*, Dr. Tanaka thought.

How come her hands were on her abdomen?

Her hands were on her abdomen!!

He had laid them by her sides after he had called the time of death, he knew he had, as it was second nature to him. A finger moved as if acknowledging his sentence.

Dr. Tanaka put a hand on her pulse and there was a faint response. He pressed the bell for the nurses' station.

A nurse rushed in, a questioning look on her face.

"Get me the Head of Neurology stat," he shouted excitedly.

Her lips were moving.

He bent closer to listen to her.

"She wouldn't leave the dolphins. She didn't want to leave the dolphins," Sam whispered.

She sighed, he checked her pulse again and it was now beating steadily.

Dr. Tanaka pressed the button for the nurse's station again.

"Get the Head of Neurology paged stat," he barked into the phone.

Awe making him forget that he had just told the nurse who had come in to call the Head of Neurology.

Chapter 39

Remi was half-heartedly listening to Yomi talking to someone on the phone when he noticed sudden movement at the nurse's station. He heard one of them gasp and say something rapidly and animatedly in Japanese.

Something was wrong, most probably another patient had gone into cardiac arrest, he thought. Three different alarms went off, consistently on the table at the nurse's station.

Remi wanted to gaze at Sam's face one last time and say his goodbyes to her privately at the hospital. Before they took her to the morgue.

Remi looked around the waiting room, Yomi was busy on the phone trying to arrange transport and flights. Bayo was sitting on his own, he was in a place far away. David and Christopher flanked Yomi, ready to help him with anything he needed an extra pair of hands for.

Remi walked over to the door and was about to go into Sam's room when one of the nurses intercepted him at the entrance.

"Excuse me Sir, you can't go in there," she said, as she pulled the blinds to cover the window in the door.

Remi looked away from the door towards the corridor and saw two doctors running, no sprinting towards where he was standing in front of room ten and watched them enter Sam's room.

Something wasn't right, he thought.

Remi decided to keep his counsel, Yomi, and the others had not noticed, or they thought all the activity was normal protocol after a death.

The phones on the table where the nurses sat were ringing non-stop. From the eerie quiet that had pervaded the room when they had been trying to revive Sam, to the current non-stop cacophony of sound.

Remi was about to see if he could find a nurse, to ask why he could not go into the room when Dr. Tanaka walked out of the room.

Remi noticed immediately there was something wrong, the doctor didn't have the somber look he had worn when he had delivered the news to them earlier on.

This time it was the look of someone in shock, deep shock, his hair was standing straight on his head.

Dr. Tanaka looked like someone who had seen something incredible, whatever it was there was a look of awe on his face.

Dr. Tanaka turned at Remi. "She said, the girl did not want to leave the dolphins."

Something made Remi shiver at that moment, something he did not understand.

"Who?" Remi asked the doctor looking confused.

Dr. Tanaka, put a hand on Remi's shoulder. "Sam, she is alive. She repeated that sentence twice, like an exasperated mum reporting her child," the doctor said, shaking his head in disbelief. "She is undergoing tests with the Heads of Neurology and Cardio, I will let you know when you can go in and see her," he said, his voice still in shock.

Dr. Tanaka continued, awe and amazement clear on his face and in his voice.

"I have heard of things like this happen before, but we have never experienced such a phenomenon here in this hospital," he continued, as he got carried away with the enormity of what he had just experienced and witnessed.

Remi watched in a shocked trance, as Dr. Tanaka pulled himself together, and watched him as he walked over to the rest of the group to deliver the unexpected but miraculous news.

It was the sound of someone collapsing onto the chairs and displacing the other chairs around it, that roused Remi from the shocked trance he was in.

Bayo had fainted on the floor, hitting his head on the sharp edge of the chair during the fall, he had cut open his head; there was now a pool of blood rapidly spreading on the floor.

Chapter 40

Dr. Tanaka quickly rushed over to where Bayo was lying on the floor and checked his pulse, it was beating strong and steady. Carefully turning Bayo over, to make sure that he was lying on his back, it was the position he needed him to be in. He needed to check his wound, there was a cut that had opened just above his temple and ended on his eyebrow, it looked like a superficial head wound but he wanted to get him on a bed ASAP, to help confirm or contradict his initial assessment.

Bayo tried to get up, "I am fine. I don't need a stretcher."

Dr. Tanaka put a hand on his shoulder. "Please let us look at this and do this the right way," he implored.

Bayo laid back down on the floor, it was obvious to everyone that he was weak.

Dr. Tanaka shouted. "Get me a stretcher and a trauma kit," to one of the nurses hovering around the waiting room.

The nurse came back a minute later with a porter who had a stretcher in tow, they carefully placed Bayo on the stretcher and moved him into room ten, which was the nearest bed to the waiting room at that point.

The trauma kit was placed on the table by the nurse as Dr. Tanaka started to take a close look at Bayo's head wound.

"It is a nasty head wound and will require stitches, but I just need to ensure he does not have a concussion," Dr. Tanaka said, as he ripped opened more sterile wipes to use on the wound.

The room was silent as Remi and Yomi stood silently watching as Dr. Tanaka stitched Bayo's wound.

Bayo was wincing in pain but was silent.

Sam was muttering on her bed.

Dr. Tanaka looked up from the stitching he was doing. "She is ok, she has been muttering a lot," he said.

"Come on Ibukun we really have to go; your dad is waiting for you," they heard her mutter in the silent room.

Dr. Tanaka looked at Yomi. "Does Sam have any children?" he asked Yomi.

Yomi was staring at Sam with a strange expression on his face.

"No," he replied, turning his attention back to Bayo on the bed. "Is he going to be ok?" Yomi asked, the concern obvious in his voice.

"Yes, he is also dehydrated so I will give him an IV and after that he should be fine," Dr. Tanaka replied, as he finished stitching up Bayo's wound. Then pressed the buzzer for the nurses' station and asked the nurse to bring in an IV for Bayo.

Dr. Tanaka then beckoned Yomi and Remi over. Remi noticed that he had that somber look on his face again.

The doctor turned to Yomi as he lowered his voice. "As her brother I need to give you the prognosis and extent of Sam's injuries."

Remi was about to leave as this was a private family conversation, Yomi's arm firmly on his shoulder told him to stay.

"Where are you taking her from here? I mean which medical facility?" Dr. Tanaka asked, looking at Yomi.

"We are taking her to New York, the hospital where she trained is waiting for her, Mount Sinai in New York, and her insurance company has sorted out all the details. We have a medical plane on standby," Yomi replied.

"Great news that is an excellent hospital," Dr. Tanaka replied, as a visible weight seemed to lift off his shoulders.

"Sam has amnesia……," Dr. Tanaka said.

"Remi come and speak to Ibukun o, she won't leave these dolphins. Tell her we will bring her back to see them," they heard her mutter.

Remi's blood went very cold, his heart skipped a beat; it was as if someone had walked on his grave, it was a feeling he could not explain. Going light-headed for a minute, he felt himself sway. There was a look of concern on Yomi's face, both the doctor and Yomi caught him as he swayed.

"Are you OK Remi?" Yomi asked

"He might be dehydrated too," Yomi said to the doctor.

Remi's heart started pumping faster than it should, it was a very eerie moment, it felt like a ghost had touched him, as the words of the man he had seen earlier manifested clearly in his head, it was as if the man was standing next to him talking to him. *Nothing is coincidence......*

"Sam has amnesia, we hope it is short term," Dr. Tanaka continued, from the brief interruption.

"Sam has been speaking a lot about a girl, I don't know if she has a sister or something? We don't know how long the amnesia will last for, but we are hoping for the best. She has been very resilient; her breathing is strong as well as her other vitals. Unfortunately, due to the internal trauma she suffered, there is a 99.9% chance that Sam can never have children. I am really sorry."

Dr. Tanaka's eyes turned to Sam as he said that last sentence.

Yomi put his hand on the doctor's shoulder. "Thank you, doctor for all you have done for her. We will have challenges ahead, for now we are happy that she is alive."

Yomi pinched his eyebrows. "I will keep you informed of her progress."

"Sam has a great love for your country, she is a top level shibari practitioner," Yomi said, as he looked towards Sam on the bed.

Dr. Tanaka looked at Sam and smiled when he heard that, his chest puffed. "Please ensure you get a second opinion when you get to America. The body has a strange way sometimes of dealing with trauma."

"I will liaise with the hospital in America regarding the best approach for her flight," Dr. Tanaka said. "I want to sedate her."

"Whoever this child is that she keeps talking about, the child is raising her blood pressure. If she is asleep, she won't get too agitated."

Dr. Tanaka walked out of the room and left Remi and Yomi alone with Bayo and Sam.

Remi stood by the door and watched as Yomi walked over to Bayo where he was lying in the bed.

"You're such a girl's blouse you know," he said, as he punched him lightly on the shoulder.

Remi saw Bayo's lips twitch with a smile at Yomi's words.

Yomi then moved over to Sam's bed and pulled the chair next to the bed and held one of her hands in his, Remi heard Yomi singing to her and he could swear he saw the ghost of a smile on Sam's lips.

Then Yomi got up and signaled Remi that they should move out of the room.

Yomi ran a hand over his hair. "This is what we are going to do. I will go with Sam to New York on the medical plane," he said.

"Please can you stay with Bayo and keep an eye on him?" Yomi asked. "The hospital should discharge him tomorrow morning, the two of you should go back to Lagos."

Remi touched Yomi's arm gently. "Of course, Yomi. Don't worry about it, I will watch out for him. That cut looks nasty."

Yomi put a hand on Remi's shoulder. "I will let you know once we get to New York how long they want to keep her in there for."

Remi nodded, as he looked towards the room Sam and Bayo were in. "Thank you," he whispered.

Yomi raked his hands through his knotted afro. "They will want to run a lot of neurological tests and I want them to check her again."

Remi turned his head back towards Yomi.

Yomi rolled his eyes. "I promise to keep you in the loop Remi, she also has two mothers I will have to deal with," he sighed, a slight smile on his face.

"Shit, I need to call them," looking reflective.

Yomi looked at Remi. "It hit my mum hard, when I told her we had lost Sam. Sam is her daughter. It was hard to hear her crying over the phone. I don't know if she has told Michael's mum," he sighed.

"Can you imagine what they put me through for the last seven days? They did not give up hope, even when I was telling them it was not looking good," he said. "They prayed on the phone, they told me not to give up. I could imagine what was going through their heads, we had buried Michael as a young adult. They would not want to do the same for Sam," his voice reflective.

Yomi continued, "I am just glad I can call them and tell them we have a miracle. I will be able to tell them she is alive and well."

"They can then sort out between themselves how they will take care of her. That's better than what we were initially facing," Yomi continued. "You also need to go back to work Remi, you can't be off for too long," Yomi said.

Yomi walked out of the room to get the wheels in motion to move Sam and to speak to his friends who were waiting for him in the meeting room.

Remi went to sit on the chair just vacated by Yomi that was between Sam and Bayo's bed.

Remi initially wanted to argue, but he knew what Yomi proposed was the correct plan of action, he would sit with Bayo. Use the time to book a return flight, catch up on work and speak to Mercy.

He checked his phone to see if she had sent him another message, he had a plethora of text messages, WhatsApp messages, emails, and a whole lot more awaiting his attention.

Remi was about to open Mercy's last text, when Bayo asked for a glass of water and complained that he had a severe headache.

Chapter 41

One month later……

Remi looked at the clock on the wall opposite his desk, it was already 7.00pm. *Where had the day gone*? he thought as he ran his hands through his hair, he was tired and exhausted.

Unfortunately, all the issues that had arisen while he was away had not been resolved or acted upon in his absence. No one wanted to risk making the wrong decision and bear the wrath of Remi Olapade, so everything had been left for him to deal with upon his return.

There was a hell of a lot to do and finish, he thought. In a way, he had been grateful for the full-on work, as it had helped keep his mind away from the mess he was currently in.

Remi needed to catch up on all his paperwork and emails before he went away again for the weekend in New York.

The last time he had been there, Sam had been very groggy coming in and out of consciousness, unaware of her surroundings.

According to Yomi's mum WhatsApp message, she was now making progress. She had started eating properly and had been asking if there was a gym in the hospital, that was a sign for everyone who knew Sam that she was getting better.

Remi had been warned that her memory hadn't fully recovered; there were still some things she could not remember. He raked his hands through his hair as his eyes dropped to the brown envelope lying on his desk. It contained the results of the prenatal paternity test he had requested from Mercy.

He had finally gone to see her two days after he and Bayo arrived back in Nigeria.

Bayo had recovered from his fall with no visible complications, apart from the scar on his face which had suddenly turned him into a babe magnet. The air hostesses had fawned all over him on the way back home, so much so, that they had upgraded the two of them.

It was a shame that such a gesture was wasted on Bayo, he had accepted the phone number the lady had slipped into his hand with the suaveness and aplomb of a seasoned playboy.

Remi had hesitated at Mercy's gate wondering how he was going to handle the situation he currently found himself in. The baby might not be his he thought, they were meant to be friends with benefits. However, the last couple of times they had been together, there had been a few mishaps that he himself was ready to attest to.

However, the fact that she had started going all clingy on him, even before the scare, had made him contemplate on whether he should continue seeing her.

Life was full of complications, Remi thought, as he drove into her compound. He got out of his car, locked it and knocked on her door.

In another life, Mercy ticked all the boxes of what he had thought he wanted in a woman. Very pretty, he could not take that away from her, roughly 5'9, very light-skinned, with 36D knockers that just made you stare at them instead of anywhere else. She wasn't thin, but was what he would describe as voluptuous, she had a reasonably small waist, wide hips and a nice arse. But for some reason at this current moment in time, it did nothing for him.

Remi heard the keys turning in the door and the door opened.

Mercy stood there looking pale and tired, which had nothing to do with the fact that she wasn't wearing any makeup.

"Hi Remi, please come in," she said, as she opened the door wider for him to step in.

He walked into her living room and sat down, sprawling on the chair with his hands on his head as he watched her.

"Can I get you anything to drink?" she asked him, as she hovered around his chair.

"I will have water, thanks," he replied.

Remi watched as she walked into her kitchen, *shit* he thought. *How had he ended up here? How had a casual hookup become so complicated?*

Mercy came back into the living room and placed a glass of water on a stool. He watched as she took a seat opposite him in her living room.

"Mercy are you ok?" Remi asked. "Are you sure you are pregnant?" he asked her.

"Remi, I have done the test three times. You remember the last couple of times we were together we had a few mishaps," as she played with the hem of her dress.

"I want to have an abortion, actually I am going to have one," she said. "I was in a state of shock and panic when I sent you that message, don't worry. I will not be saddling you with a child," looking down at her dress.

Remi hesitated, he was being given a get out of jail free card here. Relief washed over him as he heard those words from Mercy about the abortion.

Remi had initially thought she wanted to use the pregnancy as a ruse for emotional blackmail, but it seemed she wasn't willing to keep the baby, anyway.

Suddenly out of nowhere, Remi heard a crystal-clear voice in his head say, *'Nothing is coincidence, embrace the lessons,'* while he was staring at Mercy.

"Mercy that's our baby you're talking about, it would be a bit hasty for you to make such a unilateral decision," he said, looking at her in the face and holding her gaze.

Remi had blurted that out on impulse, it wasn't what he had planned on saying to her. Hoping that the softly approach would help diffuse the tense situation they were currently in. Not wanting her to do anything rash.

"Remi, I don't want a baby right now and it doesn't fit in with my plans or schedule," she said, as she played with her hair.

"Plus, I don't want the stigma of being a baby mother. Not that it matters these days, but it matters to me," staring at him defiantly.

Remi took in her words, there was no way he would marry Mercy even if the baby turned out to be his. Maybe, before the events of the last few weeks he might have considered it, but now it was totally out of the picture.

Mercy was a party girl and had never worked a day in her life as far as he could tell. How she kept herself in such a place was anyone's guess.

They had met and became friends through a mutual acquaintance at a party. Her physical attributes had initially blinded him to the fact that intelligent discourse wasn't her forte.

"Do you want to get married then?" Remi asked, staring at her.

Chapter 42

Sam walked back to her bed with one of her hands on her head. Feeling very dizzy with a horrible headache that was making her feel nauseous.

Her head started pounding any time she tried to remember things or events, it was like trying to see through thick dense fog.

The doctors had said she was trying too hard, the gaps in her memory would eventually return when they were ready to. She was putting herself under too much stress by trying too hard to remember.

Due to the amnesia and the knock on her head, they said she might also display unusual behaviour that might be different to the norm for her.

The PTSD they had diagnosed was keeping her up at night; she wasn't sleeping at all, any time she closed her eyes she experienced the flashbacks that took her back to Tokyo airport, where everything got replayed in brilliant technicolour. The bomb went off again and again in her head every time she closed her eyes.

Sam breathed a sigh of relief when she got back to her room, pouring herself a glass of water and decided to rest as she got on her bed.

Auntie Lara, Yomi's mum, had left an hour ago to rest and cook up something hot and spicy. As far as she was concerned the bland food wasn't helping Sam's situation, she needed pepper.

What Sam needed was her own mother she thought, she had never seen her mum after she had dumped her, when she was five years old. Right now, she needed someone to lash out to, someone who she could really reveal herself to, without pretending that everything was fine. Without having to box in her real feelings and emotions due to a sense of obligation. The obligation of gratitude and politeness.

Sam needed someone who would do that for her and comfort her, she wished she could have that. She had always acted like the perfect daughter, she had always done what was expected of her since Yomi's family had taken her in.

All she wanted right now, was the hugs and comfort of her mum, for her to lie beside her and comfort her and tell her that everything was going to be OK.

Sam had been dreaming about her a lot, but her face was always blurred out in a funny way. She had seen the two of them repeatedly at a beach playing and building sand castles. It triggered a deep memory from her childhood that she had buried deep down in the recesses of her brain a long time ago.

Sam had never found out who her father was either, the feeling of loss and lack of closure made her weepy. Turning on her bed she picked up the television remote from the side table, to find something interesting to watch.

Before Aunty Lara had left she had berated Sam on her appearance, she had moaned that just because she was in a hospital did not mean she should not brush her hair and add some gloss to her lips.

Sam had rolled her eyes at her.

Aunty Lara had hinted that there were some nice-looking doctors around that she had noticed and who knows what might happen, staring at her mischievously.

Sam had rolled her eyes at her, "Aunty this is not one of those doctor shows you watch where they stare soulfully into each other's eyes, this is real life."

"Such things don't happen," shaking her head.

Auntie Lara did not listen to her. Before she left, she had forced Sam to get her natural hair in a decent state, without looking like Medusa and put on the prescribed lip gloss.

Sam was busy flicking through the channels when she noticed the most adorable hunk of a black man standing hesitantly at the door. She unconsciously looked around the room, thinking he could not be coming to see her, rather someone else in the room.

The hunk was at least 6'2 with very manly broad shoulders, and um, um, um, those shoulders were to die for OMG. His biceps, oh lawd they were big, sexy, and strong.

The hunk was wearing a tight black t-shirt that did a lot for that manly chest, the t-shirt hugged a long lean hard torso. His bottom half was encased in black jeans, this guy needed to come in and speak to her and not whoever he was going to see.

Auntie Lara had been correct, there were some nice-looking men around.

Her headache pounded harder as her eyes slid down to his dick, she had to stop her appraisal of that piece of his anatomy when the man said, "Hi".

"Erm, Hi," Sam replied, as she tore her gaze away, and slowly moved it up to his face. He was also very good looking, he had stubble on his chin that her hands were itching to touch.

"Who are you looking for?" Sam asked.

The hunk took a couple of steps into the room and she noticed he had a very desirable and delectable backside, very nice to hold onto...

Sam brought herself up short regarding her carnal thoughts when she remembered the doctors saying she might exhibit strange behaviour for a while.

Was this strange?

Mmm, she could not help but admire him, whoever his personal trainer was she wanted to meet him.

Shifting her focus back to the TV, expecting him to leave anytime soon, she wasn't expecting any visitors.

"Hi Sam," the hunk said, as he took a few more steps into the room.

Sam looked at him, "Do I know you?" she asked, as she quickly pulled up the sheets to cover herself properly using it as a shield for any verbal onslaught about to drop.

"Sam, it's me Remi," the hunk replied.

She had never seen him before. *Damn,* she should have tried to look better if she knew she would be entertaining this prized specimen of manhood in her room.

"My mum's name is Remi," she replied. "I don't know who you are," a look of confusion on her face.

The hunk sighed as a sad look came into his eyes. "Do you remember Adam?" he asked looking at her.

Sam put her hands to her head as the pounding increased in severity. "No," she whispered.

"What are those names meant to mean to me?" she asked the man.

"My head hurts," she said, as she lay back on the bed, closing her eyes and the image of the man setting off the bomb came unbidden.

Sam screamed and cried, she heard the stranger drop his stuff on the table and felt him take her in his arms and comfort her.

That's what broke her, as she inhaled the smell of his aftershave, it made her feel protected and safe, as she sobbed into his shoulder. He kept on soothing her, his hands on her hair while rocking her gently and whispering in her ear, that it was all right.

A nurse quickly ran into the room, alerted to Sam's distress having heard her scream.

Moving in on her and checking her vitals. "She is getting flashbacks," the nurse said, as she turned to Remi. "She was close to the detonation, she had tried to reason with the man not to set off his vest," she continued. "I will be outside if you need me," she said to Remi, as she walked out of the room.

Sam detangled herself from the stranger and laid back on her bed. The hunk pulled up a chair next to her bed and held her hand as he stroked it gently.

She turned her head his way.

"Who are you?" Sam asked.

Chapter 43

The anguish in her question had touched Remi to his core, he felt her pain. The difficulty of not being able to remember certain aspects of your life.

Remi held Sam's hand in his hands as he tried to soothe her and comfort her. After her crying episode, she looked so small and vulnerable on the bed.

Seeing her in such a distressed state had tugged at his heartstrings, making him wish there was something he could do to help take away her pain.

The Sam he knew was tough and indomitable, not the weepy vulnerable girl who was on the bed.

Remi had taken a long time with his appearance that morning, hoping that she would appreciate the fact he had dressed the way she demanded and told him to, when she had been into her alter ego Mistress Eve.

His body had responded to her appraising glance, warming him to the tip between his legs. Noticing the appreciation and interest in her eyes as she had watched him hovering by the door.

Remi never thought in a million years that she wouldn't recognize him. He was shocked and disappointed, but he hoped he could help her regain those memories. He needed her to remember him, they had a lot of unfinished business he wanted to collect on.

Bringing himself back to reality by thinking about the mess he currently found himself in.

Remi was in love with a woman and he also had another woman carrying his baby, was he doing the right thing coming to see Sam instead of being back in Lagos supporting Mercy?

The thoughts churned through his head as he remembered the events that led up to his departure for New York.

Remi didn't know where the question regarding marriage had come from, the first evening he had gone to see Mercy.

"Do you want to get married then?" he had asked her.

"Ha-ha... OMG Remi, you do make me laugh. No, I don't want marriage. Why would I want to become shackled to a man?" Mercy had replied.

"No... but I don't want the baby....it's an irritating inconvenience," she had told him, as she stroked the armchair she was sitting on.

Remi had looked at her in shock.

Was Mercy really that shallow? How had he made the mistake of creating a baby with such an individual?

"I want the baby," Remi had blurted out.

"I want to keep it. I can't let you go ahead with the abortion Mercy. Please think about it." Remi had pleaded with her, the first time he had visited her after he had returned from Japan.

He went over and hugged her. "Please think about it Mercy."

He had kissed her on her forehead and walked out of her flat, fear and turmoil going through his mind.

Leaving her flat he had gone for a drive to clear his head, still feeling vulnerable and emotional after all he had witnessed the days before in Tokyo.

If the child was his he wanted that child, but he knew that he was also at the mercy of Mercy. The irony of the situation wasn't lost on him. He just hoped and wished that she would listen to him.

Remi's thoughts had gone to Sam at that moment when he had been driving and thinking, she was a friend that he knew he could speak to about most things.

He had wished at that moment for the opportunity to call her and talk to her, to seek her counsel, but that wouldn't be possible as she had just been airlifted to NYC.

Plus, what would he tell her anyway, a lady he had slept with might be carrying his baby?

He had laughed at the thought.

Instead, he had sent a message to Yomi who was still out there with her, to see how she was getting on.

The following week, after his initial visit Remi had gone back to see Mercy.

She had welcomed him warmly, she wasn't looking as pale as the last time he had been there.

"Two visits in less than ten days, I must be honored Remi," as she led him to her living room.

Remi cut through the preamble going straight to the point. "I want a prenatal paternity test," Remi told her, looking her in the eye.

"Sure, Remi no problem. I know the baby is yours as will be confirmed by the test," she replied.

She had been very friendly to him that night, he had expected resistance from her. But she had been pleasant to him during the time he had spent with her.

After an hour he had left to go back to his place.

Two days before he came to New York, the results had come back confirming that the baby was his.

It had been a bittersweet confirmation, some part of him had been hoping that it would not be true.

He had sent a message to Mercy to share the news of the results.

Her reply had shocked him.

Chapter 44

Please check your email, that had been Mercy's response to him on WhatsApp, when he sent her the message that the results confirmed that the baby was his.

Switching over to his email app he refreshed the screen, his heart filling with dread.

What did she have to say that could not go on WhatsApp?

Remi,

I did tell you that I was sure that the baby was yours. I never had any doubt, but you did. Which is fair enough, you did what I expected of you by asking for a test.

Unfortunately, accidents like this happen. The last two occasions we were together, the condoms malfunctioned, they were yours. If they had been my condoms, you might have thought I was playing dirty and deliberately trying to get pregnant with your child.

So here we are, we have made a baby together.

As I have mentioned before, having a baby now does not fit into my plans or my lifestyle at all.

Sorry, I am not ready to give up my plans or my life style for the inconvenience of having a baby.

The main deciding factor in helping to come to my decision is the fact that my current sugar daddy would have a fit if he found out I was pregnant with another man. One thing I can assure you of is that he will never find out about this.

So, here's the deal Remi, you're the one hung up about not aborting the pregnancy.

You want this baby, so when the baby is born, the baby will be handed over to you.

Yes, you, the father at the hospital.

I am not looking after the baby. The baby's upkeep and day-to-day care will be down to you.

I have decided that I will be having an elective caesarean at around 37 weeks, which is the earliest time I can have one. I am not going through any pushing marathon or having my nether regions stretched for your child. You will need to be at the hospital to take the baby home with you.

I will come and see the baby as I wish, after all, this is what men do when they leave the woman to care for their children.

I would advise you to start making the necessary arrangements required for having a new baby living with you. You will also need to start getting ready mentally to take on the role of being both father and mother to this baby.

Once the baby starts showing I will go on holiday somewhere where I will stay till the baby is born. You will pay me $10,000 for all the inconvenience and expenses I will be going through and incur during this time. Please note that the amount stated above might increase.

Any questions, please don't hesitate to contact me.

I hope we are clear about the next steps if I don't hear from you I will assume that you don't want the baby and I will go ahead and book the termination.

Mercy

Chapter 45

Remi gasped while reading the email Mercy had sent, forgetting where he was.

"Are you OK?" he heard Sam ask through the fog of shock enveloping him.

Even in her distressed state, *she always put other people's welfare before her own*, Remi thought.

"Not really," he replied, standing up from the chair.

Not knowing what to do, he started pacing the room, scratching his head as he paced.

"Do you want to share, a problem aired is a problem shared," Sam said, as she moved up on the bed. Moving the pillows so she was sitting upright.

Picking up a pencil and pad, it was obvious to Remi that she had unconsciously switched to doctor mode.

Should he be open and tell her?

"Someone, a casual acquaintance is pregnant with my child," he said, stopping his pacing staring at her from across the room.

"Is that a problem for you?" Sam asked.

She has gone into shrink mode, Remi thought.

"Yes, the lady in question was a casual acquaintance, pregnancy was never part of the arrangement," he whispered.

"Are you with someone else? Is that why you are so agitated?" she continued.

"Or do you want to show me what she sent you? It might help me understand her state of mind, which might help you," the compassion and understanding clear in her eyes.

Remi handed over the phone, even though he knew she did not remember him, he still wanted to be open with her.

There would be nothing to gain from keeping such information from her.

After reading the message she handed the phone back to him. "Mercy doesn't view you as a casual acquaintance, she is sacrificing a lot for you, by carrying that baby to term. She has feelings for you."

"Have you told your partner about this?" she asked.

Remi wondered how he could answer that question; he and Sam had never gone past the friend stage.

With Mistress Eve, just thinking about her got him hard.

"Um yes, I did," he stuttered.

"How did she respond?" Sam asked, making notes on the paper in front of her.

"I don't know," he replied, staring at her, as he put his head in his hands.

He noticed that she paused, a look of comprehension finally dawned on her face.

"Is there anything going on between the two of us?" she asked, the shock plain in her voice.

"I really want there to be something between us Sam, I want to be with you. But I never had the opportunity to tell you before you left for your trip," as he stopped pacing.

Her next question amused him.

"Have we been intimate, I mean did we have sex in the past?" she asked him, looking at him squarely in the eye.

"It's complicated," he answered, as he looked down at his feet.

"What do you mean it's complicated?"

"That should be an easy yes or no answer," looking at him with an arched brow.

"Damn, I had hoped if we had, it could act as a trigger," she sighed. Remi felt her eyes rake over him, sexual intent crystal clear in her expression.

Dropping the pad on the side of her bed she stared at him. "Have we ever kissed?" she asked.

"No," Remi replied.

"Are you for real? Are you sure we have met before?" she asked, incredulity in her voice.

"So, I can't use sex or a kiss from you as a trigger to regain my memory."

"Those fairy tales were all a pack of lies, anyway," as she stared at him.

"You don't want to know what it's like, talking to people not knowing who they are. Listening to them telling you what their perceived view of you is. It's soul destroying, there are things I remember, some I don't."

"Some things apparently that I never spoke about, I am talking about now," she said. "I remember rifling through bins looking for food to eat, the day my father beat my mum to a pulp."

"Apparently, I have never spoken about that," she whispered, the anguish clear in her voice.

Remi wished there was something he could do to take away the pain and anguish.

Wow, he thought, this lady had been through a lot in her lifetime, but she had risen above it and not become a victim. Yet here he was about to add more complexity to her life.

Remi's need to protect her and look after her rose to the forefront once again. But he saw the opportunity of that happening fade away.

Who in their right mind would go for a man with a baby on the way by another woman?

"You must be very serious about me otherwise you would not be here," she said, looking at him.

Sam stared at him, "Are you the Remi, my brother keeps talking about?" she asked.

Remi looked up and nodded.

"Let's take one day at a time, for now. Let's use this as an opportunity to get to know one another again, we will start with a clean slate," she said.

"I can give you advice on how to handle Mercy, from what I can read between the lines, she has suffered trauma in her life. Treat her well for the sake of your child, remember she will always be the mother of your child. The well-being of your child should be your sole priority right now," she told him.

"You need to give her all the support she needs," she continued.

"Do you have parents?" Sam asked.

Remi stared at her if he hadn't felt love for her before he felt it now.

She hadn't pushed him away, she was interested in his predicament and was offering him advice.

"Yes, my parents are still alive. Why did you ask that question?" Remi asked.

"You will need to find a trustworthy person to look after your child, when you are at work. Your parents might help you find someone to foot that bill," she told him.

Now I know why I needed someone like Sam in his life, he thought as he sent off a text to his mum.

Remi wasn't looking forward to the chat he would be having with his parents. Their first grandchild would be born into very inauspicious circumstances.

Chapter 46

Remi sat back in his seat and watched as the New York lights got dimmer as the plane continued its ascent for the flight back to Lagos. He had a lot of thinking to do as he stared at the clouds, without a doubt he wanted to be with Sam. But he realized the chances of her wanting to be with him now that Mercy was on the scene looked negligible and almost impossible.

That there was something between them was obvious, but whether it would happen was anyone's guess. Sam had been insistent on him looking after Mercy and doing the right thing.

But what was the right thing? he thought, touching the two boxes in his bag. Mercy had made it crystal clear she was not interested in marrying, she wouldn't do it for the child either.

There was no point of going into a marriage of convenience if one party was so vehemently against it. The marriage would have been a sham, one of them would eventually file for divorce once the child was born.

If he had to lay odds that person would most probably be him.

The other thing that troubled him on a strange male base level was Mercy could be sleeping with other men while his baby was growing in her.

Remi groaned at the thought and put his head in his hands, trying to get rid of that image.

Sam had not come out to say she wouldn't talk to him anymore but had insisted they take each day as it comes. The hospital had agreed she could leave that week, and they decided they would see how things panned out when she got back to Nigeria.

The air hostess came over. "Would you like a drink, Sir?" gazing at him with interest.

"Can I have two bottles of brandy, please?" Remi asked, pulling the tray from the back of the seat in front of him.

Remi's first point of call when he landed was to see Mercy, he had tried calling after her email, but she had sent a text back that she was with her boyfriend so could not talk to him.

Was that a real boyfriend or her sugar daddy, he thought. *The whole thing was ridiculous*; how in God's name had he managed to get into such a tangled web?

Remi really wished he could take the baby out and incubate it out of Mercy's womb.

But the question he could not answer was why was he so attached to this baby?

Remi had never been the broody type, men never were. But something about this child had stopped him in his tracks. The baby already had him wound around its little finger. Pulling himself out of his thoughts, he concentrated on the drive to Mercy's flat.

The email still sent shock-waves through him. Why wouldn't a woman want to keep her own child? That didn't sound right.

The other thing going through his mind that made his heart race, would Mercy take good care of herself to ensure the baby was healthy?

That was the question going through Remi's mind when he knocked on Mercy's door.

Mercy opened the door after the third round of knocks. Finally opening the door, wearing jeans and a pink t-shirt, her make-up and hair in place. Any other time he would have commented that she looked flawless, but he was not in the mood to dole out compliments today.

Even though he had to admit she looked well for a pregnant lady and hadn't started showing yet.

"Hello Remi, come in," opening the door further for him to come into her home.

"Mercy what's the meaning of the email you sent me?" Remi burst out, without even saying hello.

"Remi, I meant everything I said in there, you want the baby you look after it. I don't want it, I don't know what came over me in the first place to tell you about it as I would normally have taken care of it," Mercy replied, as she walked into the living room.

Remi blanched at the thought, how many abortions had she done?

"But how can you give up your motherly duties? That is not natural," as he paced in her living room.

"Is it natural for men to abandon their children Remi?" she asked, staring at him scornfully.

"Remi, there are loads of mothers out there who hate their children but are forced to look after them. Is that natural? They beat the living daylights out of the kids or maltreat them. Is that right and natural? So please don't tell me what is natural or unnatural," as she sat down.

"I will rent a place in a quiet location up north, as long as I have an internet connection, electricity, and water I will be fine," she said.

"What we do need to decide on though, is the hospital where I will give birth to the child. We also need to factor in how long it will take you to get there. As I mentioned you will be the one going home with the baby not me," she said, staring at him.

"Would you like anything to drink Remi?" she asked, as he continued pacing in the living room.

"No thank you," as he stopped pacing. "I need to leave now, I will be back tomorrow Mercy," as he walked out of her house.

When he got into the car, he decided it was about time to go and see his parents and face the music and their disapproval. Sending a text message to his mum that he was on his way to see them i.e. the two of them.

Pulling into his childhood home Remi sat in the car for a few minutes, while he tried to gather his thoughts, and ready himself for the verbal assault he was going to get from his parents. He used his keys to open the door and heard them talking in the dining room.

"Good evening Mum and Dad," as he walked into the room.

"Kabo Remi," his mum said, "how was your trip?" she asked, as she paused eating.

His father looked up from the paper he was reading. "Hello Remi, welcome home, how was your trip?" he asked, returning to the paper.

"It was fine, thank you. I have something to discuss with the two of you," Remi said, as he pulled out a chair near the table and sat on it facing his parents.

"Mum, I am…ehm… I am having a baby," Remi said, staring at his hands on the table.

"A baby?" His mother questioned.

"Yes, Mum. Yes, someone is pregnant with my child, I have done all the tests and the baby is mine. We had an accident, and she got pregnant," he told them.

"What do you mean, you had an accident?" she asked, shock in her voice.

Breathing deeply, she shook her head. "How can you accidentally make someone pregnant?"

"Who is this someone?" she asked him.

"A casual friend, we were never in a relationship," Remi said, as he looked up at his mum.

"Is it Sam?" his mother asked, hope clear in her voice, a wide smile on her face.

Damn, if it had been Sam, his mother would be on her phone now organizing a wedding, with the top two wedding planners in Nigeria, he thought.

"No, Mother it is not Sam," he answered her question. The disappointment clear in her eyes.

"It is someone else Mum. Her name is Mercy, she is in a relationship with someone else," he murmured, staring at the floor.

"So how does Sam fit into all of this because I am confused o?" her legs shaking on the chair.

"Kay, Baba Remi aren't you going to join this conversation? I know you are pretending to be engrossed in your paper," as she looked at him and nudged her husband in the ribs.

"I have made a mess of things Mum. I never believed things between myself and Mercy could ever become this complicated."

"I like Sam; my hope is to be with Sam if I had the chance. I want to take my chances with her, I saw her over the weekend mum. I told her about the situation I find myself in. I don't know how she took it as she hasn't fully regained all of her memory," Remi said.

His mother looked at him, consternation in her eyes. "How would you expect her to take it Remi?" her legs were moving faster on the chair.

"Who is this girl pregnant for you Remi, do you like her?" his dad asked.

"Not like Sam Dad, Mercy was meant to be a...." he hesitated, as he looked for the right word.

"A friend with benefits? Is that what you were trying to say?" his father asked him.

Remi was shocked.

His dad laughed. "You kids need to know there is nothing new under the sun, nothing. All the things you are doing we have done before and our grandfathers before us. So, remember that," as he folded his newspaper and looked at him.

"So, what do you want to do?" his father asked him. "I want to listen to what you have to say, before I castigate you," his father said.

Remi hesitated, he had been lucky to have great parents, even though he could tell they were not pleased with him, he knew they always had his back.

Which made him wonder what kind of parents Mercy had.

Pulling his phone out of his pocket, he showed his father the email from Mercy. The thunder on his father's face was not unexpected as he finished reading the email.

Standing up, his father went to the fridge and poured himself a glass of cold water. Walking back to the table he handed Remi's phone over to his mum, as expected she flew off the handle.

His mum got up from her chair, the chair falling behind her as she tightened the scarf on her head

Remi groaned inwardly, she was spoiling for a fight.

"What! I can't believe what I am reading. What kind of woman is this? Remi where in God's name did you find this woman?" his mother asked him.

Mercy was lucky she was not standing in front of his mother at that moment, he thought. She would have received a slap from his mother.

His father pulled up the fallen chair, but she started pacing the kitchen and rained all kinds of insults on Mercy's head.

"Bose, please calm down and let us talk this through with our son. The damage has been done, so let us find a way to resolve the situation we find ourselves in. Or rather Remi finds himself in," his father pleaded with his mother.

"Ok Remi, from what I can read this Mercy woman is serious. Is Sam aware of what is going on? Since this Mercy lady is not interested in you either?" His father asked, looking at Remi.

"Sam is aware of it Dad. Sam said I should concentrate on Mercy now as she is the mother of my child. But Mercy is involved with someone else too, who she wants to hold on to," Remi sighed heavily.

His mum took off her scarf and threw it on the table. "What is this world coming to? You children of today, I don't understand you."

"Remi this is a complete mess you know," his mum told him. "How can she want to hold on to her man while carrying someone else's child? I really don't understand you kids of today o," his mother added.

Tell me about it, he thought.

He had balled things up big time.

But he was determined to go ahead with it, he wanted to keep the baby.

"My first grandchild will be mired in a lot of controversy, but that child is determined to come as this Mercy girl could have terminated the pregnancy without you knowing. Why did she tell you anyway, was she trying to blackmail you?" His mother asked him.

His mum was about to go into another bout of questioning when his father interrupted her.

"Bose, now is not the time for if, why and what could have been. We need to start thinking about what Remi is going to do. More along the lines of how he is going to look after a newborn on his own," his father said, as he stared at him.

His father the eternal pragmatist, got down to business and steered them and the conversation down the path of reality, as the enormity of the task Remi was embarking on finally sunk in.

His mother reluctantly accepted the situation, she wasn't happy, but she told Remi she was happy he had taken a stand and would look after his child.

"Don't worry Remi," his mum said. "We will do what we can to help, but, that baby is your responsibility."

"If the baby is staying with you Remi, then you better get yourself ready for the arrival of your child. This Mercy woman seems serious if she wants to visit her child she will have every right to visit. I will start looking around for help. You will need a full-time live-in Nanny to help you as a single father."

"Leave it with me, I will help you find a Nanny as soon as possible," his mother said, as she pulled her two phones out of her handbag and scrolled through her contacts.

Chapter 47

Sam stood up from her desk and opened the blinds, she had closed during the session with her last patient. The sunshine spilled into the room dispersing the feeling of doom and gloom that had previously pervaded the office.

According to the notes in front of Sam, the girl sitting in front of her had been her patient for the last eight months. A group had held her in captivity under brutal conditions, she was undergoing treatment with Sam for PTSD. The poor girl had been through a lot, her only sin having been in the wrong school at the wrong time when it had been raided.

Sam did not recognize the girl. Luckily, she always kept meticulous notes, and that was what helped her continue the treatment for the girl. The fact she had kept very detailed notes on all her patients helped her get back into her work.

The intense nature of her profession had helped take her mind away from some gaps that still existed in her memory.

There were people she remembered and there were other people she did not recognize at all. Luckily her patients weren't aware of her memory lapse, she hid it very well.

However, to be on the safe side before each patient arrived she read their case files meticulously; some patient's details came back to her, others did not.

The girl said goodbye to Sam and walked out of her office.

Sam walked back to her desk, made notes in the girl's file and put it away. Sighing, she rested her head in her hands, lost in thought. One person she had no notes on, was the enigma called Remi. According to him, they had met each other at the gym which was plausible; he said she had helped whip him into shape. He looked spectacular, she had to admit. If she had done that, then she must have had the hots for him. But how come she hadn't slept with him. *Damn.*

Fantasies about running her hands down his torso occupied her thoughts a lot. Especially in the middle of the night, making her wake up hot, horny, and flustered.

Laughing softly, yes, she had to admit, he was a hunk as she packed her bags.

Going back to the gym and dealing with the hell of DOMS had been hard, but she got into a routine and was back in shape in no time. From what she could see and feel her body enjoyed it as she quickly regained her muscles.

Remi also accompanied her to the gym, they trained together, and he even spotted for her sometimes.

The look of animosity she got from the receptionist and some ladies at the gym when they walked in together hadn't gone unnoticed. Whenever she questioned Remi more intently about their so-called relationship, he always left something out. There was something he wasn't telling her, and the omission was obvious to her. Thinking he hid it well, which he did to be honest; it was just her training that helped her pick up his tell.

Picking up the piece of rope on her desk she twisted it, still in her seat lost in thought. The other issue she had with Remi was the pregnancy; it scared her. Remi had even suggested that the three of them meet but she had balked at that idea.

What would she have to say to his baby mother? She hated confrontation, Mercy had a soft spot for Remi.

Sighing, wishing she had someone she could talk to about Remi, instead, she had written to a blog on Instagram called Beyond_Intimacy asking for advice, the followers on there had been vocal. Don't do it.

So here she was, staring at the abyss and she didn't know if she should jump in with Remi or run away from him...

Physically she was attracted to Remi, who wouldn't be. But she had been frustrated that he hadn't taken the initiative and fucked her to oblivion to trigger her memory,

Something held him back, he was attracted to her, she could see that especially when he caught her looking at him, he became aroused, flustered, and looked away.

Sam sighed. Emotions had always scared her, she was being asked to take a risk and a chance on Remi.

Indecision was making it hard for her, she wasn't sure if she could or should go with him. Remi had been so patient and understanding with her, letting her know with his actions and words, that he would do anything to ensure they got together as a couple.

Remi had been with Yomi and Bayo looking for her, so she must have meant something to him, she was very grateful to him.

While recovering in New York, he had come out to see her three times, and he had been at her house every weekend since she got back. Sleeping in her guest room for goodness sake, and making her breakfast in bed.

But he never touched her, other than giving her a chaste kiss on the forehead, whenever she had been staring at his dick, which was always hard for her whenever she stared at it.

Was he worried that it might be considered non-consensual sex, if he forced his way with her?

If he wasn't hovering over her and looking after her, he was at work, or he went to see Mercy.

Mercy was still living with her partner; she did not want to leave him. From what Remi told her, the said partner was not around a lot.

We really do know how to complicate things, as human beings, she thought, as she made an intricate knot with the rope in her hands.

Putting the rope on her desk, Sam finished annotating her last patient's notes, picked up her bag and went over to her assistant to go over the cases for the day. They went over her diary and appointments for the next day, consequently she said goodbye and left to go home.

The drive home felt unusually long as she churned through her thoughts. Remi was coming over to pick her up later, so she showered and changed as she waited for his call.

Remi wanted her to go with him to interview and chat with the woman his mum had found who could potentially be his live-in nanny. Wanting her professional advice on the woman. Would she wake up and kill him in the middle of the night? Or would she end up trying to sleep with him and get her wicked way with him?

Even though he had jokingly delivered those questions, she knew he was serious and worried. Sam had laughed at him but had agreed to come over as a professional and run a few tests on the potential nanny.

So here she was nervous as hell waiting for Remi to turn up. The meeting was being held at Remi's mum's business premises, well the warehouse that was attached to it; where she had an office.

Sam felt uneasy, she had been having a strange feeling all day. Something was going to happen, she had learnt as a child to take heed of that feeling, it always heralded a major event good or bad.

The beep of her phone alerted her that a notification had arrived, it was a text message from Remi.

Remi: Hi Sam, I am outside ready when you are x.

Sam: Ok, coming out. She finished replying and put her phone in her bag.

She locked her door and stepped into his car.

"Hi," she said.

Leaning over he gave her a kiss on the cheek. "How was work today? Did you recognize any more of your patients?" he asked the concern obvious in his voice.

"No, but it's a good thing I kept good notes, that has helped me a lot," Sam replied, as she played with the strap of her bag.

"Shame I kept no notes on you Remi. I still don't know who you are," she smiled wistfully.

"You might only be interested in me because I can give you free psychological profiles," she joked with him.

He looked over at her. "What do you want to know Sam? Ask me and I will tell you. You already know that I am in a jam, with this baby coming and I have spoken to you about my ex long-term girlfriend," he said, as he concentrated on his driving.

"All I know Remi, is that there is something you are not telling me," Sam said, as she looked at him.

There, if she had looked away she would have missed it. Desire and something else flashed in his eyes when he stared at her, then it was gone.

"I have told you everything," he said, as he touched her hand resting on her thigh.

They drove in silence till they got to his mum's place.

Remi's mum had not said too much about the woman to Remi; all Sam knew was that it had taken Remi's mum two months to narrow down the search for a suitable caregiver for her grandchild.

His mother had interviewed thirty-five women and had dismissed each applicant for one reason or the other. Mostly because they would have designs on his vulnerability and rape him in the middle of the night.

Sam knew that the clock was rapidly ticking, Mercy had left Lagos and was now holed up somewhere in Kano. She only had 6-8 weeks left so Remi was getting worried, he hoped this woman would be the one.

They arrived at his mum's place, Sam went into the office and pulled out her laptop and a notepad, ready to question the lady on Remi's behalf. They had set the interview for half past five, at 5.20 there was a knock on the door.

Remi was in the main shop with his mum and had left Sam on her own for the first part of the interview.

Sam noted the woman who walked in was tall, elegantly dressed, and very dark in complexion. Sam put her to be around 40. She reminded her of a headmistress but with a warm and friendly demeanor.

Looking over her properly again Sam realized that she could not actually place her age.

Standing up to welcome the woman. "Good afternoon, thank you for coming please take a seat," Sam said.

"My name is Sam," she said, as she put her hand out to shake the woman.

"Hi, my name is Kechi Ojukwu," the woman replied, shaking Sam's hand.

Interesting Sam thought, same surname as my maiden name.

The feeling of unease she had experienced all day intensified as she stared at the woman. The woman stared at her and became still, if Sam hadn't been watching closely she would have missed it, there was something in that glance.

Dismissing the feeling of unease, she asked Kechi the questions she had prepared. Sam ran through the questions with Kechi, she passed them all with flying colors.

Remi's mother had been right, she was perfect for the job.

One answer hinted at some sort of loss, she had experienced, which was normal. *We all go through loss at one stage or the other in our lives*, Sam thought going over the answers again.

Sam could not resist, "Kechi, how old are you?" Sam asked while making notes on her laptop.

"I am 57 Sam, I hope that isn't a problem?" Kechi smiled shyly at her.

Wow. Sam was gobsmacked, her face was unlined and plump, and her figure, would give most thirty something's a run for their money, she thought.

"So why do you want this job, Kechi? It will be demanding," Sam queried her. "Do you have any children?" Sam continued.

"No, I don't have children," Kechi replied, sadness and regret evident in her tone. "But I have been looking after children all my life as you can see, I am a Norland trained Nanny. I haven't worked since I have been back in Nigeria. Traditional English nannies are not in demand here, but I took a chance after doing my research on the young man who needs a nanny."

"I will also give you my references if needed," Kechi continued.

"Yes, we will need those references," Sam replied, as she typed on her laptop.

"Please may I ask you a question, it's Sam, right?" Kechi asked.

Looking up from her notes. "Yes, sure you can," Sam replied.

Sam's feeling of uneasiness increased there was something about this woman that unnerved her, she was staring at her as if she had seen a ghost.

"Is your mother's name Remi?" Kechi asked.

Sam's heart slowed down, she heard the pounding in her head. Pushing her laptop away, she looked back up at the woman.

"Yes, why?" Sam asked, dread in her voice.

Kechi's eyes widened in shock, as a hand went over her mouth. "Oh my God, Nkechi, is it really you?" the woman gasped.

Sam's second name was Nkechi no one had ever called her that, she had always gone by the name of Samantha, which she had shortened to Sam. She knew her mum's name had been Remi Ojukwu. But the surname was a common one, she had come across a lot of them in her lifetime.

"Who is Nkechi?" Sam asked, as a headache started building on her temples, it was like the ones she had experienced in hospital while in New York.

She closed her eyes and saw the man with the vest, but she breathed slowly and willed the image away it was not real.

The woman dropped her bag and ran over to Sam.

"Are you ok, Sam?" she asked her, her hand on her shoulder.

"I am ok, thank you. It's just a bad headache," Sam replied, as a wave of nausea bubbled in her throat.

The woman went back to her seat and opened her bag. "I don't know why I had the urge to put this picture in my bag today," Kechi rummaged through her bag and pulled out a bible.

"I have spent the last twenty-five years looking for my sister and her daughter, every time I went for an interview, I always took this with me as a good luck charm." She opened the bible staring at something in the middle.

"I was getting bored at home and was contemplating going back to England when I saw the ad," she said softly, still staring at something in her bible.

Kechi took out an old dog-eared picture and showed it to Sam, it was a picture of a young woman and a child holding a cuddly toy.

The young woman in the picture was a carbon copy of Sam. The exact copy of the picture the woman was holding out to her; was in Sam's bible that resided on her bed stand at home, it was a picture of Sam as a child holding on to her favorite toy Mr. Snoopy, with her mother.

Chapter 48

Remi watched as his mum made witty conversation with one of her customers, by the time the lady left the shop she had bought three more items she did not need. Most probably the poor woman had come in to buy one thing, he watched in amusement as the woman left the shop laden with bags.

His mother was a born salesperson, he had always told her that she could sell ice to the Eskimos, she always found that joke funny.

Pacing continuously in his mother's shop, Remi wondered how Sam was getting on.

"Remi, please stop pacing. You are making me dizzy," his mum moaned.

"I believe this will be the best person for the job, she will be expensive, but I think she will be the one," she said. "She has never worked in Nigeria, all her positions have been in Europe and the Middle East, I don't know if she has looked after a Nigerian baby before," she said, as she started putting things away in preparation for closing.

Remi looked over to his mum. "Is she white? How will she cope being alone in Nigeria? She might get homesick Mum and leave," he said.

His mum laughed. "She is a Nigerian Remi, from what I can tell, so relax. She mentioned she was trying to reconnect with her family here. I did not probe any further."

"However, I will defer to Sam's expertise regarding the final decision. She will be able to detect if there is anything else we need to be worried about," his mother said.

His mother walked over and put a hand on his shoulder. "Don't worry Remi, everything will be fine eventually. It looks difficult now, but things will work out."

Remi stopped pacing; he really needed someone as soon as possible, Mercy could give birth to the baby in the next 4 weeks. He was full of trepidation about the birth and the arrival of a baby he still wasn't prepared for.

If only he could convince Sam to take a chance with him, but she had been reluctant. He did not blame her, his mother the eternal optimist had told him not to worry that things would work out for the best.

It wasn't looking that way now.

"Sam is not interested in me Mum, she thinks the whole thing is too complicated," Remi sighed.

"Remi, of course the thing is complicated, do you blame her?"

"If it was your sister would you tell her to go with the guy?" his mother asked him.

"No," he mumbled.

"Knowing you, you would be mad if your sister went with someone like that."

"Exactly, there you go, so be patient with her Remi, things will work themselves out," she told him. "You also need to factor in the memory loss Remi, you can't tell someone who does not know you to take a chance on you."

Remi looked at his watch, Sam and the lady had been talking for more than ninety minutes; what kind of questionnaire was Sam putting the poor woman through, he thought. He decided to go over to the warehouse and see what was going on.

"Mum I will be back shortly, I just need to check and see how Sam is getting on," he said, as he walked out of the door.

Remi bumped into Sam walking out of the door of the warehouse, tears were running down her eyes. It was obvious that she was upset and that she had been crying.

"Sam, what's wrong? What happened? Are you Ok?" Remi asked, worry in his voice.

"I don't know," Sam replied as she walked out of the warehouse.

Remi looked at her confused, he walked into the office and saw another lady sitting on a chair by the table wiping tears away from her eyes.

Something was seriously wrong, he thought.

"Good evening, Ma. My name is Remi," he said as he held out a hand towards the woman.

The lady looked up from dabbing her eyes and held out a hand. He looked at her, there was something about the woman that reminded him of Sam, he couldn't put his finger on what it was.

"Good evening, my name is Kechi," the woman said as she held out her hand for him to shake.

"What's going on?" Remi asked the woman. "Did you upset her?" he stared at her.

That was it, when she moved her head in a certain way, the woman could pass for a relative of Sam's, there was something about her that looked like Sam's facial features.

"Sam is recovering from a serious accident." The accusation obvious in his tone, as he stared at the woman.

The woman gasped, "Oh my god, my Nkechi, what happened to her?" She looked up at Remi as more tears fell from her eyes.

Now this is weird, Remi thought.

What the hell was going on?

Remi saw something on the table, he moved nearer to the table, he picked it up, it was a picture of Sam with a child.

His blood went cold, no one had told him Sam had a child. What had happened to the girl?

How come Sam hadn't told him, how come Yomi had not mentioned that to him either.

What other secrets would he uncover about Sam?

"Stay here," he said to the lady, as he walked out of the office and walked back towards his mother's shop.

Remi stopped dead in his tracks as he saw the sight in front of him. His mum had Sam in her arms and was comforting her, Sam was holding her head in her hands. Something must have triggered a headache, he thought.

The doctors had explained to him when he had been there; when she tried too hard to remember things a severe headache always followed, sometimes with flashbacks to the event.

Remi felt helpless at not being able to help her, he wanted to hold her and comfort her. His mum sighted him and used her hand to tell him to go away. He decided to go back to the woman to find out what had happened.

Kechi was standing in the warehouse in front of the table, she was stroking a face in the picture he had seen on the table.

She looked up as he walked in, she had regained her composure, the tears were gone in its place was the face of a calm and composed woman. Kechi reminded him of a head mistress, looking down at her students with a firm and stern gaze.

"Please can you tell me what is going on Kechi?" Remi asked, this time the conciliatory tone in his voice was obvious.

"Is Sam ok?" Kechi asked him, the play of her hands on her handbag the only thing showing that she was agitated about something.

"She is ok for now, please tell me what happened?" Remi asked her again.

Kechi sat up in her chair, straightened her back and stared at Remi.

"My father had an affair when I was younger, the lady he had an affair with got pregnant. Pregnancy was never meant to be part of the deal," she gave him a quizzical look.

Remi suddenly felt uncomfortable.

"He had never wanted it to go that far, according to him," She said. "Unfortunately, the lady died during childbirth, her family laid the blame squarely at my father's door. If he had not been messing around as a married man, their daughter would be alive."

"They decided the shame was too much and told my father to come and get his child, which was a girl."

Kechi shook her head. "My father in his infinite wisdom then asked my mother to take the child into our household and adopt her."

"Can you believe it?" she asked.

Remi shook his head, as he listened to the story unfolding in front of him.

"My mother refused, saying that seeing the child would always remind her of his infidelity."

"Even though my mother had always wanted another child it had never happened, which was why my father thought she would be keen on taking in his child."

"Men can be so callous at times, if my mother had come with the same proposition, he would have thrown her stuff out," Kechi said and sighed. "For all we know my father could have been the one with the fertility problem," she said, speculation in her voice.

Remi was shocked. It was a big ask, but then realized how different was it to the situation he was in? He wanted Sam in his life and to take care of his child. A child that he couldn't even call love-child. The thing between him and Mercy had never been love. He sighed, this was a mess.

Kechi shook her head and took a sip of water. "Since my mother refused my father's absurd request, the child was sent away to live with my father's sister."

"My auntie and my dad were not always on the best of terms, but she agreed to look after the child for a price."

"My father's girlfriend had also been a Yoruba girl, so that added insult to injury," she said. "My auntie treated the girl like her personal slave."

"It was like they named her so that she would be aware of her difference, a Yoruba first name with her traditional Igbo surname." Kechi wiped the tears from her face again. "The dog in that house was treated better than my sister."

"My Auntie hated Remi with a passion. She used it as an opportunity to pour all the hate she had for my father on my sister. I tried talking to my father, but he did not listen to me."

"My sister did not ask for the life she was subjected to," Kechi cried as she remembered something.

"I also know that my aunt's husband abused the girl as she was growing up. I found out a lot during the times I stayed at my aunt's place."

"You see, when I found out that I had a sister I ensured that I spent as many of my holidays as possible with my auntie. While I was there Remi was treated a bit better, but the fear was always there in her eyes, when I left the abuse intensified all over again."

Kechi paused and looked at the picture in her hands. "I left Nigeria and went to study in England, I wanted to be a Nanny. My father paid for me to go to England, I tried to keep in contact with my sister."

"My first job took me to the Middle East, and I lost contact with her."

"We made contact again briefly when I heard she had moved to England. I don't know how she got to England, I suspected that she must have gone with a man, to run away from the life she had been forced to live. As my father did not pay over the odds for her upkeep and education. He certainly wasn't interested in doing anything for her after secondary school."

Kechi paused her story and looked sadly at Remi. "Old sins have long shadows, Remi. Always remember that," she said quietly.

Remi watched her as he digested what she had told him so far. It made him feel uncomfortable listening to the way this man had treated his own offspring.

Kechi took a sip of water. "We kept in contact, my sister and I, she got pregnant and she named the baby Samantha Nkechi after me her Auntie."

Remi's heart skipped a beat, damn that man, he thought. Remi felt a wave of sadness; Sam's horrific childhood had been set in motion by her own grandfather. Kechi was correct about sins.

"I was going back to England to help her when I lost all contact with her," Kechi said. "I searched everywhere; it was as if she had disappeared off the face of the earth. It was also the time before social media so I could not even mobilize anyone via the internet to help me look for her."

"This is the last picture I have of Sam and my Sister. I have been looking for them since."

"She sent this to me so that I could have a picture of my niece."

"The woman in the picture is my sister Remi and the child is Sam. Sam is the carbon copy of her mother. Sam is my niece that I have been searching for, for as long as I can remember," Kechi wiped her face again.

Kechi said. "It's like nature cloned Remi and made her Sam, its uncanny."

Kechi looked away into the distance. "Without being horrible my father's only grandchild is from the child he threw away," she shook her head sadly.

Kechi paused and this time she burst into tears again.

Remi was flabbergasted, he had picked up the sadness in Sam when he had been with her in America regarding the fact that she did not really know who her parents or family were.

Sam had lived most of her young life with Yomi's family, her life before her fifth birthday had been fuzzy she told him.

Kechi looked at him, her composure once again restored and stared at him.

"What is going on between the two of you and why is there another woman pregnant with your child?" Kechi asked Remi.

Chapter 49

Remi wandered where he would or could start explaining his dilemma to the lady standing in front of him. Right now, it felt like he was standing in front of his school headmistress confessing to past misdemeanors.

Even without looking at her he could feel the disapproval that was coming off her in waves. He could not blame her, he had spoken sharply to her, when he had asked her why Sam had run out of the room.

Kechi was wise enough to know that there must be something going on between them. Plus, he had no idea what his mother had said to the lady.

Where would he start?

Remi stared at her it was uncanny; he was staring at an older version of Sam. It was obvious that the two of them were related, he hadn't seen it when he had barged into the room earlier.

But then he had been blind to the similarities between Sam and Mistress Eve, he thought wryly.

It was a running joke amongst men that look at your girlfriend's mother and you will know what your girlfriend would look like in the future. If what they joked about held true, then Sam would turn heads for a very long time.

It was strange how fate had brought them together, he thought.

If he did not have an impending birth Sam would never have met her long-lost Aunt. Life really was a mystery; his mind briefly went back to the strange man he had met in Japan.

Remi sighed and ran his fingers through his afro. He had made a real mess of things.

As his mother had mentioned earlier; if Sam was his sister and asked him for advice, he would tell her in no uncertain terms, that she should not have anything to do with such a man, damn quick.

Remi realized that he was the kind of man girls wrote to Joro and beyond_intimacy about.

He looked up, Kechi was still staring at him, waiting for him to answer her question. The disapproval was still seeping through her pores he could feel it. Remi sighed, the only way to get out of this was to tell the truth.

"Ehm, there is not really anything going on between myself and Sam," Remi said, looking at her.

"Remi, oh…" Kechi answered, as she looked at him.

Staring at him. "You have the same name as my sister," she said.

Kechi shook her head and sighed. "So, you were saying, there is nothing going on between the two of you?" she asked, raising her eyebrows.

It was obvious to Remi that she did not believe him.

"You don't act as if there is nothing going on between the two of you," she continued.

Kechi stared at him. "You're in love with her, it's obvious," she said.

Remi paused, it was an accurate observation.

"We are friends, Sam and I we met at the gym, she was um..helping me with my fitness regime," Remi quickly added.

"You don't say," Kechi murmured, as another eyebrow went up.

It was obvious to Remi from her facial expressions that her idea of fitness regime certainly didn't match his.

"So how come another woman is having your child and where is she?" Kechi probed further.

"Um, the lady having my child was not really my girlfriend. She was...," he faltered as he looked for the right word to use.

"A friend with benefits or a booty call that went wrong?" Kechi asked, an arched eyebrow accompanied the question.

Remi was silent, now was not the time to try and explain the scientific male definition of the two. He was in enough shit as it was.

"Ehm it was something like that," he said, as he sighed deeply, looking down at the floor again.

In the cold light of day, he was feeling very uncomfortable with his situation.

"So where is she then?" Kechi asked again.

"Her name is Mercy, and she currently is in Kano, awaiting the birth of our child," he said. "She does not want the child, so she is going to have it and hand the baby over to me, the father."

"I am the father," he stated, responding to the question on her face.

"We did a DNA test," Remi said, his eyes on the floor.

"But she does not want to keep her own child?" Kechi asked in surprise.

"Yes, Mercy told me men do it all the time."

"So, she was exercising her right to do the same." Remi put a hand to his chest. "Her exact words," he said.

A shadow passed over Kechi's face, her father Remi thought.

"Plus, she doesn't want her sugar daddy to find out she had a child while in a relationship with him," Remi said, as he looked down at the floor again.

Remi could not look Kechi in the eyes, he did not want to see her disapproval.

"What? Are you serious?" Kechi exclaimed, the shock apparent in her voice.

She was about to say something else, but Remi noticed she decided to keep her counsel.

"When is the baby due?" Kechi asked.

Remi felt he was in front of a headmistress, the way the questions were being thrown at him.

"Any time now, Mercy said she was not interested in pushing so she was going to have an elective caesarean," Remi said.

Remi noticed the furrowing of her brows as her eyes took on a speculative look, heaven only knew what was going through her head, he thought.

Kechi stood tall, straightened her blouse and looked at Remi.

"Here's the deal," she started. "These are my demands." she said, as she stared at him squarely in the eyes.

"One, I only work Monday to Friday evening."

"You will make sure you are home by six pm on Friday evening."

"You will make sure you, you Remi, look after your child over the weekend."

"Not your mother, not your sister, but you," she stared at him. "It's important for the two of you to bond," she said.

"Two, I return to your place by 7.00pm on a Sunday."

"Three, I need my own quarters."

"I have no idea what your house looks like, to accommodate a live in Nanny?" she asked.

Remi tried to open his mouth, she stared at him, she did not give him a chance to answer the question.

"Four, I will be paid on the third Friday of every month."

"Five, you will spend time with your child every evening."

"There are a few more things, but we will talk about those when the time comes," Kechi finished and looked at him. "Just in case you have any doubts, some of my previous charges are among the movers and shakers of the world."

"I am Godmother to one Prince, two Princesses and some of the top CEO's of global top 100 companies, in Russia and Europe."

"They look after me very well and take it upon themselves to help me if I say I have a problem," Kechi said, delivered with steel in her voice.

The not so hidden message was crystal clear.

For one brief second, a brief nano second Remi, wondered who was the boss, but that thought swiftly left his mind.

He looked at her in confusion, "You want the job?" he asked in surprise.

The vibration coming from his phone stopped him from asking any more questions.

Two text messages appeared on his phone; one was from Mercy and the other was from his ex-long-term girlfriend Janet.

Shit, he thought, as he remembered the unexpected visit from Janet the night before.

Chapter 50

Mercy wandered restlessly around her flat as she rubbed her bump. It was a hot, humid morning, and the air conditioner struggled to blow the cold air needed to cool her down. The sweat trickled down her chest and onto her tummy, leaving her feeling sticky and uncomfortable.

Driving home the fact that she was all alone in Kano as she went into the kitchen to get a glass of water. Rubbing her stomach absentmindedly as she waddled back into the small living room of her flat. The flowing dress she wore was making her feel hot and uncomfortable, she had been having what she thought were mild contractions since yesterday.

Calling upon girlfriends to compare notes was out of the picture as none of them knew she was pregnant. She had dropped off the social scene claiming she was going away to get treatment for her fibroids.

She hoped that the pains were not just phantom contractions; she wanted the real ones as soon as possible. It was a bad thing to want a premature child, but she was going stir crazy.

The isolation was boring her to tears. Being holed up in a remote area of Kano with no friends or family, other than a phone for company. She had told no one she was pregnant; moving temporarily away from Lagos in case the news got back to Frank.

Women gossiped a lot, the last thing she wanted or needed was one of the girls who wanted to be with Frank telling him what she was up to.

Any sign of weakness, her so-called friends would zoom in on Frank like a heat-seeking missile. There was no girl code amongst her so-called friends.

Frank had made it known from the very start of their relationship she wasn't allowed to see anyone else, having someone else's baby was a big no no.

The doctors had told Mercy she would have to wait another two more weeks before she could have her elective caesarean; she wanted the baby out as soon as possible. Wanting the C-section done at 34 weeks, but the doctors had refused point blank to operate on her. Saying there was nothing medically wrong with her, so she should wait until she was at least 37 weeks, then they would evaluate.

Evaluate not operate; as the guidelines for caesareans had just been moved to 39 weeks. The screams and threats she made did not work, the doctors had not budged.

How and why she had talked herself into keeping the baby, she did not know. Deep down inside her she knew why she had done it.

Feeling huge and fat as she walked around her flat, sleeping had become nonexistent at night as the baby kicked her with reckless abandon. The baby was playing football in there or the baby also wanted to get out. The kicking, in her mind was not what she expected from an unborn baby.

Was it always like this, or was it because the baby knew its mum did not want it? There was folklore in Africa that babies were old souls with powers.

Maybe the baby wanted to get out too, Mercy thought to herself. As she paced alone around her flat at 3AM.

She needed a break ASAP she thought as another twinge ripped through her tummy. Was this baby coming early or was it normal? She would have to Google that later she thought to herself.

Remi had not been in contact as regularly as she had hoped. She had been hoping that something could blossom between them after all they were having a child together.

Remi had not balked when she told him he would have to look after the baby himself. A baby just did not fit into her carefree plans now, what man would willingly run after a mother of one?

She just was not cut out for such baby rearing activities right now.

Luckily for her Frank was away, so he hadn't seen her as much which suited her fine. As far as he was concerned her fibroids had flared up again, and she was in Kano seeking treatment from one of the best doctors in the country. He was on a long-extended trip abroad, but he kept her in money so it suited her well, which is why she wanted the baby out ASAP. Frank would be back soon and he would want to see her.

Maybe she should have considered Remi's marriage proposal, after all he had been ready to marry for the sake of his unborn child. Being rich enough to keep her accustomed to the lifestyle she had grown used to.

Mercy had based her decision to keep the baby on the fact she had done too many abortions for her liking. The shock of falling pregnant again had sobered her into thinking maybe it was time to stop doing it.

If it had been Frank's child she wasn't sure what she would have done to be honest; he already had two wives. A child wouldn't have been a special thing for him, he already had nine kids from his two wives.

Two!!

And he was keeping her as a mistress, she shook her head, not that she was complaining. Just amazed about how wasteful men were.

The lifestyle Frank had got her accustomed to was something she was loath to give up. Servicing Frank a couple of times a month was a small price to pay for her own flat, car, a driver and a generous allowance.

While she was away in Kano, she had put her driver on leave with full pay, she was not sure if he was a spy of Frank.

Mercy wasn't sure where Frank got his money from; she did not particularly care. She had not bothered to probe too deeply in case he got annoyed with her.

The nice flat in the posh area of Ikoyi accompanied by a great lifestyle was all that mattered to her. If Frank stopped giving her what she wanted she would move on. Which is why she had held on to Remi, she would leave Frank for Remi in seconds if Remi responded to her subtle signs.

Rubbing her tummy as she felt the baby kick again, this time she thought her bottom would drop to the floor. Feeling no excitement at all, she wanted the baby out.

During the early stages of the pregnancy she had noticed an increase in her libido, Frank had moaned about it. The silly old man had moaned that he could not cope; he wanted a mistress, but he couldn't keep it up or satisfy her fully. It was like he could only graze the entrance of the well but not the well itself.

"Mercy, what has come over you I am an old man nau, I can't give you 2 rounds per night o," he had complained.

Not that he was with her every night in the first place anyway, the few nights he had been with her he had complained.

Mercy had thought he was joking, he wasn't, and as a result she had become sexually frustrated.

Remi who was fantastic in bed had been sporadic in his appearances. Steering clear of her, it was like once she had told him she was pregnant, he had gone off her. Moaning that he had business trips he had to attend in New York.

To help with the problem at hand, Mercy had found a nice young man who knew his way around with his decent sized joystick, who was able to go into the well as deep and as frequently as she wanted.

There was no point going without when she needed it she had thought to herself. Mercy had left one major detail out of their casual encounters, she never told the young man she was pregnant. Shame she had not been able to bring him to Kano, she sighed with boredom.

Most men would be uncomfortable being with someone pregnant with someone else's baby and who wanted sex all the time, day and night.

She winced as she rubbed where the baby had just given her what felt like a vicious kick.

One thing she promised herself though, if she had a boy, she would warn him about wasting money on run girls.

She missed her friends and the gossip. Social media had helped her stay in touch but it wasn't the same as being there and seeing things happen.

She did not enjoy being alone, she wanted company. She picked up the phone and sent a message to Remi.

Maybe the two of them being alone together for the next couple of weeks might change the way they felt about each other. She had always harboured a soft spot for Remi, if she was going to leave Frank for someone else, it would be Remi the father of her unborn child.

Chapter 51

Remi was mentally exhausted, teetering from one drama to another. Mercy wanted him to come over and stay with her. Janet's visit had been to tell him she had called the engagement off.

Janet had confessed that she had leaked news of the supposed engagement to make him jealous. She wanted them to get back together; she implored. He had told her he was in love with someone else, the two boxes in his pocket reminding him of the fact, extracting himself from her embrace.

Janet had cried and screamed that wasn't possible, until he finally came out and told her he would be marrying this new woman. She had begged him, to think about what he was doing. How could he marry someone he hardly knew, she had cried. When he had finally convinced Janet to leave, her parting shot had been she would be waiting for him to come back.

Unfortunately for Janet, it made him resolute to marry Sam. Remi did not want to think Sam might not want to marry him.

Mercy wanted him to come and stay with her so that they could bond over the impending birth of their child.

That request filled him with dread. There had been nothing meaningful between them, having deep conversations with Mercy was not something they had ever delved into. They had nothing in common other than having casual sex together.

His father had also contacted lawyers to draw up papers to ensure that Remi would have sole custody of the child once it was born. How would she react when he told her? Not that she had a say in the matter, according to Yoruba tradition it was the father who had ownership of the child not the mother.

All these things were agitating him and were putting him on the edge. He did not want to lumber Sam with the hell that was his life.

Sexual frustration also added to the mix, being near Sam and not being able to touch her, was driving him insane with want and need.

Remi sighed.

"Are you ok Remi?" Sam asked.

They were in Remi's car, he was driving them back to Sam's place, he looked over to her. "I am ok," he replied.

"What about you, Sam?"

"It has been an eventful day for you."

There were two things burning a hole in his pocket that could make the day even more eventful.

"I am ok Remi, just in shock. It's a lot to take in."

A weak smile on her face as she stared out of the window. "But I will be ok."

"I am looking forward to Kechi coming around tomorrow," she said, as they pulled up to Sam's house.

Smiling at him as she opened the car door. "Come in Remi, let me get you a drink. Thank you for bringing me home."

Sam was in a better frame of mind, but he wanted to stay with her to ensure her well-being after the shock encounter with her Aunt.

His mum had also stated that it would be a good idea for someone to look out for her tonight.

Remi dumped his keys on the worktop in the kitchen and went to the toilet in the guest room he used when he stayed over. Sam had gone upstairs to get changed out of her clothes.

Coming out of the room to get himself a glass of water Remi saw Sam by the worktop where he had dumped his keys.

Sam was standing by the worktop, holding up a gold chain.

"Remi, what is this?" she asked, holding up the nipple clamp he had kept in his pocket when they had been looking for her.

Damn it.

Remi had forgotten it was in his pocket, he normally kept it in his bag and took it out at night, before he went to bed. Turning to where she was standing he looked at her and hesitated. Sam looked so young and vulnerable in the green kimono she was wearing, wondering for a brief second if she was wearing anything underneath it.

He watched as she opened a draw and took out a strand of rope, watching in fascination as she kept on tying and untying it. Was that her coping mechanism he wondered?

How much more information could she process today without having another episode.

His mum had told him that she had cried uncontrollably, it had been hard to console her. The cry of someone grieving, that's why his mother had told him to take her home and that she would finish up with Kechi after he told his mum she was taking the job.

What a day, shaking his head in bewilderment.

"I take it the chain is not yours?" she asked him.

'Erm no,' Remi responded, raking his hand through his hair.

The rope was now fashioned in an intricate knot. "Who does it belong to or is there another woman in this complicated life of yours?" Sam asked him, staring at the knot she had just made.

Was that anger or jealousy in her voice, he wandered.

Remi paused as he honestly did not know how to answer the question. Thinking back to that last night he had spent with Mistress Eve, he wanted that back. Having finally seen the woman behind the mask, he had to admit he had fallen deeply and hopelessly in love with her, even though they had not been intimate. *Well, that was not true technically* he thought.

Remi had decided early on to give Sam time to make the first move sexually, but she hadn't. He had caught her staring at him a lot of times, but something held her back from going where her gaze went which was his dick. Plus, she had already picked up that there was something he was not telling her.

Remi took a deep breath and took out one of the items in his pocket, moving closer to where she was standing.

It had taken him half a day going around in circles with Google maps to find the obscure place he had contacted via the internet, to commission this custom piece of jewelry.

The plan had been to give it to her the first time he had visited her in New York. But he couldn't, she hadn't remembered either Remi or Adam. So, he had carried it around with him hoping and waiting for the right moment to give it to her.

Remi held out his hand. "I have been carrying this box around for a while."

He stared at her, and then looked down. "I was going to give this to you that first day I came to New York. But you didn't remember me, I have been carrying the box around ever since. Looking for the right moment to give it to you."

"Open it, please," Remi said.

"What has this box got to do with the chain Remi?" there was steel in her voice.

Something stirred in him. "I will explain, but please open it first," he replied.

The rope tying stopped as she opened the box.

Inside, was a sterling silver bracelet, fashioned with intricate knots. He had decided against gold, Sam did not come across as the gold, gaudy type. Instead, he had opted for stable, durable, discreet sterling silver.

Remi watched as she picked it up and ran her fingers around the knots on the bracelet. Attached to the bracelet was a key that was on a chain, designed in the same intricate knot as the bracelet.

Sam's eyes widened. "Remi, this is.. beautiful," she said.

He could see the awe in her eyes as she ran her hand around the knots.

Sam picked up the necklace and ran her hands through it, he could see that he had made a good choice in the design.

There was a look of wonder on her face. "It's breathtaking," her voice changed.

Remi watched as she picked up the bracelet again, it fascinated her, she noticed the inscription on the inside.

ME yours in knots forever a

He had been particular about the capitalization; the jeweler had thought it was a mistake.

No, he had sent back in his email, that's how he wanted it, waiting to see if she understood what she had just opened.

Sam might not remember him, but he hoped that she remembered her D/s life and understood what he had just given her. She went quiet, as she looked at the bracelet and then at Remi.

It suddenly dawned on her, what she was holding. Sam stared at him, realization hitting her.

Sam picked up the nipple clamp.

Remi answered the unspoken question, "It's yours Mistress," he whispered, staring at the floor.

"I have carried it around with me, from the day you dropped it at the club in Room 3."

"It was a source of comfort when you were missing and it keeps you close, even though you don't remember.. me." There was a slight catch in his voice as he looked up at her again.

Sam looked up at him, there was desire and sadness in her eyes. It broke Remi's heart to see her in such pain and so unsure of herself. This wasn't the Sam or Mistress Eve he was used to.

Her next words shocked him.

Sam dropped the bracelet on the counter. "Help me remember you. Make love to me," she said, moving closer to Remi.

The second item in his pocket would have to wait, his Mistress had put him to task, and he would ensure he did a fucking good job any submissive would do for his Mistress.

Chapter 52

The journey home from Remi's mum's place had been a reflective one for Sam.

After years of being alone and not knowing where she had come from like a bolt out of the blue, she had met her Aunt.

The irony of the situation was not lost on Sam, without Remi's complicated mess she would never had met her.

Sam still viewed him as an enigma, what had gone on between them? Remi had been with her every weekend since she had been back, and for some god known reason, he had been sleeping in her guest room.

For goodness sake why? Why hadn't he made the move to get into her bed? At one point she thought he was gay, or he had superhuman self-control.

There had been a day when she had been staring at him and had seen his reaction in his jeans. He had stared back at her, dropped his eyes, waiting for her to do something.

And those fucking tight black jeans he wore all the time were driving her crazy. The tight t-shirts he wore with them showed cased his strong shoulders and gave way to a trim waist, he wore the jeans low enough sometimes, for her to see the v of his pelvis.

Sam wanted to run her hands down that torso of his and get a feel of that nice firm arse. She would also love to get her hands around his dick. She had seen enough of it calling to her in those jeans.

She had been getting sexually frustrated with him being there and doing nothing. The more Sam tried to remember what had gone on between them, the headaches started. She decided that she would let nature take its course, a lot of her other memories had come back to her.

Sam hadn't known how to get him to move in the right direction. She knew he was aware that she found him desirable.

This had led to her having only what she could call sexmares of the hottest kind.

She had dreamed of hot steamy sex with him a few times, the sound of her cumming waking her up from her dreams. She wondered if she had been loud enough to wake him up from his sleep.

Sam sighed. She held on to those dreams as she watched him move around her house. According to local folklore, sleeping with a man in your dreams and cumming the way she did was bad.

No scratch bad, it was disastrous. It meant that you had a spiritual husband in the other realm who would not let you have peace, real relationships, or orgasms in the real world. He would be jealous of any man you were with.

It was a good thing she had never discussed this with anyone, as the first thing anyone would say was she needed deliverance from her spirit husband and send her packing to a church.

Sam didn't need deliverance. No, she needed to fuck the stud that was looking after her.

A whole raft of emotions had churned through her when she had seen the piece of jewelry on the table. Jealousy tore through her for a brief second.

Was he seeing someone else?

Sam had reacted and picked it up before she could take a step back to think why she was jealous. She had shocked herself further, by asking Remi to make love to her.

He had responded to that request from her immediately.

Those fucking sexy eyes of his had brightened, it was like she had given him his favorite sweet.

Chapter 53

Sam loosened the belt on her kimono, exposing her breasts which were taut and firm to Remi's gaze. They were silently screaming for a touch, lick anything.

The red knickers she wore were soaked, and she could smell her own arousal, from being so close to him.

Sam wanted him so badly, staring as he walked over to where she was standing, and pulled her into his arms. The first physical contact she had with him, her nipples hardened against his chest, as his warmth and masculine smell soothed and played havoc on her senses. Bending his neck towards her and kissing her bare shoulder.

There was a faint catch in his breath as he held her tight, desire smoldering in his eyes.

He grazed his mouth on the pulse on her throat as she ran her hands down his torso. He felt thick and solid, comforting her with his presence, she wanted to run her hands all over his body. Wanting to feel those muscles contract and expand as she touched them.

"Take your t-shirt off Remi," she whispered, the words out of her mouth before she could take them back.

Hesitating briefly, he took it off as she ran her hands over his muscles, and pinched one of his nipples slightly, it reacted to her touch, pulling herself closer into him, wanting to feel skin against skin.

The hardness of his dick telling Sam he wanted her too, pressing against her abdomen showing her how aroused he was. Lifting her up he carried her and headed towards her bedroom; she shrugged slightly so that the kimono was now off, and she watched as Remi feasted his eyes on her breasts.

Her nipples were calling out to be touched, he lifted her slightly to him, and sucked on one of her breasts as he walked into the bedroom.

A wave of desire jolted down from her nipples right down to her pussy that was now on fire. Her clit was swollen and heavy against the fabric of her knickers.

Remi laid Sam gently down on the bed, staring at her.

Sam watched as he quickly took off his jeans, she felt the wetness on her thighs as she stared at him.

He moved closer, bent towards her slightly and started sucking one of her breasts, sending another jolt of desire down to her pussy.

Stopping briefly, as his tongue and mouth trailed a path of kisses and sucking till he reached the honey pot between her legs.

Sam arched her back, willing him to take off her knickers that was soaked with her juices. As her clit heavy and pulsing, anticipated the touch it yearned for.

Her clit was hard, and heavy, she could feel it peeking out of her folds, no doubt waiting and expecting something to help assuage the burning want of need.

Remi teased her, he would get nearer then stop. Stopping and breathing in her scent as she lifted herself to meet his mouth, anything for stimulation.

Sam needed his touch; the agony of waiting was creating an itch and burn she could no longer bear.

Then he breathed softly over her pussy before he bit gently through the fabric of her knickers.

Sam moaned, as he gently removed her knickers and put his tongue over her swollen clit. That was all she needed as the first mini contraction swept through her.

The first orgasm wasn't enough she wanted and needed more, as she pushed herself into his head, matching every bite with a moan.

A finger went in her steaming pussy, in and out as he also sucked hard on her hard clit. She squeezed tightly on his finger trying to trap it in there, not wanting to let go.

Remi quickly got out of his boxers and hesitated, looking around her room, most probably looking for condoms. There weren't any as this would be the first time she had sex here. She wanted him so badly wanting to feel him inside of her. The echoes of the doctor's prognosis in her head.

She shook it away; she did not want to think of such things right now in the throes of passion. Wanting to stay in the moment, in his arms.

"Fuck me Remi, now," she growled.

"It's ok," she said.

He hesitated. "Fuck me now Remi."

"I want to feel you in me," she said.

He continued stimulating her clit, then moved upwards towards her.

Sam pulled him towards her and kissed him, tasting her juices on his tongue.

Straddling her his dick grazing her entrance as he used it to stimulate her clit even more, then without warning he plunged deep and hard into her.

It was hot ferocious fucking, she could feel the pent-up tension and frustration in each glorious thrust. Remi wasn't making love to her, this was pure animalistic let me fuck you hard, let me show you I exist and know how to fuck fucking.

"Sam, Sam," he whispered, as the thrust deep inside her.

Matching each thrust Sam arched her back to meet and match his rhythm, in, out, stop. Squeezing him on his arse as she pulled him deeper into her. Matching his thrusts with her own, pushing herself up to match his pace.

Sam squeezed him tight with her muscles, as his dick started pulsating in her.

She wasn't ready yet, she was close, but she wanted to see his face, with a subtle shift of her legs she flipped him over and changed position.

Straddling him, one hand twisted a nipple while she used the other one to stimulate his balls.

He used his hands to hold on to her waist to steady her, help her as she went up, down, and squeezed on him.

"Look at me Remi," she said to him, staring at him, as a wave engulfed her, shattering her body into a thousand pieces. Sam felt him pulsate underneath her as he emptied himself into her throbbing pussy.

"Mistress, Mistress," she heard him whisper as they both came together, her juices flooding his dick and the bed.

She closed her eyes as the aftermath of her orgasm swept through her, still in the straddled position, as she squeezed his dick and milked all the cum out of him.

Opening her eyes, she was in the same position, his hands were still around her waist.

It was Adam lying there gazing up at her.

Adam.

It all came rushing back, that night at the club. That had been something, he had shown her that night what a skillful lover he was.

She felt her pussy clench against his dick in memory of that previous encounter.

Remi was staring back at her intently.

Sam wanted to get up from him, instead he gently turned so that they were both facing each other on her bed.

Remi pulled her in closer into his arms.

"Please don't go," he whispered.

"I have waited for this for so long," he said kissing her face.

"I waited so long to see the woman behind the mask."

Sam tried to get up.

She stroked his face, "Adam."

"Is your name really Adam?" Sam asked him, a half smile on her face.

Remi rested one shoulder on the bed and pulled her closer to him, "Yes, that's my first name."

"You remember me now," he smiled. "You see, there is some truth in those fairy tales after all," he continued.

"Nothing like hot sex to jog the memory," as he playfully caressed her breast.

"I am not letting you out of my sight again," he said.

"I love you Sam," Remi blurted out.

Sam's heart ached at those words, she remembered the bracelet on the table. So much had changed since that last night in Room 3.

He wanted to take things further, all the way. Could she allow herself to be with another man?

The doctor's voice came back to her. *'We are sorry Sam there is nothing we can do, you will never have children. The damage from the blast was too severe.'*

The tears pricked her eyes. "Remi, I can't give you what you want," she said.

She sniffed. "It will be unfair to you, I can't have children."

"I am also older than you, it wouldn't work."

Sam disentangled herself from his arms and ran into the bathroom, tears running down her face.

Chapter 54

Remi had hoped he was making progress with Sam. *Damn it, the woman was so fucking complicated.*

The doctor in Japan, had emphatically told Yomi that it would be impossible for Sam to have children after the blast, but he had told them to seek a second opinion.

Poor Sam, she had been through a lot in her life, he felt a wave of sadness for her; that kind of news would make all women depressed.

If only there was something he could do, he wished he could take all that hurt away. Remi wanted forever with Sam, Mistress Eve. He loved them both.

Her voice, her touch, her smell, he wanted to be in that embrace forever.

Memories of their love making flooded his vision, Remi had fucked her with all the frustration and fears he had harbored since he found out who she was. The grief he had felt when they lost her, the elation when she had miraculously recovered in that hospital room. The sadness when she hadn't remembered him.

Remi wanted her in his life, he wanted to leave his mark on her and claim her as his Mistress.

Convincing her to give them a chance, was proving to be difficult, however, he was not ready to walk away from her.

The words of the man in Japan came to him, '*Nothing is a coincidence. Everything you're experiencing is meant to happen exactly how it is happening. Embrace the lessons. Be grateful. Trust me you will be fine.*'

He could understand her fears, there was IVF and surrogacy these days, if they worked together as a team, one of them would be a success.

Remi went downstairs to the guest room and had a shower, got dressed and picked up his keys. He touched the bracelet thoughtfully and left it on the counter.

The other box in his pocket could wait. He sent Sam a text to tell her that he was going out and would be back later.

His mum's sage advice and words were what he needed right now, if anyone could give him advice on what to do it would be her.

"Hello Remi," his mum said, as he walked into the kitchen, the aroma of fried plantain and jollof rice attacked his nostrils and made his tummy growl.

Remi had burned quite a few calories earlier on.

Stirring something on the cooker, his mum looked over, "How is Sam?" she asked.

'Sam is ok Mum, I think she is getting better, she finally remembers me.'

His mum smiled at him, "Remi, that's good news." She went back to stirring the pot. "How did that happen?" his mum asked.

Remi paused, no matter how close he was to his mum he would not tell her that it was a good hard fuck, that had re-calibrated Sam's brain.

No, that would be too crude.

I asked her to marry me, that wasn't true either.

Remi had asked her to make him hers. He wanted her to know he belonged to her, heart, dick, body and soul. That bracelet had been for the D/s part of their relationship.

The sign of ownership in the regular vanilla world was still burning a hole in his pocket.

His mum was busy attending to the plantain to notice he had not answered the question.

Walking over to the counter. "She won't marry me Mum, I don't know what more I can do to convince her," he said.

Remi put his head in his hands distressed.

Sighing deeply. "I was given another chance with her when she woke up after being pronounced dead," he said.

Remi's mum lowered the heat under the pan and turned to Remi.

Wiping her hands on her apron, she turned to Remi. "What do you mean they pronounced her dead?" she asked, her voice catching.

"Hold on let me put this plantain away," she said, as she emptied the plantain onto kitchen paper to soak up the oil.

"Mum, by the time we found Sam, she had been in a coma for a few days."

"When we got there, something happened and she flatlined, they tried to resuscitate her, but they couldn't."

"We were ecstatic that we found her, only for tragedy to strike minutes later," Remi said.

The memory returned vividly, and his voice shook slightly. "The doctor came out and pronounced her dead. I can never forget it, it was 14.14pm, Lagos time," he felt the tears prick his eyes.

Remi shook his head and blinked. The aroma of the plantain was too hard to resist; he went over to where it was draining and put one in his mouth; as he paced around the kitchen.

Remi realized his mum was engrossed in what he was saying otherwise he would have been told off for eating the plantain before dinner was served and pacing. The pacing always made her dizzy.

Chewing on the plantain. "I was going to say goodbye to her when all hell broke loose," he said.

"Sam came back from the dead, muttering something about me telling my daughter to leave the dolphins, that we will bring her back."

Remi come and speak to Ibukun o, she won't leave these dolphins. Tell her we will bring her back to see them, the words echoed eerily in his head.

There was a look of shock and something he could only call awe or wonder on his mum's face.

"The doctor had to sedate her, he said whoever the child was, was raising her blood pressure to dangerous levels."

Another piece of plantain went into his mouth. "It was strange Mum, a lot of strange things happened that day," he said.

Yep, his mum was deep in thought, at this rate he would eat it all and she wouldn't notice.

"Remi, did Sam mention a name? What were her exact words? Can you remember?" his mum stared at him.

"I will never forget it Mum."

'Come on Ibukun we really have to go; your dad is waiting for you.'

"Then before they finally put her under she repeated." *'Come on Ibukun we really must go; your dad is waiting for you.'*

His mum shook herself as if there was a chill in the room.

"She also said, Remi tell Ibukun we will bring her back to see the dolphins, but we must go."

"Dolphins?" his mother asked.

"She kept on saying Remi, come and speak to Ibukun, she won't leave the dolphins."

His mum came over to him, the look on her face, one he had never seen before.

It was either she had seen a ghost or had just been told some earth shattering news.

"Don't worry Remi, things seem impossible now, but they will work out."

His mum was rubbing her arms, the goosebumps there for him to see.

"You will be having a girl with Mercy, there is a connection between Sam and that child," she said.

"Sam is meant to be your wife."

"Mum, please that's your superstition at work."

"Really," she said.

His mum was quiet, a troubling look on her face. "Think about it Remi, she had to drag that child away. Sam sacrificed her life to drag your child away."

"She dragged her away from danger, she mentioned your name," she said, rubbing on her arms.

"Sam and your daughter have met in the spiritual realm," his mum said. "They say, I mean the elders and the custodians of our culture, say some children will do anything to come to earth if they have a mission to fulfil. This is something I know is believed in other cultures too. Which is why there is also a saying and prayer in Yoruba, let my own heavenly child come to earth. Remi it seems your daughter is one of those who will do anything to come to earth. Whatever her mission is, it's important enough for her to have showed her face to Sam."

"For all we know your daughter and Sam could have been mother and daughter before," his mum said, a reflective tone in her voice.

A chill went down Remi's spine as he remembered what Sam told him, her father had beat her mother to a pulp. But her mother had managed to drop off Sam at Yomi's mum doorstep.

"I really hope that Mercy has not endangered the life of your child," she looked at him, the question obvious on her face.

Remi's blood went cold when he remembered the note Mercy had sent to him, for them to spend time together.

Would she willingly harm their child if he did not show up?

"The veil between the living and the dead can be very thin at times, and it's only those with special awareness, that can see what is going on," his mum whispered.

Remi stopped pacing and stared at his mum.

"If dolphins had not been involved I would have agreed with you, that things might be hopeless," rubbing her arms again. It was obvious his mum was spooked by what they were talking about.

"According to local folklore and the elders, the dolphin represents renewal and rebirth."

"Trust me, there is a connection between Sam and your child."

Remi was silent.

What if what his mum was saying was true, a lot had happened that day in Japan that he would never forget. The man in the Arsenal top, the same man had watched over Sam and spoken to him. It was only now, speaking to his mum that he had figured that out.

Stating the obvious he sighed. "Mum, she won't marry me. Sam says the fact that she is Igbo and older than me is a problem."

"She is looking for every excuse to keep me away."

Remi wasn't ready to tell his mum what her greatest fear was, being barren.

"Remi, if Sam was from the moon, she is welcome into our family. I like her a lot."

"Being older than you is not an issue either." There was a short pause. "I am older than your dad," she said.

Remi looked at her in shock.

"Mum, you're just saying that to make me feel better."

His mum shook her head. "Remember when you were young, we never let you children see our passports? We told you it was because you would lose them, it was really because you would figure out the age gap that was why."

"I am four years older than your father. It did cause a lot of problems for us, but things have changed." She smiled at him. "Look at Harry and Meghan, look at Macron. Don't worry about it."

"Go and bring Sam's friend and your child home, then you will see everything will fall into place."

"All that is happening is meant to be, it's a rocky path now, but you will get there."

His mum walked over to the counter. "By the way, why did you finish all the plantain?" she asked, as she picked up the knife to make some more.

Chapter 55

Sam cried silently in the bathroom she was so anxious; before she had gone to Japan she would have locked in the bracelet on Remi's wrist in seconds. Now she wasn't sure. She did not want his pity.

With Michael they had both known having a child would be unfair, Michael's genetic disorder would be inherited by the child and would not live past the age of two.

They had decided when the time came for them to have children they would adopt. That had been different, they had always known that the odds were stacked against them.

However, fate had dealt them a cruel blow, Michael's condition had deteriorated, and they had moved so that he could die at home near his family.

This was different, Remi was what most girls would swoon over, he was intelligent, confident, caring, and sexy as hell.

He could have any woman he wanted, why would he want one that couldn't give him kids.

Nigeria was a place that if you did not have kids after marriage you were deemed to be a failure. The blame was never laid at the man's door, it was normally deemed to be the woman's fault, and, in this instance, they would be correct.

The sudden vibration startled her out of her reflections, she picked up her phone.

A text message from Remi.

Sam I am going to see my mum. I love you Sam, remember that. Back soon xx

The sound of the door slamming behind Remi echoed in the house.

Feeling thirsty, Sam wiped her eyes and went downstairs to get a glass of water. The bracelet was still on the counter she picked it up and opened the box.

It was beautiful, Remi had put a lot of thought into the design.

It had been etched with the Gordian knot, the chain that held the key had been fashioned in the same design. It would have cost him a fortune, as she gently caressed the necklace.

Sam was in love with Remi, she could not deny that, but she was full of self-doubt. Remi's baby would not be an issue, she could deal with that, being barren was harder to bear.

Box in hand, Sam went back upstairs to lie down, a wave of drowsiness came over her, she needed to sleep.

She was back on the island, she hadn't been back there since the accident when Michael had led her and a young girl off. Yomi had told her what the doctor had seen, and she had remembered in vivid detail, her conversations with Michael.

The clouds were overcast and grey their miserable countenance out of character from the way she remembered the island. The sea reflected the drabness of the clouds and took on its grey hue, the waves were fast and choppy, she could taste the sea water at the back of her throat, a storm was brewing. The sand that had been white was now green and dark, populated with long pieces of seaweed. On the horizon lightning flashed in the distance, the tide was rapidly inching closer inward.

Sitting all alone not too far from where Sam was standing was a child, she looked around.

Where were the parents?

The waves would sweep the child away at any minute, it wasn't safe, she walked over.

Sam bent down and asked, "Are you ok?"

The child looked up, she looked familiar, her face was tired and sad. Her dress tattered and grey.

The child's eyes were dark and frightened, she looked up to Sam, "Why don't you want to help me anymore?" she asked.

Sam looked at the child again, it was the girl she had been seeing in her dreams, there, she wore a bright yellow dress and had looked happy, healthy, and pretty. The child she had left the island with.

Now she looked emancipated and ill, there was a red mark around her neck. Had she been caught in the seaweed?

"What happened?" Sam asked, "What do you mean?"

"You promised to help me, so I told the others to stay in a safe place until I came back for them when it was suitable to do so." the child said, as she looked towards the distance.

"What others?" Sam asked, "do you have brothers and sisters?"

Two faint dots were present further along the sandy shore. Sam was worried that she wouldn't be able to get to them before the tide swept them out.

Sam picked up the child in front of her, her body was wet, cold, and frail. She embraced her and said, "I will look after you don't worry."

"Let's go and help your siblings, you are safe now," she said, as she took off her jacket to wrap around the child. The sea calmed and she noticed the sky suddenly brightened, the seaweed..

Abruptly Sam's eyes opened, the dream disappearing like the slithers of the seaweed on the seashore, she was in her bed, it had been so real.

She looked at her hand it was wet, the smell of seaweed pervading the air in her bedroom.

Chapter 56

Remi headed back to Sam's house; deep in thought, his mum's words were resonating in his head. Could Mercy have harmed the child while he had been absent?

Keys in hand, he opened the door to Sam's house, she had given him his own set of keys when she came out of the hospital. They were practically living together as a couple, yet she did not want to make it formal.

The living room downstairs was quiet and empty when Remi walked in, he wandered into the kitchen to see if she was there; it was empty. The bracelet was no longer on the counter, she must have picked it up and placed it somewhere else. His next stop was her bedroom, he walked upstairs; the door was ajar, she was lying on her bed curled up against a pillow fast asleep.

The box with the bracelet was on top of the bible she kept by her bedside, the one with the picture of her mum. That gave him hope, she might just be considering his proposal.

He sent her a text to say he was going up North to see Mercy, he wanted to ask Kechi to come along but then he remembered that she was visiting Sam the next day.

He dialed Kechi's number and made the arrangements for Kechi to meet him in Kano two days later.

Chapter 57

Remi got on the last flight of the day to Kano, his mind churning through the conversation he had with his mum. He sent a text message to Sam to check how she was, hoping that she would respond to him.

Mercy in her infinite wisdom had ensured that the flat she rented was close to the airport. Ten minutes after landing Remi was knocking on the door of Mercy's flat.

"Hi Remi, please come in," Mercy said, as she invited him in.

Pregnancy suited Mercy her skin glowed in the sunshine, her cheeks and neck were fuller than the last time he had seen her. Her eyes however told a different story, they looked tired, hollow, and haunted.

Remi took all this in as his eyes discreetly wandered down to her tummy, the pregnancy was there in full bloom. Her belly was huge underneath the flowing dress she wore, from his limited experience the baby looked like it was ready to drop.

Seeing Mercy so obviously pregnant with his child was a strange feeling for Remi, this woman was carrying his first born and yet he felt nothing for her at all.

The attraction and lust that had led to their sexual encounters had disappeared into the mists of time.

Remi walked in, the place was small but tastefully furnished as he looked around following her into the living room.

"Can I offer you water or anything?" Mercy asked, looking around the living room.

Mercy rested a hand on her back. "You definitely chose the right time to visit Remi."

"This child won't stop kicking," she winced, her hand going over her tummy as she sat down. She could not sit properly as she held onto her tummy while perching on the edge of the chair.

"The kicking has been ferocious for the last couple of days," she said, as she put her head in her hands.

"All I get is kicking all the time day and night. I have not been able to sleep," she said. She looked up at Remi, in the light of the living room he could see her eyes were red from lack of sleep.

Remi got up, guilt gnawing at him. "Is there anything I can get you Mercy?" he asked.

Mercy pointed to the sofa. "Please pass me the pillow, I need to place it on my back," she said.

Remi got up and gave it to her. "You're looking well Mercy; how have you been coping?"

Feeling guilty, Remi said. "I'm sorry that I have not been around a lot, business kept me away from seeing you as much as I wanted to."

Looking around it was obvious to Remi that the allowance she had asked for had been well spent, she was living in comfort. That comfort wasn't helping her now as he watched her wince in pain. This baby has already cost me a lot of money, he thought.

"How much more time do you have to wait for the C section?" Remi asked, looking around the room.

"I wish I could have it now Remi, I am tired of being fat and uncomfortable," she winced in pain. "I also need to go back to Lagos soon, Frank is coming back."

Remi wandered how Mercy had managed to pull off a pregnancy under the nose of her sugar daddy. The treachery of the whole situation wasn't lost on him, he wished he could cut ties with Mercy, but that would never happen. They were now tied together for ever due to the impending birth of their child.

"I have a few weeks to go before the C section evaluation," she grimaced, as another wave of pain shot through her. "They want to wait as long as possible before they allow me to have the C-Section." She gasped in pain.

Mercy moved the pillow behind her back trying to find a comfortable position as she winced again and doubled over in pain.

Remi jumped up. "Mercy, are you ok?" he asked, concerned.

Mercy groaned in agony. "Argh, oh my god, this is too much," she screamed, her cries were harrowing to Remi's ears.

"Remi, I can't take this pain anymore, it's been like this for days. I really think something is wrong with the baby," she said, breathing heavily, as sweat poured down her face.

Fear pierced Remi's heart, he had come this far he did not want to lose this baby.

"Remi, Remi, please, take me to the hospital," she screamed, "I can't take this pain anymore," Mercy screamed again in agony.

It was obvious to Remi that something was wrong as his mum's words echoed in his brain. Picking up his phone he dialed an Uber and five minutes later they were in the car as they rushed Mercy to the private hospital she had registered with, situated five minutes away from her flat.

Mercy had ensured that all the important things needed to facilitate the birth of their child like the airport and medical centre were within reasonable driving distance.

Remi felt helpless as he watched Mercy wince and moan in pain. All he could say to her was pele, and hold her hand all the way to the hospital as she continued to scream in agony. The whole thing unfortunately, made him realize that he felt nothing for Mercy. Where had the feelings of sexual attraction gone? If it had been Sam in the Uber in pain, he would be cradling her in his arms and kissing her forehead to help ease the pain.

He shook his head sadly. Remi, on advice from Mercy, had called ahead to the hospital to explain what was happening. By the time the Uber pulled up at the hospital entrance, a doctor with a wheelchair was awaiting their arrival, his badge read Dr. Peters.

"Good evening Madam," he said, as he helped Mercy into the wheelchair.

Dr. Peters led them into a room where he got Mercy on a bed, ready to examine the baby's vitals.

Turning to Remi, the doctor said. "I need to check to see how the baby is positioned in the womb and if there is any dilation of the uterus."

Remi watched as the doctor pulled on his gloves and turned to examined Mercy, the expression on the doctor's face changed, it had gone from neutral to pensive.

The doctor pulled off his gloves and turned to Remi. "The baby is in a breech position. I need to perform an ultrasound to make sure the baby is not in any distress, in cases like this the umbilical cord can create unexpected problems."

Remi's heart beat faster, he watched as the doctor wheeled the ultrasound machine next to Mercy's bed. Here he was again in a hospital, facing another life-threatening situation.

Dr. Peters sighed as he placed the ultrasound probe on Mercy's belly. "It is what I feared," he said, as he looked down at Mercy on the bed. "The umbilical cord is around the baby's neck. The baby is distressed, that is why the kicking has been so ferocious. It has been trying to escape the noose around its neck. We will need to operate immediately I'm afraid, one wrong move on the part of the baby and it can end up being fatal." he said, looking Remi in the eye.

The doctor looking concerned turned his gaze to Mercy. "Madam, you should have come to the hospital earlier," he said, as the doctor shook his head.

Remi noticed the concerned tone in the doctor's voice, it sent waves of panic down his spine.

Remi touched Dr. Peters arm. "Will the baby be ok if she comes out this early?" he asked, looking towards Mercy's belly.

Dr. Peters looked up at Remi from the chart he had written on. "We are past thirty-six weeks, so it should be fine. But we need to operate immediately, the way the umbilical cord is wound around the baby's neck is giving me cause for concern," he said.

Dr. Peters picked up the phone and told the person on the other end to get the theatre ready for an emergency C section.

"We need to operate immediately," he told the person on the other end.

Remi remembering all that he had been through with Sam in Japan felt a deep sense of dread returning. Please God let her be ok he said, as he prayed for the safe delivery of Ibukun his first born. He hadn't even stopped to think his child could be a boy; he had experienced too many strange things to think otherwise.

Remi's heart flipped unexpectedly, he understood the danger the baby was in, if they were not careful the very thing that had given it life would end up taking it away.

Mercy held on to Remi's hand. "Remi please don't go away," she screamed, as the pain got worse. "Please don't leave me. Oh my God Remi, I can't stand this pain, why did I go ahead with this," she cried in agony.

Remi walked alongside the doctor holding Mercy's hand as they wheeled Mercy towards the operating theatre.

The doctor looked at Remi. "Are you coming in to give support as we perform the C section?" He asked.

Remi hesitated. "Yes, I would like to be there," he said, as he squeezed Mercy's hand.

A nurse gestured over to Remi as they entered the theatre and gave him the scrubs and hat required before entering the operating theatre. By the time he got to Mercy, she had been given her anesthetic and a tent had been put over her tummy while the doctors got ready to perform the c section. All kinds of thoughts were going through Remi's mind, mainly how he had created a baby with someone like Mercy. He looked on as the doctors frantically worked on getting his daughter safely out of the womb.

Mercy was calm, the drugs had numbed the pain, her agony now a distant memory.

Remi looked up and watched as they passed the baby over to another table where they were tasked with cleaning out the airways and waiting for the baby to cry. He watched as they pressed his daughter's chest waiting for her to respond to the light and air for the first time. The worried look on one of the nurse's faces made Remi's heart contract in fear.

Was there something wrong with her?

"Come on Ibukun," he muttered under his breath, remembering his mum's words.

"Come on Ibukun, Sam is waiting for you," he did not know why he said it, it just popped into his head, as he watched the nurses and doctors press her chest.

Had she been strangled by the cord or had she been deprived of oxygen as she came out. Wild thoughts ran through Remi's mind until after what seemed like an eternity he heard her cry.

He took a deep breath as he felt water on his cheeks, the situation had been so tense, he had not known that he had been crying. He wiped his eyes, straightened his shoulders and turned to Mercy with a smile on his face.

"She is ok," he said, breathing a sigh of relief.

Mercy looked at Remi. "How do you know it's a girl?" she asked.

"Trust me Mercy, our baby is a girl," Remi responded.

Remi watched and waited patiently as the nurse cleaned up his baby and finally handed over his child to him wrapped in a blanket.

"Your daughter will have a lot of hair," the nurse said, as she handed the baby to Remi.

Holding his daughter in his hands for the first time filled Remi with a gamut of emotions words could not describe. She looked perfect as she laid quietly in his arms; her complexion light caramel, smooth, and soft, with a full head of wavy jet black hair, she looked beautiful as he touched her cheek tenderly. Holding her like this made him realize that he was looking at a mini version of his mother, the resemblance was uncanny.

It was while he was getting accustomed to the family resemblance that he noticed a red welt around his daughter's neck, it was red, horrific, and raised, something must have been wound around her neck to leave such a horrific mark.

The sight dismayed Remi, what had happened to his daughter?

The nurse sensing Remi's dismay said. "That is where the blood pooled, when the cord got around her neck. It should fade away with time," she said, as she continued clearing up the operating room.

Remi looked at Ibukun again and touched her cheek, poor thing. Wondering how it must have felt for her, trying to escape the stranglehold of the cord his heart constricted in fear.

Had there been any lasting damage that the doctors were not aware of? He fervently hoped there was nothing wrong with his daughter. The looks the nurses had exchanged when they were trying to get her to cry had not gone unnoticed by him. He knew the score if things went wrong with her supply of oxygen; he had witnessed the aftermath of such events in children.

Remi looked over to the doctor. "Will she be ok?" he asked, staring at the red welt around her neck.

"As long as she meets all her developmental milestones, she should be ok," the doctor said.

Remi felt a wave of anger, but he did not know who he could direct it to. Who was to blame for the baby moving into the wrong position? Mercy, the baby, fate? All the questions rattled through his brain as the hopelessness of the situation overwhelmed him.

The doctor put a hand on Remi's shoulder. "I understand how you feel, but we got to her in time, she should be ok. Keep a vigilant eye on her for the first three months," the Dr. said. "If you think she is not making the progress you think she should be making, see your pediatrician immediately."

The doctor paused. "To be on the safe side get her registered with a pediatrician immediately and ensure you go for weekly development checkups for the first three months. That way you will pick up any anomalies sooner rather than later. Congratulations on the birth of your daughter," the doctor said and walked out of the theatre.

Holding the baby in his hands Remi went over to Mercy on the bed. "Mercy, meet our daughter," Remi said, as he put the naked baby on her chest.

Mercy looked at the baby, resting on her chest, without touching her. "She looks a lot like you Remi," she said, wearily.

Mercy stared warily at the baby and finally picked her up from her chest. "She is all yours Remi," she said, as she handed the baby back to Remi. "I told you that I am not looking after the baby that is your responsibility," turning her back to Remi and closing her eyes.

Remi was speechless, her reaction shocked him. "Don't you want to hold your child Mercy? She is your daughter for goodness sake," Remi said. "Mercy aren't you going to breastfeed her?" he asked, as he held his daughter in his arms.

Remi took a deep breath to calm his anger. "What is wrong with you Mercy? How can you be that heartless to your own child?" he asked, pacing the room with his daughter in his arms.

He was seething, he had expected to see the maternal side of Mercy after their child had been born, women fell in love with their children once they held them in their arms. Mercy's reaction to the baby was proving to be an anomaly. What had happened to her to make her so cold and unyielding? He looked down at his innocent daughter, a pawn in Mercy's grand scheme of material survival. What would have happened to his daughter if he had not stepped in and taken responsibility of his own child? He did not want to think what the answer would be.

Mercy turned around on the bed and stared at him. "Remi I am not breastfeeding her now or ever. She will make my breasts sag and I don't want that. I didn't do all I did to look after myself to ensure I did not get stretch marks to then end up with flat boobs," she said, as she shook her head. "No can do. I told you once the baby was born, I will hand over the baby to you, Remi. You better ask the nurses to show you how to mix formula, she is your responsibility now," she said, as she closed her eyes once again.

Chapter 58

Remi returned to Lagos two days after the birth of his child with Kechi in tow and went straight to his parent's place for his mum to give his daughter the traditional first bath. Kechi had left him there and had gone to see Sam.

The baby's first bath was a tradition in Yoruba families, the duty for this normally fell to the eldest female member of the family. In Remi's case, this duty had fallen willingly to his mum. The bath involved liberal amounts of palm oil rubbed all over the baby's body; it was meant to remove dead skin cells and help moisturize the new skin coming through. The palm oil was applied to the body of the baby using a sponge, and washing it off using black traditional soap, all the while stretching the baby's limbs, in a ritual the West had termed baby yoga.

Necessity made Remi adapt quickly to the needs of his daughter, days after his showdown with Mercy at the hospital he had become an expert in preparing formula and changing nappies; a lot had changed in those two days. The reality of his rash decision to keep his baby finally sunk in, here was another human being, dependent on him for food, love, and shelter.

It was a daunting and sobering prospect for Remi.

He had sent a text to his mum from the airport they were en route, so he wasn't surprised to see his mum run out of their house before his car had pulled up near their front door. She had been so excited to meet her granddaughter for the first time, the inauspicious circumstances of her birth forgotten and cast aside as she fussed over her. His father had taken one brief look at the baby and said she was her grandmother's grandchild, the resemblance was strong. Knowing when he was not needed, his father had wisely and swiftly left Remi and his mum alone and retired to another area of the house.

The welt on Ibukun's neck had shocked his mother. "Remi, oh my god what happened?" she asked.

Without waiting for a response, she had gone into prayer thanking God that her grandchild had survived such a traumatic birth and had told Remi that she would investigate oils and creams that could be used to get rid of the red welt around her neck. She had given him the look of I told you so, as she fussed over the baby.

Remi followed behind her as he recounted the experience they had gone through and the fact that Ibukun was a breech baby.

The breech word stopped his mum in her tracks and she stared at him after he finished. "This child is special you know Remi, she is an Ige and an Aina combined," she stared thoughtfully at Ibukun lying in her arms.

Remi stared at his mum blankly.

His mother sighed and shook her head. "When a child is born feet first its preordained given name is Ige in Yoruba land. You understand what I mean by preordained name?" she asked.

Remi shook his head.

His mum rolled her eyes and sighed. "You children of nowadays, you don't know your culture any more. Some children due to the nature of their birth are given the names that relate to the event of their birth, not the names their parents might want to give them. Case in point with your daughter, when a child is born with the umbilical cord around its neck it is Aina. She is Ige and Aina and even has a birthmark to show for it."

"But we must be thankful that she made it, this red welt looks like that cord was around her neck for a while," his mother murmured, a worried look on her face.

Looking down at Ibukun again. "Wow Remi, this is your daughter o," she went on, "she is the spitting image of you." She shook her head in awe. "No one can doubt that you are the father."

Remi smiled and laughed. "Mum the baby looks like you, it's like I am carrying you in my arms when I look at her," he said to her.

It was strange how the birth of his daughter suddenly made him realize how much he looked like his mum, something he had never thought of.

Four days after arriving back from Kano, Remi was back at his parent's house waiting for the elder his mum had contacted, to arrive and do the traditional naming ceremony for his daughter. He had already told his mum that his daughter's name would be Ibukunola, that name had been preordained when Sam had come back from the dead. He did not know what his parents would name the child, but he had also carefully chosen two more names for his daughter.

Remi looked thoughtfully at Ibukun lying quietly in his Mum's arms, she had taken Ibukun off him when he had arrived earlier on to dress her in the naming ceremony clothes she had bought for Ibukun. His mum had commissioned a family aso ebi for the naming ceremony, he and his father had been roped into wearing the clothes she had sewn for them. There was no escaping his Mum once she was on a mission.

"Mum I am worried about Ibukun," he said, as he waited for the inevitable telling off she would give him. He had said his daughter's name out loud before the naming ceremony, he hoped his mum would not castigate him or say there was some unknown tradition he was breaking resulting in dire consequences...

"She does not cry, I mean babies are meant to cry right, nonstop, aren't they? She doesn't, she just stares at me and it is unnerving. The first night I took her home, Mum, I swear something, or someone tapped me on the shoulder to get up and feed her. I walked over to her cot and there she was wide awake but just staring into space, she was not crying."

"Then she moved her head slightly and looked at me, it was like her eyes were boring into my soul, Mum. She scares me sometimes, her gaze is like that of an old spirit, looking at me and finding me wanting." He shook his head, as he tried to shake away the strange feelings running through his mind.

"I now wake up automatically to feed her between 2-3am, and when I get to her cot she is awake," Remi sighed.

"She is not drinking as much milk as I would expect her to either. Based on what the nurses gave me as a guideline in Kano. Unfortunately for her, if she is being fussy and wants breast milk that is all I have. I can't breastfeed her." Remi sighed deeply.

His mum touched Ibukun's cheek. "According to the elders and local folklore Remi, during the first seven days of a baby's life the doorway between the spirit world and this world is still wide open. That is why you hear of strange occurrences of a few babies speaking in those seven days telling the parents or family who they are or where they came from." She looked up at him. "That was why some babies died before the seventh day if they found their new home wanting."

What she left unsaid worried him, would his daughter find her new surroundings wanting. Was she missing her own mother? Or had she felt the rejection from her own mother, that day in the hospital. These things he would never know as his daughter was not one of the anomalies who spoke words in the first seven days. Instead she just stared and scared the shit out of him.

Remi shook his head, clearing away the strange thoughts. Mercy had been discharged from the hospital four days after the birth. Remi had not heard from her, he was still in shock regarding the way she had reacted to her own daughter.

Remi knew his mum wanted to ask him about Mercy, but for some reason she had kept her counsel. Which was very unlike his mother, she normally called things as she saw it.

His mum looked at him thoughtfully. "I noticed the same thing too Remi, I mean her quietness. When I was giving her the bath and stretching her, I was expecting screams of indignation. Most babies cry as if something is happening to them or the world as they know it is coming to an end. But I did not get that reaction from her, all I got were some soft anemic whimpers and that was it. She is too quiet for my liking o."

Remi chuckled inwardly, his mother liked the word anemic when she described people. Using that term on his daughter was worrying as that meant there was something wrong.

"What did the doctor say? You mentioned that it took a while for her to cry when they took her out," his mother asked.

Remi stood up and started pacing in the living room. "They said we should get her registered with a pediatrician asap and go for weekly checkups," Remi responded.

"I am worried that she might have been deprived of oxygen before we got to the hospital, that mark is so red and vivid Mum," Remi said. It was the main thing that worried him and kept him up late at night after he had fed her.

What his mother said was true, Remi had noticed that she was too quiet, he had decided that he would consult Sam when she arrived. He had already hinted to her that he thought there was something wrong with Ibukun in texts they exchanged daily. He had asked if she could have a look at her, Sam was a doctor after all, and before doctors specialized they rotated around all areas of medicine.

He had invited Sam to come and meet Ibukun that evening after the naming ceremony. She had not been around since he had been back with the baby, even though they texted every day. Remi missed Sam, and he had told her so, but she had refused to come and see him and said he needed time to bond with his daughter.

Remi also needed and wanted her support, with all the attention needed and time that would be taken up by his baby being on the scene he did not want Sam to slip away. Remi was trying his damn best to keep Sam on his side.

His mum must have noticed his agitation. "Remi don't worry your daughter will be fine, it might be a bit uncertain now, but she is strong. Let me look after her this weekend, so that you can get some sleep and prepare for your return to work," she said.

A sudden wave of tiredness swept over him, his mum was right he needed to catch up on sleep, he was back to work the following Monday.

Remi went over to his Mum and hugged her. "Thank you, Mum, I really appreciate it," he said.

There was a soft knock on the door and Remi watched with interest as his father came into the living room they were in and placed salt, sugar, honey, water, palm oil, bitter kola, kola nut, pepper and dried fish on a table.

Remi asked. "Dad what are all the things you have laid out used for in the naming ceremony?"

His father looked towards the items on the table. "Remi the naming ceremony is a very important tradition in Yorubaland, as we believe a child lives out the meaning of their names every day of their lives. That is why parents are given seven days to think carefully about the names they want for their children."

His father paused and smiled. "Take your name for instance, Oluwaremilekun. It means God comforts me."

"Now back to our naming items," he said, as he pointed towards the table.

"Water it is very important, it symbolizes that your child will never be thirsty in life. Water is everlasting and has no enemies."

"Palm oil, it symbolizes that your child will have a life of love and no friction. Palm oil is used to lubricate and soothe the body."

"Bitter kola, it symbolizes that your child will have a long life. Bitter kola lasts a very long time."

"Kola nut, it repels evil spirits, it is chewed and spat out."

Pausing looking at Remi, hoping the significance of the ceremony was clear.

Continuing, "Sugar & honey symbolizes that your child will have a sweet and happy life. Honey and sugar are sweeteners."

"Salt symbolizes that your child's life will be full of flavor, happiness and substance. Salt is a preservative."

"Fish symbolizes that your child will remain in its natural environment; that of its parents and will find its way in life even in tough times."

"Pepper is full of seeds and fruitful. Your child's life will be fruitful."

His father finished talking as he laid and arranged the items carefully out on the table. The Elder had called and had told his Mum that he was fifteen minutes away.

Remi's dad turned towards him and placed a hand on his shoulder. "Since the mother of the child is not here, it will fall to you Remi to taste some of these things on behalf of your daughter," he said, as he stared at Remi.

"Remi my son, I hope you have put a lot of thought into the names you want to give to your daughter?" he asked, as he walked away.

The words stayed with Remi as he watched his father leave the living room, most probably to go and get changed. His mother would have a fit if his father was not in his aso ebi. He stared thoughtfully at his father's back; he had put in a lot of thought into the other two names he wanted for his daughter.

Remi heard the doorbell ring, the murmurs at the door heralded the man had arrived to name the baby. The naming ceremony would take place with just Remi the father, holding the baby, the Elder had been briefed that the mother was not on the scene. He had been wise to keep his counsel as Remi's mother had not entertained any detailed questions about Mercy's whereabouts.

The ceremony was kicked off with a short prayer, after which the Elder went into the significance of the naming ritual; and why it was so important.

Just before the man had arrived his mum had written down the names they wanted to give his daughter. She had folded the sheet of paper and handed it to Remi.

The Elder finished his sermon and turned to Remi. "Where are the names you want to give your child?" he asked.

Remi pulled out two sheets of paper from his pocket and handed them over to the man.

The Elder cleared his throat. "The baby's names from henceforth will be Alexandra, Ibukunola, Enitan, Kikelomo Akanke Olapade.

Ibukunola since it was the name Sam had called out to him when she had come back from the dead, it meant blessing.

Enitan came from his parents as his mum was convinced that there was a mystery surrounding her coming to earth. He couldn't roll his eyes at her prognosis, too many strange things had happened in getting Ibukun to where she was.

Akanke her Oriki, also came from his parents, he smiled it was an apt name for her. It meant one who is especially cherished or pampered.

Remi had given her Kikelomo – children are meant to be loved and looked after. He would ensure that she did not miss out on the love she deserved due to the way her mother had treated and abandoned her.

Alexandra – because he wanted her to do great things and it was the same initial as his first name Adam.

Remi smiled inwardly, if his daughter lived up to the names she had been given, she would end up being one spoilt Daddy's girl.

Remi watched as his mum and dad nodded and smiled in agreement to the names being given to their first grandchild.

As the oil, sugar, and salt were placed on the baby's tongue Remi said a prayer and thanked God for all he had. The words of the mystery man in Japan came back to him *'Nothing is a coincidence. Everything you're experiencing is meant to happen exactly how it is happening. Embrace the lessons. Be grateful. Trust me you will be fine.'*

Remi was grateful, as he absent-mindedly touched the welt around his daughter's neck. What story are you trying to tell me Ibukun? He wondered as he looked down at her dozing in his arms. He would be happy and grateful if Sam accepted his offer to become the next Mrs Olapade, he sighed as he watched the Elder and closed his eyes as the man led them in the last prayer of the ceremony.

Ibukun had been so quiet during the naming ceremony, it was unnerving that even the Elder had even commented that this was the first child that had been this quiet while being wide awake during their own naming ceremony. Remi watched as the Elder and his father walked out of the room, leaving Remi with Ibukun in his arms and his mother in the room.

The doorbell rang again, they were expecting friends and family to stop by, to eat, drink, and celebrate the arrival of his baby, Remi looked up and saw Sam walk into the room.

It was at that second that Ibukun suddenly jerked violently in his arms and let forth the most heart-rending cry he had ever heard; it sent a shiver down his spine. Ibukun finally cried for the first time since her birth at the top of her tiny lungs. It was a cry of pain, heartache and frustration, it was hard to describe but it was spooky. She continued with her violent spasms as the crying continued. His mum was right, there a lot was going on here that he knew nothing about.

Remi looked up, his mum was staring at him, but from her eyes and facial expression she was telling him to just watch what was about to unfold as Sam rushed in and picked up Ibukun from his arms.

Chapter 59

Sam switched off the engine of her car and gathered her thoughts, the gateman had let her in with minimum fuss once she had mentioned her name. This would be the first time she had been invited to Remi's parents' house. The house in question was huge, Remi came from some very serious generational money. What her friends in America would call trust fund money. His maternal grandfather had been one of the foremost doctors in America before coming back home to Nigeria to retire. It had not been a real retirement as he had opened a chain of private hospitals that attracted the rich and famous from all over Africa. Unfortunately, his first child and daughter Remi's mum, though academically brilliant, had not been interested in medicine, but her first and only boyfriend she had brought home to her dad had been studying medicine and Remi's grandfather had been impressed, even though she was older than her boyfriend. He had left control and the legacy of his medical empire to his daughter and her husband but had left his daughter with majority control.

Sam had never met Remi's Father, even though Remi had mentioned on numerous occasions that his dad was keen to meet her, so they could talk Dr. to Dr. She pressed the doorbell; a handsome and older version of Remi opened the door.

"Good evening, you must be Sam? Please come in," he said as he held out his hand.

Sam bent downwards. "Good evening Sir, yes, it is Sam," she said, as she stood up shaking his hand.

Sam looked around the hallway in awe as she entered, the house was huge. She knew they were rich, but this made her self-conscious of her humble background.

Remi's father pointed her to a door. "Remi and his mum are in there, I will pop in later. I need to entertain the guests," he said, as he smiled at Sam.

The nerves fluttering in her chest were cast aside as she walked towards the door. Sam had made a promise, she needed to see the child, from what Remi had told her he was concerned about her progress, she was not as responsive as he expected and wasn't eating as much as she should.

Sam had made a promise to Michael that she would look after the girl, and after the last encounter she had with the child, she wanted to make sure the baby was all right.

Sam knocked on the door and as she put her foot over the doorway and walked in, Ibukun let out a loud ear-splitting scream for a baby. It was harrowing; it was a cry of frustration, pain, and sadness, this wasn't a cry for hunger she knew instinctively something was wrong. Sam knew why and understood the heartache behind that cry, in her misguided notion of letting the father and daughter bond, Ibukun must have thought she had left her again.

Swiftly and briefly greeting Remi's mum, Sam turned towards Remi and Ibukun. The baby would always be Ibukun in her heart, she did not know what names Remi had given his daughter.

Ibukun was still screaming along with the violent spasms and jerking as she approached Remi. There was a puzzled look on his face.

"Remi, please let me carry her," Sam said to him, as she held out her hands.

Sam looked down at the baby in his arms, she was staring at a mini version of Remi; the resemblance was uncanny.

Remi passed over Ibukun to her and Ibukun immediately grabbed hold of Sam's index finger. Her hold was strong and firm. Her screams turned into whimpers and soon after that she started kicking Sam ferociously aiming for her stomach, her brow was sweaty, thinking she was hot Sam took off her clothes leaving her in her nappy. That is when she saw the red welt on her neck and another ferocious kick from Ibukun landed on her abdomen. A wave of indescribable pain washed over Sam, she winced. It must have been obvious because out of the corner of her eye she saw Remi approaching, but his mother put a hand on his arm. Telling him to wait.

Ibukun kicked her again as she held on ferociously to Sam's finger.

Sam touched the red welt. "I am sorry Ibukun, I should have come earlier," she whispered, as the tears fell down her face.

Sam wiped away the tears on her face and noticed that Ibukun had also stopped crying and kicking, and was now gurgling and smiling at her, her hand still firm on Sam's finger. The gurgling from Ibukun went on for a while, it was strange, it was as if she was trying to tell her something.

Sam watched as Remi's mum came over to her and sat next to her on the sofa, she made no move to take Ibukun from her.

"Sam, are you all right?" she asked, her voice low and soft.

Sam looked up at her, there was knowledge and deep thought in her eyes. Remi's mum said. "I noticed that you were in pain when she kicked you. Are you ok?" she asked Sam again.

Sam looked down at the baby gurgling and smiling at her. "It must have been my ovaries reacting to such a cute baby," Sam said, joking, trying to make light of the strange thing that had happened between her and Ibukun. The pain was similar, but at a higher intensity to what she had felt when she had woken up after the bomb blast in Japan, she had eventually found out it was because her uterus had been scarred beyond repair. The words of the doctors an echo in her brain. *'Sorry Sam, you will never have children.'*

Remi's mum smiled. "She was most probably kicking your ovaries into shape and getting your womb ready for her brother or sister," she said.

Sam looked down and away from her gaze, how could she tell her that she could never have children. Would Remi's mum still be as accepting of her as she was, if she knew the truth? The best gynecologists in the world had told her it wasn't possible. Sam shook her head and chased those cobwebs away.

Remi's mum continued. "Folklore has it that children born with their feet first have special healing powers."

Ibukun must have agreed with what her grandmother was saying, as her gurgling increased in intensity at that moment repeatedly, as she smiled at Sam.

Remi's mum laughed suddenly. "Remi I can see you rolling your eyes at me."

Sam looked up at Remi, he had been rolling his eyes; she smiled weakly at him.

Sam tried to pry Ibukun's hand off her finger as she gave her a quick examination. From what she could see there was nothing wrong with the child if anything she was developing quickly, her reflexes were quick and strong. She finished and handed her back to Remi. Ibukun started screaming at the top of her lungs, only this time there were no tears. This time even Sam knew it was a scream of indignation.

Sam laughed at Remi. "I don't know why you were worried, there is nothing wrong with her," she said, as she watched Ibukun wriggle in Remi's arms.

Remi handed Ibukun back to Sam. "She might be hungry let me get her bottle," he said, as he walked over to a table in the corner of the room.

Sam looked down at Ibukun, she had stopped crying the second Sam had carried her.

Remi's mum who had been watching the whole thing laughed. "Sam you have yourself a fan," she said. "Right, I will leave you three and attend to our guests."

His mum turned to Remi. "Don't forget what I said about dropping her off for the weekend," she said, as she walked out of the room.

Chapter 60

Remi had just finished brushing his teeth and was walking back into the bedroom ready to switch off the lights when his phone beeped. He had been looking forward to a night of uninterrupted sleep, without having to wake up to warm up bottles or change dirty nappies.

Yawning, he went over to the bedside table and picked up the phone. It could be his mum, looking at the notification page. This would be the first time Ibukun had stayed away, and he was nervous. Understanding how most mothers felt leaving their babies with relatives for the first time, he was missing her gurgling and baby smell.

The notification was from the email app and from someone he had not heard from in a while.

The subject line read *Instructions*, his heart beat faster, his dick hardened and there was a flutter in his stomach when he saw the name of the sender. He had been waiting for this email ever since Sam had returned from America.

Be in Room 3 tomorrow at 9.00pm. Mistress Eve

Remi fell asleep with a smile on his face, his dreams dominated by the woman in the mask. The next morning, Remi woke up to a plethora of pictures of Ibukun on WhatsApp from his mum. Each one had a different caption, he never knew his mum was so savvy with technology. One message from his mum got him laughing, she said Ibukun had not stopped talking; she was going on about something, but she was happy, reveling in the attention of her grandparents. Remi was still curious to understand what had happened between Sam and Ibukun. Ibukun's demeanor had transformed after that evening. She had increased the uptake on her milk and whenever he mentioned the word Sam, her eyes lit up. The brightness of the mark around her neck had dimmed, with time he hoped it would disappear.

Remi spent the rest of the day tidying up the house and catching up on work emails, his mind occasionally wandering to Mistress Eve and their evening ahead. While lost in thought thinking about Sam, he contacted one of his old school friends who was good at locating things; he needed his help.

By the time he left for The Lekki Club that evening, realization dawned on him, that in his haste and excitement he'd forgotten to email Mistress Eve about a pass.

When he got to the gate, the burly gateman asked for his ID, and waved him in after handing over an envelope with his name on it through the car window.

Memories of his previous encounters flooded his mind as Remi opened the door into Room 3, the entry code was different, as it had been every time he had been there.

The handwritten instructions in the envelope had been simple, be naked, blind-folded, hard, and kneeling upright by the door, and wait for his Mistress. Casting his eye over the room he looked for a place close by to keep the box he had in his pocket, determined to leave Room 3 without the contents of the box.

The room was just as he remembered it from the last time he had been there. The plants, the walls, were all the same, the only thing different was the full moon reflecting through the glass ceiling, it cast a magical and eerie feel to the surroundings. The lights were off; the moonlight the only illumination.

Remi cast his eye around as he gently massaged the oil on his wrists and ankles. The instructions had been to do his dick last. From what he now knew about the club, *she* could be watching what he was doing. It was while he was sensually oiling his dick that he noticed a pole towards the back of the room; he had never noticed it before. Was it new? Could it have been a new addition? It looked like what dancers used for pole dancing. It must be new he thought, even though he hadn't been to the club since Sam got back.

Thoughts of Mistress Eve filled his head making him harden in anticipation, as he continued to massage his dick, imagining her hands on it instead. It stayed hard in his hand; his instructions had been to keep himself hard. If she came in and he was flaccid, she would mete out her own form of punishment. He could not wait to see her, he would endure anything tonight he knew her mask would come off.

Remi had chuckled when reading the instructions, Mistress Eve had a quirky side as he picked up the blindfold, the darkness that followed helped keep his mind and thoughts on how she had fucked him for the first time in her house when she had regained her memory. His dick hardened, his balls heavy, when a light breeze brushed against his torso, the temperature had changed, someone was in the room.

A faint whining sound filled the room as he knelt upright moving his head trying to figure out where the sound was coming from, something was moving or being opened.

"Nice to see you made it Adam," she said, her American accent on. The voice sending a shiver of excitement down his spine, she was in character.

Remi wandered if the tattoo was also in place, he shook his head, chai, this woman had fooled him for so long with her disguise.

He needed to find out how she did it, she must have fooled a lot of the club members too. As he imagined what she was wearing, a dress, skirt, shorts? Was she naked under her clothes? With her dark, smooth, soft skin, gleaming with cocoa butter.

"Get up and walk towards my voice, and keep your hands behind your back," she said.

Remi stood up trying to establish where her voice was coming from. It sounded like it was right in front of him, so he walked towards her.

"Stop, you're walking in the wrong direction," she said. Her voice sounded like it was coming from behind him, it confused him.

Pushing him gently, he felt a cold long surface on his back as she moved his body into a steel column. The pole he had seen in the room earlier.

"The last time you were here Adam, I asked you a question; that you purposely omitted to answer. I used the word omitted, as I find it hard to believe you would disobey your Mistress," she said. Pulling each arm up and clasping his wrists to the pole with metal handcuffs. She cuffed his feet to the bottom, making him feel like the Angel of the North.

Remi wriggled his hands on the pole, the whining sound had been the other parts opening. His arse cheeks split by the pole his legs now slightly spread eagle. Feeling more like the Vitruvian man, arms up, legs slightly apart, the only thing missing was the circle, he sighed. *What did she have in store for him tonight*, he thought?

The sting of the whip on his arse; was sharp, harsh, and immediate. His body stiffened, this wasn't the sensual lash whips she had given him in the past.

"Do you remember the question Adam?" she asked the steel back in her voice.

This was his Mistress back to true form, something had pissed her off, Remi thought.

Remi moved his head towards her voice. "Mistress what was the question, I don't remember?"

Her response was another lash of the whip, he winced, shit that hurt. This time he could feel the strength in the delivery, steeling himself he realized that he was in for a bumpy ride tonight. Mistress Eve was on a mission as his brain churned through memories of their last night at the club.

"The question I asked you Adam," she said, as she whipped his balls harshly. "Was, did your previous Domme's share you with anyone else?" she asked him the question again.

Remi hesitated, when he had purposely omitted to answer that question he had not known Mistress Eve studied people for a living, he had purposely and knowingly deflected. It wasn't his fault as he had been too busy watching her put her hand in her leggings; he remembered one of the other conversations she had with him that fateful night.

*'Think about this carefully Adam before I see you next week. **I don't share**.'*

A lot of things had happened after that, the most monumental one, Ibukun. But he had sorted his harem out as per her instructions, he never wanted one again.

He felt the lash of the whip again on his arse; she wasn't being light handed today.

"Adam I am waiting," she said, pinching his nipple harder than usual.

He whispered. "Yes," he heard her sigh.

"Was it that difficult to answer my question Adam?" she asked, as the whip went over his arse again, the blood flowed to the surface awakening the multitude of nerve endings in his body.

She used her soft hands to soothe the spot she had just whipped. A groan escaped Remi's lips, her touch was soft, smooth, and gentle.

He was hard again, damn it. He could feel the pre-cum dripping out of him.

"What would you do if I asked the other person, the man or the woman in this room to suck you off like this?" she asked.

Remi gasped, the tongue on the tip of his dick was so unexpected his leg jerked in shock. He hardened involuntarily, reacting to the gentle blow of breath as the lips of the unknown person opened to take his dick deep into their mouth. Groaning as the length of his dick was licked all the way down to his balls, and the tongue came back up and took his tip back into their mouth.

"Don't you want to fuck that wet, moist, warm mouth around your dick Adam? Don't you want to feel that tongue on your tip?" he heard her whisper, turning his head to figure out where her voice was coming from.

Remi panicked, was there someone else in the room? Would she bring another person into their scene because she thought he enjoyed it? Panic consumed him, pulling violently against the cuffs on his wrists, a sharp pain manifested, the metal cutting sharply into his wrists, the pain momentarily numbed by the panic in his chest.

"No, please," he groaned. "Please Mistress, tell the person to stop. I don't want you to share me out, please," his voice cracked, trying to stop his body from reacting to the sensations he was feeling.

Struggling violently like a caged animal his bonds too tight, they kept him in place. "Please," he cried, scared.

No, no, he didn't want it, he'd had his fill of threesomes, he did not want that with her.

What he wanted with Mistress Eve did not involve that, he wanted to be all she needed.

"No, please stop," his voice cracked again, pulling violently against his chains. "Please Mistress, please tell the person to stop," he begged.

"Are you hungry Adam?"

"Yes," he said.

Remi heard a click of fingers and the mouth on his dick stopped, he slumped against the pole. Panic still running through him as he took a deep breath to calm himself down.

"Adam, your dick behaved otherwise, while being licked and sucked off."

"Why?" she asked.

Remi tried to figure out where her voice was coming from, he moved his head slightly to the left.

"Why did you ask me to tell the person to stop?" she asked.

Remi wished he could see her through his blindfold, he wanted to be her submissive, wanted to be enough for her that she would not need to have another submissive. Remi finally acknowledged his jealousy, and insecurities, the thought of her playing Domme to another man or woman filled him with anxiety and dread.

Things had happened so fast in their relationship he hadn't thought that far about that part of the D/s lifestyle. Mistress Eve in her infinite wisdom, had laid her cards on the table that night before leaving for Japan. No wonder she had been insistent on getting an answer to that question.

Did he like to be shared?

It was strange how things changed. In his previous experimentation as a submissive, the bonds, the harnesses had been hard limits for him. Trusting no one enough to tie him up. Group sex and sharing had never bothered him then; but now with the woman of his dreams, D/s sharing had now become a hard limit for him with his Mistress. He had never been open enough to experience subspace with them either; he was truly and permanently attached to Mistress Eve.

"It's a hard limit," he whispered.

There was silence. "I thought you told me you did not have limit's Adam?"

"Mistress I don't share, I want to be your one and only submissive," he said, pulling at his chains again. He was ready to do her live D/s shows if she wanted, as long as he was her subject.

"That's a bit forward of you Adam don't you think? I decide whether I share you with anyone else or if I want to have another submissive serve me. If that is my wish you will have to obey me," she said.

Remi pulled at his chains again, a brief sliver of pain passed through his wrist, he wanted to see her face.

Damn it.

He felt her breath on his chest, "You don't want to share your Mistress with another submissive and watch as she plays with him for her pleasure? While she watches him jerk off, or anything else she might want him to do?" she asked, as she raked her nails down his chest.

Remi felt another searing wave of jealousy run through him as he pictured her with another man, doing what she was putting him through with someone else. His body tensed as she took his nipple in her mouth and bit down hard on it, teasing it to harden on her tongue. His dick getting harder than it already was.

"Answer me Adam," as her hands went further down and clicked a ring around the base of his dick.

"No, Mistress, I want to serve you, and only you. I want to learn so that I can be enough for you," he whispered, as she pumped his dick.

The ring was doing its job keeping him hard, he groaned, moving her hand down to his balls, towards his taint massaging him gently and rhythmically. Remi shuddered, damn it, he never even knew the area existed until she came along. He was losing control over his body as the need to cum intensified.

He felt her whip on his dick, he jerked, it was painfully hard, he really needed to cum soon. The deadly cocktail of pleasure and pain was driving him crazy, his dick was going to explode.

She went back to whipping his arse, then soothing his warm arse with her hands.

"Please, Mistress," he groaned, pulling at the cuffs holding him on the pole. "Please Mistress, I can't control myself," he whimpered. The urge to cum was all-consuming.

"Adam, stop pulling on your cuffs," she said, unlocking the cuff on his right hand, and rubbed oil on it and clamped it shut again.

"Adam," whispering softly into his ear.

"Yes Mistress," he groaned, as sweat poured off his shoulders.

"I don't share Adam, if I catch you sharing my property around, there will be hell to pay. You will not sit down for a week," she said, as a hard lash landed on his thighs, he shuddered, he was getting so close, he was about to lose control.

So, who the fucking hell had been giving him the blow job, he thought.

"Do you understand me Adam?" she asked.

"Yes Mistress, I understand," he whimpered.

She pumped him again with her hand as he felt his control crumbling away.

"What do you want right now Adam?" she asked, as her hands brushed his tip.

Remi groaned, a fire raging between his legs, he did not know how much longer he could keep.

"Please Mistress," Remi groaned.

"Is this what you want Adam?"

Before he could answer, the unexpected touch of her lips on him had him jerk to her touch. The soft, warm, moist action was too much for him, his body was on fire, the need too great as she massaged his taint, and balls, he growled, he knew it was her as he couldn't hear her voice. Jerking forward, trying to put as much of his dick into her mouth, hoping to feel his tip at the back of her throat. Damn it, the witch knew how to give head, she had watched him long enough to know just where to apply the pressure. He couldn't control it anymore, the tingle and tightening of his balls jerking him deeper into her mouth.

"Cum for me Adam," she said, blowing on his dick as she placed a finger softly on his ring.

Remi lost control, his groans echoing through the room as he erupted in her mouth, hot pulsating gushes as her mouth and lips sucked him dry. Closing his eyes pulling his body back together as the euphoria he experienced the last time he was in Room 3 returned. It was intense as dizziness consumed him, making him slump onto the pole.

"I wanted your dick in my mouth since your first strip tease Adam," she said, raking her hands down his torso.

"You have such a lovely body," she whispered, "I can run my hands down your body all day."

"I am all yours Mistress," Remi said, he wanted her arms around him.

Damn it, Remi chuckled, even though he now knew who she was, the woman was a witch.

Sam brushed against him and the blindfold came off, Mistress Eve was standing in front of him, licking her lips, the mask in place, with the rose tattoo, and wearing the rope necklace he had given her.

Did that mean she was ready to give him the bracelet? Pulling at his chains, he wanted to get down. Remi smiled, hopefully she would give him the bracelet as well.

Mistress Eve was one sexy woman, he thought, staring at her, she was incredible. Moving closer to him, she took off the cuffs on his wrists, pressed a switch next to the pole and the leg restraints fell away.

Remi wanted to taste her; he dropped to his knees and buried his face in between her legs he was about to put his hands on her waist, when he noticed the bracelet on his right wrist. His wrist was bleeding probably from when he had been struggling with his restraints. Breathing a deep sigh of relief, his fears allayed. She had done it; she had finally collared him with the bracelet. Mistress Eve had accepted him as her submissive.

"Excuse me Mistress," he said, as he stood up walking over to his folded clothes. He did not want to give her a chance to argue with him.

Remi walked back box in hand, dropped back on his knees, his head near her legs, her musky feminine scent calling to him. His mysterious sexy Mistress.

"Mistress Eve, will you marry me?" he asked, as he handed over the box to her.

Remi watched her eyes as she opened the box, there was worry he understood why, but there was also happiness and mischief.

Chapter 61

Sam looked down at Remi kneeling in front of her with love shining in his eyes. Remi her darling, was complex and submissive. That was what fascinated her and it's who she had fallen in love with. Remi was the most alpha man you would come across; confident bordering on arrogant, assertive and protective, yet loving and caring.

Sam was looking forward to waking up next to him every morning feeling those sexy lips on her pussy. How she was going to get that dick in her mouth without giving up her position of control during their D/s play was something she still needed to figure out. As a Mistress, her submissive should never see her on her knees giving a blow job.

Well, that was why she had a lifetime to figure out the mechanics of that conundrum, she chuckled.

But he needed to fuck her. Watching his dick harden and him losing control had created a fire between her legs. She had cum just watching as he had struggled against her first attempt at giving him head.

She had needed to find out what made her submissive happy. Time to get to understand limits and such had not been on their side, because of her accident and having Ibukun. If Remi had been into sharing, she'd have been willing to compromise her limits for his needs. However, most things had worked themselves out.

Damn it, she thought. *Remi was so fucking sexy and he was all hers to tie up forever.*

Her hands were shaking as she opened the box. The ring was beautiful, simple, and elegant. The diamond glistened like tiny stars in the moonlight gloom of the room.

There was a brief sliver of doubt, but she pushed the thoughts to the back of her mind and proceeded to pull his head into her pussy. She was horny as hell.

"Remi, on one condition."

"Anything you want Mistress," he replied, as he breathed lightly onto her pussy.

"We need a locked playroom. I can't have Ibukun walking in on you tied up on the ceiling," she sighed, desire raging through her.

"I will call my architect immediately Mistress. Are you sure you don't want a dungeon instead?" he asked just above a whisper, as his fingers slid up her leg.

Sam put a hand on his shoulder. "Remi," she started, watching him lean forward into her pussy as it called to him.

Finally looking up at her. "Yes Mistress," he responded, as his fingers moved surreptitiously up her thigh.

"Yes, Adam Remi I will marry you," she murmured, putting her hand out for him to place the ring on her finger. The ring fit perfectly. How had he known her ring size? She wondered.

Moving his head slightly, he kissed and bit down gently on her clit as he slid the ring on. Then he stood up and kissed her on the mouth; her juices and his salty juices mingling on their lips and in their kiss.

Pulling her into his arms while touching her mask, he asked, "Mistress Eve, please can I take it off?" as his hands went up to the back of her head.

Sam stood still watching as Remi towered over her, his hands untying the string holding the mask in place.

Simultaneously, she pulled the straps off her dress and stood in front of Remi naked, save for her rose tattoo. There was a brief glimpse of confusion on his face, as his brain processed the tattoo with Sam, the woman without the mask.

Sam chuckled at the look on his face. "Remi," she began, taking his hand to her dripping pussy. "Fuck me now, or I will tie you up on that pole again and whip you."

Sam watched him smile that cheeky sexy smile of his. Needing to feel Remi in her soon, she grabbed hold of his dick and it was hard. She ran her other hand down his muscular torso as she moved in closer, breathing in his scent. His aftershave was driving her crazy. She pinched his nipple as he carried her to the bedroom attached to Room 3 and gently placed her on the bed.

Remi stared at the tattoo on her chest. "How do you get this tattoo off?" he asked, as he bit gently on her nipple.

"If I tell you Remi, I will have to kill you," she murmured, as she grazed her thigh on his chin.

Damn, Remi was so fucking good, she thought as she felt her juices flood his tongue.

"Kiss me Remi," she whispered, as she watched him move up towards her on the bed. Her hand went to his dick. It was rock hard and pulsing in anticipation of entering somewhere hot, warm, and moist.

"Where do you want this Remi?" she whispered, as she watched his face. Her fingers swirling around his tip.

Using her feet, she drew him in between her thighs as she watched his face smolder with desire.

"Fuck me Remi. I want to feel that hard dick of yours in my pussy. Show your Mistress you know how to fuck," she commanded, staring at him while twisting her nipple.

Needing no more incentives, he stared, caressed her face, and without warning thrust deep and hard into her.

Sam gasped at the suddenness of his action. Her body adjusted to every artful stroke and she whimpered for more. More, deep, slow thrusts. He teased her incessantly. Her pussy, slick with her juices, clasped on tight to his dick, not wanting to lose the feeling of fullness she was currently experiencing. Remi was on a mission to show her he knew what to do to satisfy her. He used one hand to stimulate her clit as he thrust even deeper inside her. As he hit against her g-spot, Sam felt the orgasm approaching and the spasms built up within her.

"Look at me Remi," she gasped as she tried and failed to control the spasms ricocheting through her body. She squeezed harder on his dick.

"Oh my God Sam, I'm cumming," he groaned, as he plunged deep into her again. His dick pulsating against her walls as her pussy contracted against his dick and the orgasm ripped through her body.

"Oh my God Remi! Oh yes!" she screamed, as she felt her juices flood over his dick.

"Hold me," she whispered. She felt lassitude take over.

Sam felt Remi pull her closer into his embrace and wallowed in the afterglow of her orgasm, crossing her legs over his thighs, and locking him in position. She felt him stir, his head resting on her breasts.

Looking up at her, he asked, "Can we go back to my place tonight? I want you to see your future home," he said, as he maneuvered her to face him on the bed.

Chapter 62

A couple of days later, Remi stared at the DHL packet the driver handed over to him. The call he had placed to his friend Jeremy Fox 'the locator' in London had yielded results. While cleaning Ibukun's bottles he had come up with an idea on what to get Sam for a wedding present.

Sam carried around a lot of melancholy because of the losses she'd suffered throughout her life. Closure regarding the fate or whereabouts of her parents would help her come to terms with her background. Jeremy had gained the nickname 'locator' amongst his friends at the school they had both attended in Scotland. When Jeremy set up shop as an investigator and security expert, Remi hadn't been surprised.

Remi opened the envelope and pulled out the contents. The drop of water on the paper made him realize he had been crying while reading the report Jeremy had put together. Drying his eyes, he went into Ibukun's room. Kechi was getting her ready for bed and would then leave for the day, for her apartment in his vast compound. He appreciated her presence in Ibukun's life. The thought hadn't occurred to him yet to end the contract they had both signed. *Mum was correct*, he thought as he stared at Ibukun. *She had orchestrated a lot of things,* and a cold shiver went down his spine.

Ibukun wasn't asleep when he picked her up to kiss her good night. She gurgled at him with eyes boring into his soul displaying knowledge and wisdom beyond her age. He hoped that she no longer had memories of her previous life. His mum had been right; some children came for a mission and he was now certain Ibukun was one. Holding her tight, he thanked God that he had made the impulsive decision to keep his child.

Remi turned to Kechi. "Please, can we have a chat?" he asked, laying Ibukun back in her cot.

"Please sit down Kechi," he continued, handing over the brown envelope.

Remi decided he would say it in the presence of Ibukun. Hopefully, this would close any pathways or whatever his mum called it, for good. Ibukun had achieved her mission and the messages were now clear.

Remi took a deep breath. "Kechi, I was thinking of what to get Sam as a wedding present and it stumped me. So, I had an idea to see if I could find out what happened to Sam's mum, your half-sister, hoping it would give her closure. I know it's something that bothers her and has shaped her into who she is today."

Kechi was sitting upright and still in the rocking chair in Ibukun's room. She was now staring at the envelope Remi had given her.

Remi stared at the envelope, too. "I thought I would speak to you first before Sam," he paused. "Kechi, Sam's mother is dead. However in her last will and testament, she wanted you to have custody of her daughter Samantha Nkechi, whom she named after you," Remi's voice softened.

Remi moved closer to Kechi's chair. "The father of your sister's child, Sam, had been her uncle. Your aunt's husband, he had raped her repeatedly. She ran away from her aunt's house after meeting a man who promised to marry her and take her to England. He did, but he was controlling, abusive, and violent. He eventually found out that Sam wasn't his and he beat Sam's mother to within an inch of her life. Despite her life-threatening injuries, she took Sam to the social worker who had been trying to convince her to leave her husband. The social worker was Yomi's mum." Remi's voice cracked. He came over to where Kechi was sitting and held her hands. They were shaking as the tears rolled down her face.

Ibukun made a sound from her cot, then was quiet again.

Remi continued, "She ran away to a shelter where she became ill from the injuries she had sustained. Hoping to get better, they told her that the prognosis was not good. She left a letter to her daughter explaining it all and that she would be back to look after her. Her last words had been, 'please tell Sam I am sorry. Please let her know I loved and cherished her despite being the child of rape,'" he finished, as the tears fell down Remi's cheeks.

The whole thing was so heart-breaking to Remi. Sam's mum had been a victim due to the unfortunate circumstances of her birth. A baby losing her mother to childbirth and subsequently discarded by her father, then put in a place where her uncle had raped her repeatedly.

That old English saying was true, *"Old sins cast long shadows. Innocent people suffer because of the sins of people they don't know. Sins have unintended consequences."*

"Kechi, I am truly sorry," Remi muttered, handing her some tissue while he blew his nose.

"What is so spooky Kechi, is that your sister died on the same day and month as Ibukun was born. Ibukun was not due at that point. She forced herself out of her Mother's womb on that day," he whispered, as Kechi stared at him.

Kechi got up and went to pick up Ibukun. She held her close and kissed her forehead with tears sliding down her cheeks. She knew without responding to the job advertisement to look after Ibukun. If she had never taken the initiative, she may have never found Sam.

Remi watched as Kechi put Ibukun back in her cot, walked over, and hugged him.

"Thank you," she whispered, her voice shaking. "Thank you, my son." With that she walked out of the room.

Chapter 63

Remi chuckled to himself as the words he had uttered about paying four times the masked lady's bride price had come back to haunt him.

Before he had received the news of Sam's parents, his family was already trying to understand and navigate the political family landscape of whom they would be going to for the Introduction. Sam had been brought up by Yomi's family, was the daughter-in-law of Michael's family, and had just recently met Kechi, her Aunt. As with most modern families, the ladies, mainly Yomi's mum, Michael's mum, and Kechi had brokered a deal on how to resolve the issue. There would be two introduction ceremonies.

The Introduction in Yorubaland is the literally the introduction of the entire family of the proposed couple to one another. It is also the ceremony where the groom's family officially asks for the bride's hand in marriage and pays the bride price. Remi wondered what would happen if in one of the ceremonies, they refused his offer. He fervently hoped it would not happen.

Kechi, now acting as Sam's mother, decided to make amends with her own father so that he would see his only grandchild marry. She told Remi that her father's sister had passed away due to hypertension after her husband was sent to prison for raping his own daughter. She still wanted them to do it at Sam's grandfather's place so that Sam knew where she came from. It would help Sam heal and have closure knowing her heritage.

Remi had gone to Sam's office the day after breaking the news to Kechi. Sam had taken it well. She had also cried and finally told Remi what Michael had said about her and Ibukun. Confirming what he had suspected all along. Yes, Michael had been the man in the Arsenal shirt.

Sam had hugged him and said, "Oluwaremilekun, I love you. Thank you. You truly are my comfort."

The weekend before the wedding, the families went to Owerri to do the first Introduction with Sam's grandfather on Thursday. They conducted the second one with Yomi's family on Saturday.

Chapter 64

Remi watched Sam walk down the aisle with tears in his eyes. She looked spectacular. Her white, off the shoulder dress contrasted beautifully against her rich, dark, smooth skin.

Convincing Sam to have the whole big Nigerian wedding had been a struggle. It had been the reason for their first major argument. He had come to realize that Sam hated attention and crowds. She liked solitude; she thrived on it and considering what she had been through it was not surprising. She had allowed him and Ibukun in at least, and for that he was grateful.

Mistress Eve on the other hand, once in character, could deal with big crowds and the attention. Once he came to understand the two personas he was dealing with, he had managed to get her to say 'yes' to the big Nigerian wedding, while she had been on top fucking him. One just had to know what to do to get the job done. He smiled and shook his head in amusement at the memory.

Remi had wanted the big Nigerian wedding. For him, it would be the only time he got married and he wanted to show Sam off. His mum, bless her, had arranged the whole thing with input from Yomi's mum and Kechi. Sam had been more concerned about who would be looking after Ibukun, and ensuring that Ibukun had her own aso ebi.

Ibukun was the most beautiful baby Remi had ever come across. Yes, he was biased as her father, but she was lovely. Once he and Sam had moved in together, she began to thrive. He was now buying milk and nappies at a phenomenal rate. Kechi predicted that she was going to be brilliant. However, Remi wondered if he would be eaten out of house and home before that time.

Ibukun was still being looked after by Kechi. He was so happy how everything had finally come together for them. Remi's mind briefly went back to the night before the wedding when they had slipped away to Room 3. Mistress Eve had shown him in no uncertain terms who would be the dominant one in that part of their union.

Anyone looking at the innocent, demure young-looking Sam in the dress would not know who she really was. Remi stroked his silver bracelet thoughtfully. Most people thought he was older than Sam; she had just been blessed with good genes.

Remi was surprised people had not moaned that the bracelet did not go with his outfits. He would not have been able to take it off anyway. The key now belonged forever to his Mistress, Sam. And there she was beside him, with Bayo, his best man, handing over the rings.

After the wedding, as they were getting changed for the evening festivities, Remi walked over to Sam and pulled her into his arms. "Mrs. Olapade, you looked stunning today. I have made a slight change to our honeymoon plans," he said. Placing his hand under her chin to kiss her on the forehead, he continued, "Don't worry, I am not leaving Ibukun behind. We are having a layover for two days in London, then we will fly to the Maldives as planned."

"Any particular reason, Mr. Olapade?" Sam asked, as she rested her hands on his chest.

Remi hugged Sam tighter in his arms. "I love you Mrs. Olapade. We are going to London first so that you can go to your mother's grave. If you need to talk to her, you now have somewhere to go. You now have another place to add to your yearly trip. When we get there, you can decide what to do with her headstone. I did not touch it."

Chapter 65

Sam put her hand to her head and closed her eyes briefly. The pounding in her head increased in intensity as well as the accompanying nausea she always had with migraines. The migraines were getting worse by the day and it was also affecting her memory, causing her to forget things; small stuff like where she left her keys or Ibukun's bottle. Things like that never happened to her. Remi had seen the funny side and had joked that she was getting old. She had threatened him with the whip. His response had been, 'anytime Mistress,' as he winked at her over dinner. She shook her head in amusement at the memory.

The whole thing was a concern to her. She was worried it might be due to something undetected from her accident. Brain injuries had a sinister way of creating other problems that could lay dormant for years. She did not want to worry Remi, as he would get his father and the whole medical society of the country to check her out.

Her reflection in the mirror showed baggy eyes and dark circles. She was insanely tired. Ibukun was teething, cranky, and as a result, she wasn't sleeping properly at night. Ibukun, just the mention of her name made her heart swell. They had decided they would wait until Ibukun was at least one before they started looking at options regarding another baby. It would be madness to have two children under the age of two.

She powdered her face, took two Ibuprofen dry, and left for work.

***

Remi took a sip of his coffee half listening to the Project Manager who was walking the board members through a slide deck on Risk. He had just finished lunch with Ibukun and Kechi. Kechi had started a weekly routine of bringing Ibukun over for lunch and he now looked forward to it. His team, now fully paid members of the Ibukun fan club, fussed over her every week. She put on her cutest smile while reveling in all the attention. Remi sighed, trying to take his mind away from the death by powerpoint unfolding in the boardroom.

Instead, he took his mind back to the blow-job he had received while blindfolded from Sam that morning. He was at the most crucial part of the mental replay when his executive P.A. walked into the boardroom with a solemn look on his face as he headed directly towards Remi.

The P.A. handed him a note.

The hospital just called. Sam collapsed and lost consciousness at work. They need you to come down immediately.

The coffee spilled over the table as Remi tried unsuccessfully to keep his hand steady on the cup. Memories of Sam's stay in the hospital flooded his mind. His P.A. waved him away, as he grabbed tissues from a side table to clean up the spilt coffee.

Oh my God. Please, let her be okay, he prayed.

Remi did not want to think that he had been living on borrowed time with Sam. He had noticed that she had been very tired lately, putting it down to Ibukun's teething. Normally, Ibukun was well-behaved, especially around Sam. But it was the small things that she kept forgetting that had him worried. Remi joked about her memory loss, acting as if he hadn't noticed so he would not alarm her. When he had discussed it with his dad, he had told him that brain trauma sometimes created other issues that don't come to light until later.

Pulling his phone out of his pocket, Remi sent a text message to Kechi to meet him at the hospital.

"Excuse me, I'm sorry I have to leave; family emergency," he stated, before walking out of the board room to head for the hospital.

Remi could feel his heart beating faster as he rushed to the hospital; memories of her stay filled his mind as he remembered her death in Japan.

Remi was speaking to the receptionist when Kechi turned up with Ibukun. Bending down, he picked Ibukun up from her pram, hugged her, and carried her as they walked down the corridor to Sam's room.

A tall slim doctor named Akinyemi by his name badge was coming out of Sam's room. The pepper spray hair and jovial looks reminded him of Dr. Richard Webber from his favorite tv show, Grey's Anatomy.

The doctor looked towards Remi and smiled. "Mr. Olapade?" he asked, putting a hand out. "I see you have been a busy young man." He touched Ibukun's cheek gently. "I don't blame you. You have a very beautiful wife." he said, patting Remi on the back.

Remi looked at the doctor confused. "Is my wife ok?"

Dr. Akinyemi smiled at Remi, "Of course. As we all know, Sam never stops. She works very hard; however, she might need to slow down a bit. Her body is telling her to. You do know that doctors make the worst patients," the doctor shook his head, while smiling at Ibukun. He pulled a pair of gloves out of his pocket. "We were waiting for you to arrive so that you would be here for the ultrasound. Your wife is pregnant."

Kechi and Remi looked at each other. It was impossible and the shock was obvious on their faces.

Dr Akinyemi sighed, "Yes, I know. Sam told me that it was impossible, so I did the test three times. Sam is indeed pregnant. We just need to see how far along she is." He put his hand on the door handle. "I am hoping the migraines and forgetfulness are due to the pregnancy. However, if what they said is true, then we will need to monitor this pregnancy carefully."

Remi was shocked. The best doctors in the world had said the damage done was too severe. Ibukun gurgled and was wriggling, trying to get out of Remi's arms as the door opened. She wanted to be with Sam.

Sam was on the bed with an intravenous drip hooked up to her arm. For a brief second Remi's fear for her health re-surfaced. He went over to hug her, as Ibukun wriggled out of his arms to hug Sam. Stepping back Remi watched in amusement as Ibukun put her finger on Sam's cheek. Sam closed her eyes while holding Ibukun close and he heard her whisper "thank you". A shiver went down his spine as Ibukun turned her head towards him and stared at him. Her eyes were sad, but happy. Then the moment was gone as she started gurgling happily; her eyes crinkling with contentment. It was spooky.

Kechi moved forward to take Ibukun out of Sam's arms to make way for the doctor. Ibukun put her hand to Kechi's face, the same way she had done to Sam's face and went quiet.

Dr. Akinyemi wheeled the machine over to Sam's bed and a feeling of déjà vu came over Remi as he remembered the last time he had been in the same position, in another hospital with Mercy.

Remi moved closer to Sam and held her hand, squeezing it and kissing her on the forehead. The room suddenly was eerily silent, as all eyes bore into the doctor; breaths expectant, as three people waited on the result of the ultrasound. There was a look of concern on Dr. Akinyemi's face as he studied the image on the screen. He put the probe down and placed more gel on Sam's stomach. The same look of concern returned to the otherwise jovial face.

Dr. Akinyemi pulled off his gloves and swiveled in his chair towards Sam and Remi.

There was a weak smile on the doctor's face. "You certainly don't do things by halves, Sam," the doctor murmured, as he stared back at the screen. "Congratulations! You are having twins."

Ibukun jerked excitedly in Kechi's arms and let out a loud cooing sound. Kechi stared at Sam and Remi in shock.

"Look at the two heartbeats," the doctor said, as he pointed to the screen.

A wave of light-headedness came over Remi, the voice was crystal clear. *'Remi, nothing is a coincidence. Everything you're experiencing is meant to happen exactly how it is happening. Embrace the lessons. Be grateful. Trust me you will be fine.*' He looked around in shock. The voice was so clear, so near it was as if Michael was in the room with them. Looking at Sam, he noticed she was staring at the door. Had she seen something?

With tears pricking his eyes, Remi bent down and hugged Sam. Words could not describe the gamut of emotions he was feeling. He was grateful. Sam wasn't ill; she was pregnant. He would now have three children under the age of two, but he had learnt to embrace the lessons. They would be fine if he survived another two lots of Ibukun in the house, drinking milk like there was no tomorrow. He smiled, gratefully, as he walked over to Kechi and Ibukun. He held on to her. His mum had been right after all.

THE END